LILY POND
FORGED ALLIANCE

HOWARD A. W. CARSON

ISBN-10: 1500987646
ISBN-13: 978-1500987640

DEDICATION

For my brother John, without whose insistence and encouragement
I would not have written this story.

PRAISE FOR LILY POND - FORGED ALLIANCE

The book <u>LILY POND</u> – <u>FORGED ALLIANCE</u>, by Howard A. W. Carson is an extensive labor of love where through fantasy he allegorically expresses the need to avert environmental disaster by people "uniting" for the common good.

His mythical characters (frogs, pixies, fairies, nymphs, imps and ancients) make colorful characters described through creative adjectives bringing them to life.

Reading his book made me wish Walt Disney would pick up his story and turn it into a classic two-hour cartoon that children and adults could enjoy together.

Mr. Carson is a natural born author, and for fans of the Hobbit (and similar novels) this book will be greatly treasured.

Perry Milek:
(Author of "Landlords Survival Kit", "5,000 Years of Graffiti, Humor, and Philosophy", "The Best of the New Beatnik Poets" and eleven other books.)

I was progressively drawn into the flow of [the] story. There is a well-balanced meshing and a consistent harmonious mix between dialogue, narrative and character development.

The use of simple language to describe a subject which has become unnecessarily complex is refreshing . . . crisp and quaint.

Dr. William Cohen, PhD.
University of Tübingen, Germany

Howard Carson's fantasy Lily Pond-Forged Alliance embraces the reader with exciting, colorful, vivid descriptions of new places, exciting events and unique personalities.

The story allowed me to really live in the communities and environments while experiencing the personalities as I travelled with the characters throughout the story.

This fabulous fantasy refreshed me as I perused the pages. Let yourself enjoy this flight of fantasy as you read and experience this adventure.

Noreen Teachout
BS, MA, Education
National Who's Who Writer

ACKNOWLEDGMENTS

Christine Brown, whose help was instrumental to being published.
Shirley Poliquin, whose support and encouragement and early
editing was indispensable.
My best friend Karen and all my family and friends that supported
my efforts by believing that I could and would accomplish what I
set out to do.

INTRODUCTION

In today's world the threat of global warming has caused a division of opinions and that division poses a dire threat.

For centuries the five factions of Lily Pond had at best a tenuous relationship amongst themselves. Despite their differences, practicality dictated the need to trade with one another; but when one had a need for more land, battles would break out along the borders and the boundaries of Lily Pond would ebb and flow.

At times the forest would expand to the water's edge and into the fields. At other times the pond would spread into the forest and fields, even pushing up into the rolling hills. Then there were times the fields would force the other areas to recede. And so the process continues as it has for so many generations.

Now, the sometimes reluctant neighbors; the five factions of this world, consist of the Water Nymphs that live in the city at the bottom of Lily Pond, the Forest Fairies that dwell in the fairy cities of the Endless Forest, the Southern Field Fairies living in the villages and the granite city that rises high out of the southern fields and the Eastern Field Fairies who make their home in the cities of the orchards and villages of the fields of the East.

The Rolling Hills Pixies make up the fifth faction. Mining the rolling hills of the West they also operate the grain and lumber mills along the winding creek.

In the midst of all these factions are the Frogs. Uniquely located and properly equipped by Nature herself, the frogs had become intermediaries, transporting goods and bringing the battles to conclusion. For this reason, the frogs became citizens of the five domains with no boundaries for them to adhere to.

And so it is that the five factions and the frogs work and live together keeping the balance in their world.

But now, unseen forces beyond this realm are about to change everything for the inhabitants, especially for one common leopard frog named Croaker.

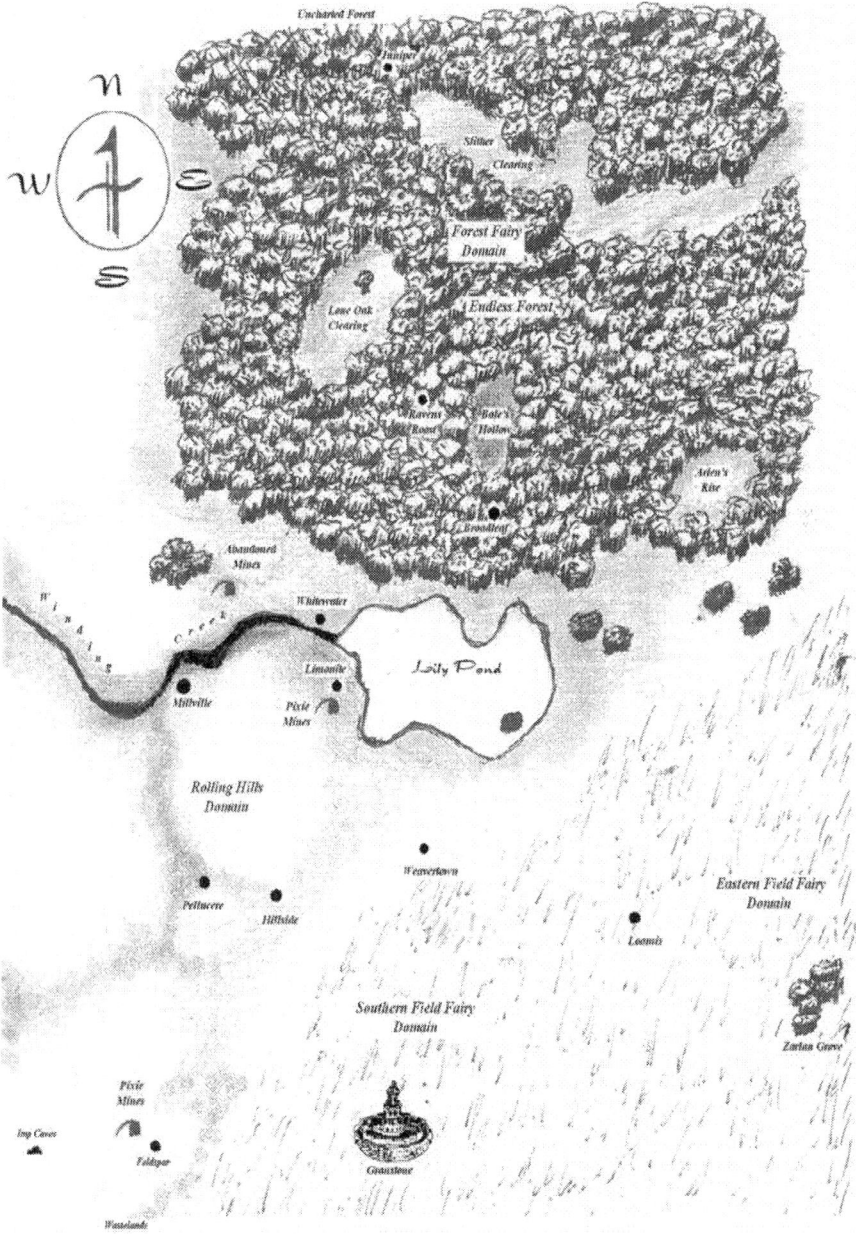

PROLOGUE

The sun had already sunk behind the rolling hills of the West and the dim gray light of dusk was fading fast. Above, glimmers of stars were beginning to appear a few at a time like tiny lamps being lit to ward off the inky black of night. From out of the hills an evening breeze as soft as a whisper flows across the land and rustles the grasses as though thousands of tiny feet were gently rushing over them. Down the hillsides and along the winding creek the breeze rushes to the waters edge, where cattails gently sway, onward across the waters of Lily Pond to the shores of the Endless Forest where it enters and darts among the trees.

Slowly a chorus builds as the evening creatures start to stir. Louder and louder the voices of the frogs call out. Their calls are for Gribit, the great sage bullfrog.

"Please, tell us again about Croaker," they say.

The night shakes with the boom of Gribit's voice, thundering from his lily pad far out in the pond.

"Grrr-ib-it, Grrr-ib-it," he begins, "not long ago it started this way..."

CHAPTER ONE

The day was still young as the sun rose higher above the eastern horizon and cast its warm rays on the western bank of Lily Pond. A young frog approached the waters edge at the end of the worn path through the tall grasses. He was making his daily visit to his favorite swimming spot at the southern tip of the western shore. Life was still relatively easy for him, as most of the harsh realities of the world had not been imposed on him yet, but destiny was about to mature him beyond his years.

"Hey there, Croaker. First time I ever beat you here," he heard Webber's voice as he appeared through the grasses to the ponds edge.

"Well, it will be the last," he shouted back a jovial challenge to his friend.

He and Webber had been friends since they were tadpoles and had shared many experiences together.

"There is no sign of Old Big Fin," Webber said, looking toward the water.

"Good! Maybe we can get a swim in without that old bass trying to have us for breakfast," Croaker replied. "Nearly got us a few times, that old boy did."

"Yes, but it was easier to hide from him when we were still tadpoles," Webber recalled, "But now it is a race for life whenever he comes around!"

"He has taken to lying under the roots of that big old tree at the waters edge," Croaker nodded in the direction of the forest shore, "He can lay in ambush there."

"Some say they have seen him go up Winding Creek as far as the rapids," Webber noted, "I think that swimming against the current is how he stays so strong."

"I think he might be trying to catch Pixies that get to close to the waters edge." Croaker chuckled as he found an agreeable spot to sit.

"Yes, the mill workers *do* tend to get careless when they are always pulling pranks on each other!" Webber laughed.

The two young frogs sat sunning themselves in the morning rays while a gentle breeze blew softly across the water carrying on it the murmured sounds of life about the pond.

"Hi Croaker, hi Webber, how is the water?" It was Lily Pad and her sister Lotus.

"We have not tried it yet, been enjoying the sun," Croaker replied.

"We would have been here sooner but we had to stop on the other side of the clearing for a while." Lily said, relief in her voice and a look of concern on her face.

"Why?" Croaker asked, concerned by the tone of her remark.

"We saw a slither going through the open area toward the forest on our way here. I do not believe he caught our scent. He just continued on in the direction he was going," she explained.

"A slither!" Croaker said looking about anxiously in the event it might have changed directions. He knew how dangerous they were and that Lily and Lotus had a close call. "There have not been any around these parts for a long time."

"We better let Gribit know about this." Webber said, "Everyone must be warned!"

"I will swim out to his pad so he can sound the alarm," Croaker agreed, rushing to the waters edge. With one giant leap Croaker launched himself out into the water, creating a splash as he went under. Returning to the surface he heard Lily frantically shouting his name, he had been in such a hurry that he hadn't stopped to check the water first.

Lily had seen the rushes move and a small wake on the surface of the shallows just as Croaker had jumped in. It was Old Big Fin looking for his breakfast.

"Old Big Fin…Old Big Fin!" Lily shouted, frantically trying to warn Croaker.

The old bass had gotten between Croaker and the shore! There was nothing to do but try for the pads further out in the pond. Quickly, Croaker dove to see where his adversary was and to his horror almost ended in the old bass's mouth! Kicking hard, Croaker dove deeper and made a series of quick turns, first one way then another.

Nearing some thick grasses, he swam for them frantically going side to side, up and down, barely avoiding the fish's jaws time after time! Doubling back over Old Big Fin's head, he narrowly avoided being caught only to have to repeat the maneuver moments later as the fish came at him again.

Tired as he was, Croaker kicked harder and dove deeper into the depths of the pond. Ahead, the stems of the lily pads came into his view. Kicking with all he had, Croaker made his way to the surface as he reached them, breaking the surface of the water as if he had been flung from a catapult and sent flying through the air! Soon he was tumbling across a giant pad finally slamming into something firm that didn't move on his impact.

"That was quite a demonstration you put on their young one," a deep voice said.

Panting from exhaustion, Croaker looked up to see what he had landed against.

"I am sorry Gribit, Old Big Fin almost had me for his breakfast, I needed to get to you as soon as possible and made the mistake of not checking the water first," Croaker explained, heart pounding like a drum.

"What could be so important for you to take such a chance?" Gribit asked.

"There is a slither in the area," Croaker answered, having regained his wind.

Gribit wasted no time and bellowed out an alarm for all of Lily Pond to hear.

The murmur of life about the pond came to a sudden halt, replaced by the warning call of Gribit, carried on the once whispering breeze, echoing from the rolling hills to the edge of the forest and through the nearby fields.

"If the slithers have returned we will all have to be on guard!" Gribit said, his eyes searching the shore, "I wonder what brings them back after all this time?"

Croaker's eyes followed Gribit's, watching the creatures scurry as the alarm spread through the domains of Lily Pond.

"Where did you see it?" Gribit asked, returning his gaze to the young frog.

"I did not see it myself. Lily and Lotus saw it on their way to the ponds edge." Croaker informed him, "They were fortunate it did not catch their scent."

"I am glad you came to tell me, but next time, use a little caution; you should always *look* before you leap."

Croaker winced from the comment and a smile came to Gribit's face, "That was some leap you made there, one for future stories," he said, softer now.

But Croaker was not pleased that Gribit derived so much enjoyment from his ordeal with Old Big Fin and returned his smile with a scowl!

"Come now Croaker, flying without the benefit of wings! That has to be some kind of accomplishment!" Gribit chuckled.

◆ ◆ ◆ ◆ ◆

Lily, Webber and Lotus all relaxed when they heard Gribit's warning call. They knew that Croaker had made it to Gribit's pad.

"I am going to kill that idiot!" Lily said, angry with Croaker but relieved he was all right.

"Yes, he has a tendency to act first and think later," Lotus chimed in.

"Do not forget the reason for him doing that," Webber was quick to point out, "You two were lucky to evade that slither."

The sisters sat quietly looking out on the pond wondering when Croaker would return, their heads hanging for their criticism of Croaker's actions when all he did was what was necessary.

Slowly the sounds of the pond world begin to return to normal, though all were now aware of the new danger at hand.

"Have you girls ever been to the little pool at Bale's Hollow?" Webber asked, breaking the silence, "It is on the southwest edge of the hollow."

"Have you?" Lotus asked back, alarmed, "What would make you venture that far from Lily Pond?"

"I have been learning the trade routes," Webber explained, "I am in line to be the trade liaison between the Forest Fairies and the Water Nymphs," he said proudly.

"I would have never guessed that you would receive such an important position," Lotus said, impressed by this revelation.

"I still have a lot to learn yet," he continued, "and then I still have to do scribe duties first. That is part of the learning process as well."

"How long is the learning process?" She asked.

"At least a year," he replied, "and then I still have to meet the Forest Fairy King, Fernon, as well as all his City Regents for their approval."

"How many regents are there?" Lotus asked, her curiosity now in full gear.

"I have been told there are thirty between the southern border of the forest and the northern tip of Slither Clearing. Beyond that I have no idea."

"That sounds like a tremendous responsibility," Lotus replied.

"The nymph Queen, Isalia, has approved me for her part, although I still need the fairies approval of me as well."

"I do not believe you will have any problem there." Lotus smiled.

"Neither do I," Lily interjected.

Intimidated by the whole process, the girls' comments bolstered Webber and set him more at ease. Even the Queen's approval had not entirely put his doubts to rest.

Now his mind returned to the present situation. "I wonder how long before Croaker gets back?" he thought aloud.

◆◆◆◆◆

King Arklan paced back and forth on a plush moss green carpet as the sunlight radiated through the multi colored panes of his study window, casting a kaleidoscope of color that splayed across the room lending a jeweled appearance to all its contents; from the walls to the oak bookcases and the polished oak desk that sat at the prominence of the chamber.

As he paced he thought about the news he had just received from the outpost at the southwestern edge of his domain. Arklan found the scouting report to be very disturbing due to the implications of this event, some which could not yet be fathomed.

The messenger waited patiently for the King's reply. Though he was tired and hungry from his hurried journey, he was ready to leave again if necessary.

"Should I inform the other realms? And what would be the best way if I do?" Arklan spoke his thoughts aloud though they were meant only for him. The possible scenarios of the report were of great concern.

Finally deciding what needed to be done, Arklan called out, "Sergeant of the guard. Send me another messenger immediately and see that this one gets food and rest before he returns to his post. That will be all."

"Yes, Your Majesty." the sergeant said, motioning the messenger to follow as he turned and left through the door and down a broad hallway in the direction of the guard station at the head of a spiral staircase. The two guards standing their post came to attention at the Sergeant's approach.

"Have a messenger report immediately to the King's study." He ordered one of the guards. "And take this man with you to the mess hall and see that he gets fed properly; when you are done with that return here to your duty station."

"Yes, sergeant," the guard said.
"Follow me please." The guard instructed the messenger as he led the way down the spiral stairs that had been carved in the granite. The messenger followed closely behind his escort, descending several levels to the military quarters located deep within the great city of Granstone, palace of the King of the Southern Field Fairies.

Granstone's splendor was second to none. Standing in the southern fields it was a mountain in a sea of grasses, visible from all directions. Had it been in the forest it would have stood twice the height of the tallest tree with the breadth of all Zarlan Grove.

When the new messenger arrived at the study, he found King Arklan at his desk writing.

"Your Majesty," The messenger said, his head slightly bowed.

"I have an urgent message that I want you to carry to Lily Pond," the King said, stamping the Royal Seal into place. "Take it directly to the frog sage, Gribit, and wait for his response," Arklan said as he looked up, a deep furrow over his brow.

"This message must be delivered at all cost," he continued, "but use caution in its delivery. It must not fall into any others hands. Until we have more knowledge no others can be trusted with its contents."

The messenger took the message from Arklan with a sense of honor that he had been chosen for this task. From the look on the King's face he knew this had to be very important, as he himself would have to cross borders to deliver it. All other messages going to another domain would be passed on to a messenger of that domain or delivered by frogs.

The messenger bowed, no words necessary as he turned and left hurriedly through the door to the hallway.

Arklan once again pondered the information he had received and the possible implications as the feeling of unease grew stronger within him.

"Your Majesty, the trade liaison from the Rolling Hills has arrived," the voice of a young boy interrupted his thoughts.

"Are all present?" he inquired.

"Yes, Your Majesty," the boy responded, head bowed in respect.

"That will be all," the King gestured with a wave of his hand, dismissing the page.

With a bow and a turn the young page went scurrying off to the great hall to inform the trade delegation that the King was on his way.

"Sergeant of the guard!" Arklan called out.

"Yes, Your Majesty," The sergeant replied as he appeared through the doorway.

"I would like to see the commander of the scouts. Have him report to me at the great hall where I will be in trade negotiations. He is to interrupt when he arrives, but tell him to be discreet about it," he instructed, returning the sergeant's bow with a nod and waiving him on.

Arklan entered the great hall through his private access. Looking out to the large half round granite table, which mirrored the hall itself, he saw the delegation all raise to their feet at his approach, bowing their heads. Behind them, three steps down, sat row upon row of oak trimmed granite seats gradually rising toward the rear of the hall. The rows followed the same arc as the table and the hall. Aisles, like spokes in a wheel divided the rows into three sections. Two inner aisles as well as the two outer aisles stretched from the table to the back of the hall. Halfway back the rows were sub-divided by three additional aisles so there were six sections in the back of the hall.

At the rear of the hall, an entrance for each aisle, each entrance was flanked by sculptures of fairies emerging from the granite walls with arms stretched wide and high, fingertips reaching to touch its companion's, forming arches over the

15

entrances. The open wings of the fairies melting into the walls behind them while their heads had crowns of small globes from which emanated a blue white light.

Above the table hung a large chandelier of oak adorned in the same way, the globes strung together like beads to form three rings. The higher outer ring was the largest with each ring progressively smaller than the last and each dropped a level lower. Thus, the Hall was immersed in a bright cool light.

As Arklan took his place, at the center of the straight side of the table, the rest of the delegation took their seats again.

Behind the King, ornate glyphs were carved in the granite wall. The glyphs depicted the everyday life of the fairies as they worked at harvesting, weaving and other daily tasks of life in this society.

Looking around the table at the liaisons for each of the domains with their scribes, the King turned to his Deputy of Commerce. Time was of the essence and Arklan dispensed with the usual introductions.

"Braylor, you may start by stating what we have available for trade," the King prompted his deputy to begin.

"Yes, Your Majesty. We currently have 50,000 baskets of grain, 5 storage houses of grass stalks, 10,000 baskets, 10,000 grass mats . . ." The deputy laid it all out as he thumbed through his ledger book.

At first bewildered by the lack of formality, the liaisons went to work while their scribes recorded the transactions, each having been told the needs of the domains they represented. The negotiating began based on what was available from their respective domains.

The process had barely begun when a page quietly approached Arklan. Bowing slightly, he extended his hand palm up in the direction of an anteroom.

The chamber fell silent at the interruption.

"Continue, no need to stand," the King said as he stood, "urgent business requires my attention. I shall return shortly," he informed the delegation, hurrying off to the anteroom.

"Your Majesty, you sent for me?" the Commander said, bowing when Arklan entered the room.

"I have orders for you," Arklan said, "I want you to execute them without raising alarm."

"Yes, Your Majesty," the Commander replied with a puzzled look on his face.

"Double all patrols throughout the domain," Arklan ordered, "something strange is happening in the southwest; I want to be prepared for anything. What I am about to tell you cannot be repeated at this time."

Arklan explained the message he had received from the southwest outpost then quickly returned to the delegation.

◆ ◆ ◆ ◆ ◆

"Three of our scouts have not reported in! All within the last two days?" King Fernon shouted, "Just where did these disappearances take place?"

"One to the west, one south and the other east," Fernon's Commander said.

"By Bale, who is playing at what?" Fernon exclaimed.

"We have no idea who is behind this," the Commander replied thinking he himself had been questioned, "These disappearances are spread so far apart it does not make sense."

"Until we learn what is going on, we are not going to be caught off guard if this is an attack on us. I want the army on full alert," Fernon said as he sat at his desk and wrote out orders, handing them to his Commander, "Deliver this to General Oakon."

"Yes, Your Majesty," the Commander nodded as he accepted his orders.

"And tighten security at the border check points!" Fernon added as an after thought.

"Your Majesty, may I recommend that *all* patrols consist of two scouts?"

"Excellent suggestion! Inform me immediately of any developments," he said, releasing the Commander to carry out his orders.

Fernon's apprehension was evident. Who could be attacking his domain? In the past he would have known by the location of the skirmishes, but this time something was different.

As he sat at his desk, in his palace among the high limbs of the ancient oak that stood in Lone Oak Clearing, he puzzled over this new situation. He felt sure he could rule out his cousin, King Arklan, because Lily Pond lies between their domains; *As for*

Isalia, she would have come in force to claim new lands for her domain. Could it be the Pixies? That rabble of confederated cities had basically no central command structure and only city militias. If it were not for the frogs, they would not even be able to negotiate trade agreements. If they wanted land they would just try to move in. That left Airlein, of the Eastern Field Fairies, but if she wanted land she would be looking more toward Arklan's domain for those since his land was more suited to her needs.

Uneasy thoughts raced round in his mind as he tried to make sense of it all.

"Page!" Fernon called while pulling at a bell cord.

"Yes, Your Majesty," came an immediate reply as the young page emerged through the entrance to the library.

"Bring me a goblet of berry brew, I have developed a headache," the King ordered.

"Yes Your Majesty, will there be anything else?"

"No, just the brew." He answered, waving the page on his way with an annoyed gesture.

The Sun was nearing its zenith and the warmth of the day with the sun's golden rays filled the room. In other times Fernon would be enjoying this moment in his favorite spot, looking out at the open area around the ancient oak to the surrounding forest that was his domain, entranced by the azure skies and the billowy white puffs floating effortlessly through that endless blue.

But now, the breezes carrying the perfume of clover and violets rising from the ground below didn't register. Now Fernon's thoughts were occupied by the suggestion of war; *a possible war, yes, but with whom? Had more than one of the domains made an alliance against him?* He must know. Somehow he had to discover who or what was behind the disappearance of his scouts, scouts that had been reliable by all accounts.

When the page returned with the brew, Fernon commanded, "Have Obrin report to me at once." He wanted to consult with his Chief of Security, his head of intelligence, about the actions he had decided he should take.

"Have him bring four of his best agents with him," he added, then with an after thought, "Bring up a cask of the berry brew with five goblets."

"Yes, Your Majesty," The page replied, happy the King was now in a somewhat better mood.

Fernon knew that what he wanted to do could have major consequences, but his need to know took precedence over any potential misunderstandings by the other domains.

"Am I interrupting anything?" Queen Nedalia said as she entered the library.

To all appearances, Nedalia virtually floated across the floor, her tall slender body accentuated by the slight breeze coming through the window, fluttering the rainbow-hued gossamer dress she wore, as she moved to her husband's side. Her silver blond hair glistening whenever the sun's rays touched it as she crossed the room, and her gentle smile added to her demeanor of royal grace.

The presence of Fernon's wife's brightened the room beyond what seemed possible; an elixir to Fernon that immediately put him in an even better mood.

"When Obrin gets here you will have to leave," he said with disappointment in his voice, "But for the moment you are here."

Nedalia crinkled up a frown when she heard Obrin's name. The mention of it usually meant something was amiss, and this worried her.

"Is it anything you can talk about?" she asked, half afraid of what he might tell her.

"I will tell you what I can later," he replied, not wanting to worry her with his apprehensions or the conclusions he had come to.

"Do I need to worry about the children?" she asked.

"No, some events have taken place that need to be looked into, that is all," he tried to put her at ease.

With that, Nedalia began to relax, the smooth features of her face returning as her frown faded. The two sat in each other's company drinking in the world outside, a momentary reprieve for the worried Fernon.

Obrin's voice interrupted their tranquility, "You sent for me Sire?"

"Yes, come in," Fernon said as Obrin appeared at the doorway, then nodding to Nedalia, "I am afraid we have to be alone now."

21

Without saying a word Nedalia rose and left as gracefully as she had arrived.

As quickly as she had left the room Fernon's mood reverted to what it had been before her appearance.

"Where are the agents?" he asked Obrin.

"I sent word for them. They should be arriving . . ." he was cut short as the page entered the library with a cask under his arm and a maid carrying the goblets followed closely behind.

"Just leave those," Fernon told the page.

The maid and the page placed these items on the round table in the center of the library then left, turning to bow before exiting.

"As I was about to say," Obrin resumed, "they should be arriving at any moment now."

Fernon supplied Obrin with the details about the disappearance of the scouts and what his conclusions were.

"I thought that is what this might be about," Obrin said.

Fernon wasn't surprised by the comment, he knew that very little got past Obrin.

"Since you asked for four agents, I made sure that one of them was my best *female* agent," Obrin said, "I am assuming you will want her for Lily Pond?"

"Yes," Fernon said, "If one or more of the domains are up to something we need to know just what it is. Since I can not rule out my cousin, I will need the fourth agent for his domain."

Walking over to the table, Obrin's four agents arrived as they were filling their goblets.

◆ ◆ ◆ ◆ ◆

Croaker had spent the morning with Gribit and it was now after the mid-day.

"I think I should get back now," Croaker said.

"Yes, I believe that old fish has left the area by now," Gribit agreed, "Of course, if he did not he would be starving by now," he added with a grin.

Croaker didn't appreciate the humor. He had no desire to be anyone's meal.

"That is not funny Gribit," Croaker frowned.

The drone of beating wings stopped Croaker, as he was about to jump back into the pond; a fairy messenger was crossing the water. Croaker and Gribit looked at each other with the same thought; *why was a fairy chancing entry in the nymph's domain? And why was he headed for them?*

"Sire," the messenger addressed Gribit as he landed next to them, "a message from King Arklan. I am to wait for your response."

Gribit accepted the message and broke the seal. Reading the contents he stared off into the southwestern distance.

"Croaker, I think I just received an answer to our early morning visitor," looking at him with concern, "I believe I have a job for you, will you take it?"

"Yes, of course," he said without even asking it's nature, knowing that the task must be very important and that it was an honor that Gribit had asked *him*.

"I need to know that I can count on you!" Gribit continued.

"You can," Croaker reassured him.

Gribit turned to the messenger, "Escort my young friend to Arklan's court. He is to be my personal liaison and to receive all intelligence on this matter."

After making sure the messenger understood, he added, "And tell your King that I will have conference with Isalia."

"Croaker, come over here for a moment," Gribit motioned to the furthest point of the pad.

"Read this," he commanded.

As Croaker read, astonishment showed on his face.

"Keep this to yourself until we know more, understand?" Gribit cautioned.

Croaker nodded.

"We do not want undue alarm," Gribit pointed out, "I am sending you because if there are any important changes or new information that I need to know about then you can deliver it to me. I would hate to think of the possible problems should another fairy enter this domain and happen to be seen; or worse, captured."

Gribit instructed the messenger to wait in the tall grasses at the shore's edge until Croaker could swim over.

"Stay alert," Gribit cautioned Croaker, "I fear there is much danger about."

And with that Croaker dove into the water and swam off.

❖ ❖ ❖ ❖ ❖

At the northwest outpost a signalman took down the message being flashed in the sunlight from the agent's high vantage point a little south of Arlen's Rise. After receiving the message and handing it to the messenger at his side, he said, "Take this immediately to the outpost Commander."

"A message from our forest agent sir," the messenger handed it to the Commander and waited for his next orders.

After reading the message, concern shown on the Commander's face. Hastily placing the message in an envelope and sealing it, he handed it back to the messenger.

"See that Queen Airlein receives this immediately, it is urgent!" he stressed.

"Sergeant of the guard!" the Commander called out.

"Yes Sir," came the reply.

"Double the guard immediately until further notice!"

The Sun was nearing the western horizon and the breeze carried on it a damp coolness as storm clouds were building in the west.

Airlein sat close to the water's edge of her pond in her palace garden at Zarlan Grove. She had taken time out from her busy schedule to relax in the sun's warm rays and enjoy the fragrances of the garden.

She could have been a flower herself, long golden hair that tossed as the breeze built to a gentle wind. She wore an emerald green gossamer dress that as the wind blew, accentuating her sinewy body, clung tight to her. Her face bore the angular features that were a trait of all fairies. Her high cheekbones and long slender nose where accentuated by her almond eyes of compelling cobalt blue pools that contained a sparkle from deep within to rival the stars at night.

The serenity of the moment was broken at the sound of hurried footsteps stirring the stones of the garden path. Looking in the direction of the sound, Airlein watched the messenger approach. Reaching her side he dropped down to one knee and bowed his head.

"Your Majesty, an urgent message from the Commander of the Northwest outpost," he informed her, handing her the sealed envelope.

Airlein rose to her feet as she read and without looking at the messenger said, "Have General Broadstem and his staff report to me at once in the war room."
Then, unfurling the nearly invisible wings tucked closely to her back, she ascended to a balcony high above in the giant walnut tree that housed her palace and canopied her garden below. Because of the urgency of the matter she had chosen not to take the stairs that spiraled up the trunk of the great tree.

The sky was darkening now as the rain clouds in the west approached, blocking out the sun.

The war room was bright; blue-white light radiating form lanterns that hung from sconces on each of the six walls of the

26

large chamber. General Broadstem and his staff had arrived, finding Airlein standing at the hexagon table in the center of the room, studying the relief map of Lily Pond and the surrounding domains.

The map was covered with small colored carvings of military assets, both hers and those of the other domains as her intelligence agency had reported.

A cadre of two Intelligence Staff were busy moving around the table, updating any new information as it came in.

"Your Majesty," General Broadstem said as he and his staff entered the room.

"I have just received word from our agent in Endless Forest that Fernon has just put his entire military on full alert," Airlein informed them, "Do we have any idea why he would do that?"

"No, Your Majesty," Broadstem said with surprise to the news while surveying his staff with a questioning look.

"Then we must assume that he intends to invade one of the domains," she surmised.

"That *would* be the logical conclusion," Broadstem replied, "and if that is the case then we should put our troops on full alert as well in case he intends to invade us."

"I agree," Airlein nodded, "and I think that we should have our intermediary contact Gribit as soon as possible to try and get a full understanding of this action," Airlein concluded, adding, "We should not jump to actions other than defensive ones based on the little information we have."

"I will get the orders out immediately," the General said as he dispatched one of his staff.

"I will talk to the Ambassador when I leave here," Airlein continued, "I hope the frogs have more thorough information."

After discussing their resources and how to deploy them, Airlein dismissed the group and returned to her quarters ringing for a page when she entered them.

She felt as though a great weight had been placed on her shoulders; the responsibility for so many and the anticipation of events that had not yet taken place; events that had the potential of bringing heartache and misery to her citizens.

"I would like to speak to the Frog Ambassador in my study as soon as possible," she ordered the page when he entered.

"Yes, Your Majesty," the page said, bowing as he left for the Ambassador's quarters.

CHAPTER TWO

Driven by the gusting winds, the rain pounded down on Croaker and his guide. Blinding flashes of lightning streaked across the blackened skies, pitch forking, appearing to Croaker as though they were illuminated thorn thicket branches. Finally reaching the edge of the northern village of Weavertown, they plodded along the now muddy road to the outpost checkpoint.

"We can find shelter and food at the local inn," the messenger told Croaker.

"I could use a warm up." Croaker said, "This rain is cold, not warm like the pond water,"

The messenger only smiled, having put on his hooded rain slicker that he carried in his hip pack when it first started to rain.

"I will see if we can find you a slicker when we get to town," he offered, "and a hip pack as well."

Croaker noted that the messenger's slicker was extremely light in weight and was made of fabric woven of spider silk, it had been dyed raw umber brown to blend with the grasses. The slicker, two layers thick had a very thin coat of bees wax between the layers to ensure it kept the water out. Until now he hadn't given it much thought, but this was exactly how the translucent dome that protected the underwater city of Lily Pond had been created; *The time and labor it must have taken to construct it,* he thought, *and the trade negotiations with the forest fairies for that fabric. The nymphs must have given a lot in return!*

"I would appreciate that," he said, accepting the messenger's offer.

At the checkpoint the messenger left Croaker to talk to the Commander of the outpost. When he returned they continued on to the village.

Shortly after going through the checkpoint they passed several houses while making their way to the inn. Weavertown was a typical field-fairy village. The houses were of pole and beam construction with walls, both exterior and interior, and roof of woven cattail leaf. The roofs and exterior walls were thatched over with grasses and the windows were made of the translucent spider silk fabric and were shuttered on the first floor.

As they walked along the cobblestone streets, Croaker noted that the cobblestones were granite; it had been quarried from Granstone at the time of great city's inception. He watched as the rain splashed off the stone, pounding distorted ripples in the small pools that had formed in the worn, uneven places.

Lightning flashes caused strange shadows to appear and disappear like ghostly figures scurrying about the village as they approached the local inn.

Entering the inn, the atmosphere was warm and cozy. Croaker was glad to be out of the cold rain, enjoying the feel of the wood plank floor beneath his feet.

Looking around the main room he saw a fire was burning in a stone fireplace at the far end. Lined with clay brick, a warm light enveloped the room from its fire joining with the light of the bees wax candles in the lanterns that hung from sconces.

In front of the long wall across from the entrance, stood a bar with tall stools.

An elderly fairy stood behind the bar, serving up drinks, and engaged in jovial conversation with the two patrons seated there. Croaker smiled as the barman noticed him and continued surveying the room.

At the other end of the room a door led to the kitchen and next to it stairs leading to the guest rooms on the next floor. There were six tables, each large enough to seat four, spread throughout the room. Seven fairies occupied the room besides himself, the messenger and the innkeeper. A young couple sat at the table near the fireplace and three field hands sat at the table next to the bar while the two that were carrying on the conversation with the barman sat on stools at the opposite end.

Now all but the young couple had turned to see who the newcomers were.

"How can I help you, sires?" the innkeeper asked, breaking away from his conversation.

"We will need lodging for the night and food," The messenger said motioning Croaker to take a seat at the closest open table, "We will also need a slicker and hip pack for my companion if there are any available."

"You are in luck sire, I know the general store has a couple slickers for frogs in stock, I will get one for your friend in the morning. They are harder to come by the closer you get to Granstone. Your chances of finding one in that direction are not as good," the innkeeper, elaborated, "I guess that is because we are so close to Lily Pond. More demand you know."

"Thank you," the messenger replied and took his seat, "Could we have food and drink now?"

"Two house dinners for our new guests!" He called out to his wife who was in the kitchen. Then bringing them two goblets of berry brew, "Enjoy, sires, it is imported from Zarlan Grove," he said as he set them on the table, adding another comment before he left, "I am afraid you will have to share the last available room we have."

"That is quite alright, oh, and bring me a domain voucher. I will sign for everything," the messenger told him, "Wait, in the morning we will need some smoked fish jerky and roasted nuts to replenish our tack."

"Yes sire," the innkeeper agreed and went to retrieve a voucher from behind the bar.

It wasn't long before the innkeeper's wife arrived at the table carrying a large tray of food. As elderly as her husband, she still possessed the grace, both in movement and appearances, of a much younger woman. Setting down the tray on another table, she deftly placed the plates, platters and bowls in front of the two new guests and set the tray of food before them.

On the tray was a feast of barley broth, roast grasshopper thighs and grilled mushroom steaks accompanied by a berry brew and mint sauce. There were sautéed chives with roasted pine nuts and a large loaf of bread and bowl of honey.

"I hope this meets with your approval, sires," she smiled.

Croaker stared, stunned at the bounty, unable to speak.

"This will do very nicely, thank you," the messenger told her with a smile while looking at Croaker's reaction from the corner of his eye, "Eat up, Sire Ambassador, you are after all a guest of the King."

Sire Ambassador! Croaker hadn't even considered having a title, but he was representing Gribit and would have access to secret information.

"I guess that is exactly who I am now," he whispered his thoughts to himself, pleased by the title.

◆ ◆ ◆ ◆ ◆

Though the storm raged above the waters of Lily Pond the city deep below maintained its perpetual calm. The great spider-silk dome glowed a pale iridescent green as light from phosphor deposits at the bottom of the pond emitted their constant light.

At the center of the dome was the palace of Queen Isalia with apartments for the workers extending outward from the palace. At the periphery of the dome were the military quarters.

Though this was a female society, the warriors were the most ferocious fighters in the realm of Lily Pond and the surrounding domains. Their society was formed by the offspring of fairies and pixies, who being always female, were rejected by both those societies.

Being a single sex society presented an unusual problem, how to perpetuate itself. The solution lay in other smaller domed areas in the pond, where they kept captured fairies and pixies as breeders in order to maintain their numbers.

After Croaker had swum off, Gribit swam to the depths of Lily Pond entering the dome through one of the many tunnel entrances of the city.

Now, as he sat in the meeting chamber that looked out over the city, he and Isalia were discussing the message that had been received from Arklan.

"That is ridiculous," Isalia retorted, "the very idea of Toads and Slithers joining forces! Next you will be telling me they plan to invade one of the domains."

"If this sighting is accurate, then it is not impossible," Gribit responded, "and as I said, a slither was sighted in this domain early this morning."

Isalia was thinking deeply about what Gribit had just said. She rose and walked to the edge of the chamber.

The pale green light of the city cast its hue on her alabaster skin and white gossamer gown. Her ebony black hair framed her face as the lines of concern that were forming at her forehead deepened.

Isalia had many of the fairy features, although, like all nymphs, she was of a stockier build and shorter than the fairies, a pixie trait.

She thought about the different possibilities that could develop. No matter which domain were attacked, providing this was the case, it would not be good for Lily Pond. She would surely have to form an alliance with that domain, or if it were hers then she would most likely need the assistance of the other domains. This was a position she hadn't found herself in before and the prospect did not please her. The current balance was tenuous enough.

Turning back to face Gribit, "I can not take any action without knowing the complete situation," she informed him.

"I am aware of that Your Majesty. That is why I sent my young friend Croaker to Arklan's court," he explained, "He is to inform me of any important developments as soon as possible."

"Are you going to tell the other domains what *might* be happening?" she wondered with concern of saying anything that was speculation.

"No, I am going to have the ambassadors send back written sealed reports right away if anything out of the ordinary happens in their domain," he said, trying to set her at ease.

"That in itself could cause alarm," she pointed out, "They will be wondering what you think might be happening that would warrant secret reports from their domains."

"I know that, but we have to get a handle on everything that is happening as soon as possible," he emphasized.

Isalia knew that Gribit had taken all into account and based on the sketchy information they had she now decided what action she should take.

"I will have to put my military on alert because of this you know," Isalia was stating the obvious.

"I would expect as much," he replied, knowing that was the only logical step for her to take.

Isalia reached for a cord near the entrance of the chamber. Shortly after pulling on it a dark hair girl appeared, bowing as she entered.

"Your Majesty rang?" the young nymph asked.

"Yes, show our guest to his quarters and attend to his needs." Isalia ordered the girl.

"Yes, Your Majesty." The girl acknowledged, bowed and motioned to Gribit to follow her.

"I will have someone wake you early, you can wait till then to send your messengers to contact the ambassadors," the queen told him as he followed the girl toward the door.

"Thank you, Your Majesty, and good night," Gribit replied, bowing and then disappearing through the entrance.

◆ ◆ ◆ ◆ ◆

Croaker woke to the sounds of the movement throughout the inn and the smell of breakfast being cooked in the kitchen below. The pale glow of day's first light was cast upon the room through the second floor oriel; a small bay window that was typical of the houses in the village.

As Croaker propped himself up from the bed with his elbow, the messenger entered the room, "It is about time you woke, Sire Ambassador, " he said with a smile, "the innkeeper has gone to the general store to get our supplies. Breakfast is waiting for us."

As they descended the stairs Croaker noticed that the field hands had just finished their breakfast and were exiting through the front door of the inn, to their jobs, as the innkeeper's wife emerged from the kitchen with a tray in hand.

"Sires, your breakfast is ready," she said looking up at them as she passed by the stairs. "We have an oat porridge, bread and honey, sassafras tea and if you like I can bring fresh eggs," she continued while she set their places at the nearest table.

"That will be fine," the messenger said, glancing at Croaker and seeing him nod in agreement.

As they sat and ate, the messenger talked about the journey and how long it would take them to reach Granstone, "We should reach the city by the mid-day. King Arklan will be expecting us about then. I had another messenger sent ahead to inform him that we were coming when we stopped at the checkpoint last night."

Before they had finished their meal the innkeeper returned from the general store with all their new supplies.

Croaker examined his new slicker, folding it and placing it in the new hip pack along with the tack and then belted it around his waist.

"It feels a little strange," he commented to the messenger.

"You will get accustomed to it soon enough," the messenger smiled back, "We should get started now."

Thanking the innkeeper and his wife for their hospitality, the travelers exited through the door to the still wet streets and turned south, leaving the innkeeper and his wife to speculate on why a King's messenger and a frog would be traveling together.

As they walked down the granite cobblestone, a low fog hung just above the ground and the smell of the damp air from the night's storm filled their nostrils. Songbirds were chirping their morning songs in the calm morning air as the land around was slowly coming to life and the light of the day was taking on an orange-yellow glow as the sun was peaking above the eastern horizon. When they reached the edge of the village the cobblestone gave way to the furrowed ruts, now with standing water, of the road south.

◆ ◆ ◆ ◆ ◆

The iridescent green glow was beginning to fade as the pale light of the sun filtered down to the depths of the domed city. The rhythmic sound of the pumps around the city, though barely audible, vibrated like heartbeats throughout the early morning quiet as they brought the fresh air to the city through the hollow reeds that stretched high above the waters surface.

Gribit was beginning to wake when the young nymph knocked at his chamber.

"Sire, it is time for you to rise," her gentle voice brought him the rest of the way to full consciousness.

"Thank you!" he replied.

"Your breakfast is ready, Sire," she informed him, "Would you like me to escort you to the dining area?"

"No, that is not necessary. I know my way around, thank you."

"As you wish Sire," she said.

Gribit could hear her footsteps as they faded away from his door.

After freshening himself at the basin in his chamber Gribit made his way down the long hallway, passing several doors that led to other chambers along the way, his nearly silent footsteps echoing off the smooth limestone walls as he padded his way to the dining area.

Approaching the entrance he could hear the clanking of dishes and the many voices of the workers as they ate and conversed in preparation of their day's work.

Entering the large open room he searched out an empty table and sat down. Noting his arrival a kitchen nymph immediately brought his breakfast to him.

"What would you like to drink with your meal?" she asked.

"Just some hot tea," he replied, looking up and giving her a smile, "Oh, I would like paper and pen," he added.

"Yes Sire, I will see to it at once," she said with a slight bow.

Walking across the room she stopped to talk to another nymph and then continued on to get Gribit his tea as the second nymph exited the room.

While he was still eating, the second nymph reappeared through the doorway with a broad flat wooden box in hand. "Your paper and pen, Sire," she said as she handed the box to Gribit.

"Thank you," he said, then after wiping his mouth with his napkin, "will you please wait a moment?"

Opening the box he took out a sheet of paper along with a quill and removed the stopper on the stone bottle of ink that was also within. Quickly jotting down the names of three frogs, Gribit handed the paper with the names to the nymph, "Have someone locate these three and have them report to me in the meeting chamber as soon as possible."

"Yes, Sire," she said, sensing the importance of the task from the urgency in his voice.

Collecting the box, she turned and hurried off through the doorway once again. Making her way through the palace to the messenger quarters, she presented the note to the Commander and explained Gribit's request.

Soon three messengers were on their way, a single frog's name in each of their possession, headed for the tube lifts to the

40

surface. Entering a tube they stepped on the wooden platform, that fit snug to the circular wall, then signaled the operator to close and seal the entrance.

Calling through a voice tube to the surface, the operator informed her counterpart that passengers were on their way. Pumping the nearest of two handles, water flowed in under the platform and began to lift it toward the surface with each stroke of the handle while the partner lift descended. As the operator pumped she watched an indicator gauge, to know when the lifts had reached their destinations, allowing her to open the entrance to the companion lift for its next use.

Reaching the surface, the messengers stepped out on to a large, floating dock that appeared to be an island a short distance off the southeast shore of Lily Pond.

The dock was moored to the twin lifts with a float collar around each and this also allowed the top section of the lift to rise· and fall with the changing depth of the pond. On the opposite end were another set of twin lifts and on the shore side were the stables where the messengers' steeds were housed.

Mounting their steeds each left in search of the frog assigned to her.

◆ ◆ ◆ ◆ ◆

When Croaker hadn't returned and the storm clouds had begun to roll in, Webber, Lily Pad and Lotus grew concerned. Webber had swum out to Gribit's pad only to find that both Croaker and Gribit were nowhere to be found. Now it was a new day and still no word from either of them! As Webber approached the shore through the grasses he found Lily Pad and Lotus waiting there.

"Any sign of him?" he asked.

"No," Lily replied, showing concern, "We have not heard a sound from Gribit's pad."

"Maybe you two should go home for now; I will swim out to Gribit's pad and come tell you anything I find out as soon as I know."

Although they weren't happy about the suggestion they agreed, weaving their way through the tall grasses as they left.

Remembering the experience that Croaker had the previous day, Webber looked for signs of Old Big Fin before entering the water. As he swam out to the lily pads he saw nymphs in their outrigger canoes seining for shiners that would later be filleted and smoked for jerky, in the smoke houses along the shore.

In the shallows a crew of nymphs were busy harvesting cattails for the leaves and cotton. This would have been by all accounts a normal day if it weren't for the fact that Croaker and Gribit had gone missing.

Webber had scarcely reached Gribit's pad when he noticed the iridescent colors of the giant dragonfly and a nymph messenger, riding in the saddle behind its head, approaching him from the shore where he and the girls had parted.

"Sire, are you Webber?" she asked as she landed next to him, "I was told he would be here by one called Lily."

"Yes," Webber responded with a puzzled look on his face.

"I have a message from the Sage, Gribit, for you Sire," the nymph continued, "He would like you to report to him in the meeting chamber of the palace."

"Do you know why?" he asked, mystified but happy to know the old frog's whereabouts. *Croaker must be there as well*; he thought.

"No," she answered, "I only know that it is urgent and he would like you to go there immediately."

Webber knew that Gribit wasn't in the habit of giving commands unless they were necessary.

"Tell him I am on my way," he told her and then thanked her for the message.

Watching the nymph and her dragonfly shrink into the distance toward the floating dock, Webber thought about the girls; *they would simply have to wait until he returned to get the news of Gribit and Croaker's whereabouts.* Jumping into the water he swam to the depths of Lily Pond and the tunnel entrances of the city.

◆◆◆◆◆

Fernon woke in a sweat, his heart pounding.

"Are you alright?" Nedalia asked, reaching out her hand and gently brushing his forehead.

"Yes, I was merely having a bad dream," he reassured her.

"Is it because of the things that have been happening?" she asked.

43

"I am afraid so," he replied, "My actions could have dire consequences if I am wrong."

"Does this have anything to do with Obrin?"

"Yes, but I cannot tell you what it is at this time," he said, afraid he had already said too much.

"I am sure that you are doing what is best for our citizens," she smiled at him.

Though she wanted to lighten the burden he carried, she understood the need for security. She still resented being left out, even if it was for her own sake. Sometimes Fernon treated her like spiders thread!

"That reminds me, I have to travel to Broadleaf and inspect the warehouses there," he said as he swung his legs over the side of the bed, "there is a shipment of goods coming from Arklan's in a couple of days and the scribe will be at Broadleaf sometime later today. He will have the inventories of items to be shipped out to the other domains."

"I do not see why the frogs could not handle it by themselves," Nedalia said, disappointed that he had to leave. Time together was precious and there had not been much of late. The time of trade negotiations was always busy for Fernon.

"I am sure they could," he acknowledged, "but the citizens will expect to see me there," then smiling added, "I am sure they would like to see *you* there as well."

"I will have the nanny watch the children," she said, surprised but happily accepting his invitation.

After freshening up for the day, Fernon and Nedalia descended the staircase from their chamber to the common room and into the dining area. Taking their seats, a kitchen maid approached the table to inquire what they would like for breakfast. As the maid left for the kitchen the nanny and two children entered the room.

"Good morning father. Good morning mother," the boy and girl said.

"And a good morning to you children!" Fernon smiled back.

"Come, give us a hug," Nedalia opened her arms.

"Good morning, Your Majesties," the nanny bowed before making her way toward the kitchen to have her breakfast with the rest of the staff.

"Nanny! The King and I are going to Broadleaf this morning so you will be in complete charge of the children until our return," Nedalia told her before she had left the room.

Stopping near the exit to the kitchen, the children's nanny acknowledged the order, "Yes, Your Majesty."

"See that they do not miss their studies. I do not want them to think that this is a vacation from them while we are gone," Nedalia said, looking at the children as she did. "Yes, Your Majesty," the nanny responded, bowing and exiting to the kitchen before the Queen could add any more tasks for her.

After breakfast, Fernon called the Commander of the Guard, having him assign an additional six troops to accompany him to Broadleaf. With all that happened he wanted to be prepared for anything, especially with the Queen in attendance.

◆ ◆ ◆ ◆ ◆

Airlein had already finished her morning meal after seeing the ambassador off for Lily Pond to speak to Gribit. She was returning to her chambers when General Broadstem met her in the corridor.

"Your Majesty," he said with a quick bow, "I believe you should come to the war room with me. There have been some new developments."

"What kind?" she asked.

"In the past few minutes we received word that Arklan has increased all his patrols," he answered.

"First Fernon and now Arklan? I wonder if Arklan's is a response to Fernon?" she speculated.

"Arklan's increase of patrols is throughout his entire domain," Broadstem replied.

"Let us have a look at the map," Airlein said as they entered the war room.

They had just started to analyze the map when a messenger entered the room carrying a message from one of Airlein's scouts in the west. She looked bewildered as she read the message.

General Broadstem read the concern on her face as she read the words on the paper.

"It seems that one of Arklan's messengers was seen leaving Lily Pond with a frog in his company prior to the rains. They were headed toward Granstone," she said.

"A fairy is able to enter and leave Lily Pond?" the General was incredulous! "It would appear that Isalia is involved in these happenings as well!" he concluded.

"I think we definitely need to hear from the frogs before we can come to any conclusions," Airlein said.

"Nonetheless, it would be prudent to move reinforcements along our northern and western borders," he suggested, looking down at the map.

"I will take that under advisement, but for now increase the patrols in those areas. I think we should increase them in the south as well. I have this feeling . . . we should not neglect that area," she ordered.

The General nodded, accepting the orders.

"I can also increase our strength at Loamis," he said thoughtfully, "We should be receiving our trade goods soon and the warehouses are full with goods to go to the other domains."

"A good suggestion," Airlein said, nodding.

"I will send one of my agents to see if he can get any information from the scribe when he arrives at Loamis," Broadstem offered, "He may have seen or heard something at Arklan's palace."

"The frogs are well trained to keep things to themselves," Airlein reminded him, adding, "I for one, am glad that they are."

"If the negotiations broke down we would know for sure that something is amiss," he replied.

So far, no one really knew what was going on and fear and speculation were already spreading through the five domains, threatening to cause the panic they all wanted to avoid.

"I would not expect that. If negotiations broke down I am sure we would have been summoned. On the other hand, if someone was up to something they would want everything to appear normal," she pointed out, "That is what I would do."

"Well something is happening and someone knows what it is," Broadstem said, his frustration showing through.

"I do not mean to tie your hands, but I have to approach this from a diplomatic view and not just a military one!" she reminded him.

"Yes, Your Majesty, though at times the two are the same," Broadstem said as he bowed and left the war room to carry out his orders.

Airlein stared at the relief map mulling over the information she had. She had a foreboding that *something* was looming on the horizon, that was greater than anything they had seen before and caution was the only way to approach it.

◆◆◆◆◆

Emerging from the tunnel entrance, Webber found himself in a small quiet pool at the inside edge of the dome. From the pool ran a small incline that reached the streets of the city and at the top of the rise stood a sentry, waiting for his approach.

"Sire frog, can I assist you?" she asked pushing the tall wooden staff she held out and pulling it back in salute.

"I am to meet Gribit, the Sage, in the palace meeting chamber. Can you direct me to him?" he asked.

"Yes, Sire. Go to the main entrance of the palace, near the city's center and ask the sentry there for a guide. She will take you the rest of the way," she instructed, pointing the way.

"Thank you," he replied, leaving in the direction she indicated.

The streets were four rings of decreasing size and spoke connectors that decreased, by half in numbers, each consecutive ring toward the center of the city.

As he walked, Webber passed between the gardens bordering the limestone buildings, giving splashes of color in the flickering, muted light. The buildings stair stepped a level at each ring with elevated enclosed walkways over the street, connecting them to one another. Overhead, he saw the arches that formed the skeletal structure to support the fabric of the dome in the event that the air pressure failed to. Looking behind him, Webber could see the translucent tunnel domes, leading to the buildings outside the main dome, which housed the tube lifts.

Reaching the inner ring street, he crossed and ascended two steps to the palace approach, which funneled into a broad courtyard. At the far end of the courtyard stood two sentries, one on each side of the large, arched, palace entrance.

"I was told I should ask for a guide to take me to the meeting chamber," he told one of the sentries, introducing himself.

"Corporal of the guard!" the sentry called out.

A young military nymph appeared at the door.

"Yes," she said.

"Sire frog wishes an escort to the meeting chamber," the sentry informed her.

"Sire, follow me please," the nymph said, motioning to Webber as she turned and headed in the direction from which she had come.

Finally arriving at the meeting chamber, Webber found Gribit standing at the opening that looked out over the city.

"Sire Webber. To see Sire Gribit," the escort announced.

Turning from the balcony, Gribit replied, "That will be all for now," dismissing the escort and smiling at Webber.

"You made it in good time," Gribit said, motioning Webber to take a seat.

"I was at your pad when the messenger found me," Webber replied.

"You were at my pad?" Gribit asked, curious. One did not encroach on another's pad in Lily Pond.

"I was looking for Croaker," he said, "Lily, Lotus and I were concerned when he did not return yesterday."

"Ah! He is alright," Gribit, informed him, "I sent him on an errand."

"Then Croaker is not here?" Webber asked, "Where is he?"

"I sent him to Arklan's court," Gribit answered, "But now to you. I have a task for you as well."

"What kind of task?" Webber asked, wondering how long he would be gone, "Is it the same as Croakers?"

Dismissing the question of Croaker, Gribit looked into Webber's eyes.

"I need you to travel to Millville. When you get there, deliver this message to the ambassador," He said, handing him a sealed envelope, "Haste is of the utmost importance."

"I will leave immediately, just as soon as I tell Lily and Lotus about Croaker," he said, turning for the door.

"No!" Gribit's tongue shot out, whapping Webber's head and stopping him in his tracks, "Go without stopping for anything. I have made arrangements for a gray bush-tail mount from Isalia's south shore stables. Not a word about Croaker to anyone! And this message is to fall into no other hands than the Ambassador's. Is that understood?"

Sensing the gravity of the situation, Webber nodded, rubbing his head as he turned back around, sheepishly. His eyes still held many questions.

Bush-tails were usually reserved as scribe mounts and as teams for the wagons and carriages, which transported goods and liaisons from one domain to another. As Webber tried to sort things out he wondered why he was being sent to the Rolling Hills when he had spent so much time learning the routes of the Endless Forest. Things were happening so fast that Webber didn't even associate Lily and Lotus's encounter with the slither to what was happening at the moment.

Gribit could see that Webber had questions, "Remember haste and caution, there is danger out there that is not yet fully understood."

As Webber was leaving the room two other frogs entered with their escort and were announced to Gribit. He surmised that they had similar tasks to perform. Head still spinning from Gribit's tongue; he hoped they would be wiser.

Retracing his steps, Webber left through the tunnel entrance he had arrived in as he began his journey to the capital city of the Pixies.

CHAPTER THREE

The sun was higher in the sky and the ground fog had burned off as Croaker and the messenger neared the crossroads that led west, to Hillside, trade hub of the Pixies, and east to Loamis, the trade hub for the Eastern Field Fairy domain. Approaching them from the south were two frog riders on their bush-tail mounts.

"Good morning Sires," one of the riders, said.

"Good morning," both Croaker and the messenger responded.

Bringing their mounts to a halt, the other rider asked, "Where do you hail from?"

"I am returning from the outpost at Weavertown," The messenger quickly said, "I met Sire frog at the village on his pilgrimage to Granstone and so we decided to travel together for the company. Will you be stopping there?"

"No, I have to be in Broadleaf this day and my friend has to be in Lily Pond," the rider replied.

"Any news from Granstone?" the messenger asked.

"None to speak of," the rider said, "But we must be off now."

"May your journey be swift and safe," the messenger said.

"And yours as well," the rider said as he reined his mount to proceed.

Croaker and the messenger watched as the two riders disappeared into the distance of the road north before returning on their way. Though neither party had given much information, a lot had been said in the protocol and the messenger's deliberate lie.

"Why did you say we met at the village?" Croaker asked.

"I did not think it wise to let anyone know that I had been sent to Lily Pond," the messenger said.

"Do you know the contents of the message you delivered to Gribit?" Croaker asked warily. Perhaps the messenger knew more that he was telling.

"No, but it must be very important or else I would not have been sent directly to the Sage," he replied.

"Yes, you are right about that," Croaker said, keeping his suspicions to himself. No one seemed to know what was going on but everyone seemed nervous about it.

The two continued on, neither wanting to speak about the message anymore. As they walked, the messenger thought of an apparent need of Croaker's and how he could resolve it for him.

"When we get to Granstone I will see that a bush-tail is available for you, Sire," the messenger said.

"I would not know how to ride one," Croaker admitted.

"That will not be a problem, Sire," the messenger assured him, "We have instructors that can teach you in a very short time."

Croaker knew that what the messenger said was true. His friend Webber had been trained after he was selected to the trade liaison corps. He said it had been easy to learn.

"I guess I should learn, I will need the speed if I am to deliver information to Gribit in a short time," he reasoned.

Reaching the crossroads, Granstone loomed higher in the southern horizon. Croaker was beginning to appreciate the scope of the city's size. In all the stories he had heard about Granstone, he had not been able to truly grasp its grandeur.

"We are right on schedule to reach Granstone at the mid-day," the messenger noted.

"I am looking forward to it," Croaker replied, excited by the prospect.

As they continued on Croaker gave thought to how the recent events had made such big changes in his life. He was now a frog of responsibility and he was looking forward to his new additional challenge of having to learn to ride a bush-tail.

◆ ◆ ◆ ◆ ◆

It was nearly the mid-day on the road that led southeast from Lily Pond, just north of Loamis, when Gribit's messenger to Airlein's domain encountered the carriage carrying the ambassador on his way to see Gribit. Reining in his mount, the frog messenger greeted the carriage driver, "Is that the Ambassador you carry?"

"Yes, it is," the driver replied.

Moving to the carriage door the messenger leaned over, "Sire Ambassador, I carry a message for you from the Sage, Gribit."

"Thank you," the ambassador said, taking the message from the rider.

"Are you continuing to Zarlan Grove or returning to Gribit's pad?" the Ambassador asked as he read the message.

"Neither Sire, I will be returning to the domed city to report back to Gribit," the messenger said.

"Gribit is with Isalia?" the Ambassador looked up with surprise.

"Yes, Sire."

"Driver, we will be going to Isalia's southern shore stables," the Ambassador directed.

"Thank you," he said to the messenger, "Inform Gribit that I am on my way to discuss matters with him."

"Yes, Sire," the messenger said as he turned his mount around and was off for Lily Pond.

"Continue on," the Ambassador commanded.

◆◆◆◆◆

Webber had ridden throughout the morning and was now headed north toward the mouth of the Winding Creek. He was entering the pixie town of Limonite, a mining town near the pixie mines. Stopping at the local stables to rest his bush-tail, he looked for the local inn. A gruff looking pixie, his face soot smudged and wearing a leather apron, had been working at the forge when he

56

arrived. Seeing Webber, he set down his bellows and approached him.

"Can I be of assistance Sire frog," the smith asked.

"Give my gray some feed," Webber replied, "I need some refreshment, could you direct me to the inn?"

"Yes, Sire frog," the pixie said, "You will find it at the end of the street and one block south."

"Thank you, please have him ready to leave when I return," Webber asked as he looked about the town, "Where are all your citizens?"

"You will find most of them gathered at the inn," He replied, "They are having a town meeting."

Webber crossed the street and headed west. As he walked down the boardwalk he passed several kinds of stores and offices. The buildings where constructed of different materials. Some were brick; others were of stone while yet others were of wood. They all had woven cattail leaf roofs that were thatched with grasses and windows of multi pane glass. To Webber it reminded him of a patchwork quilt but laid out in a functional pattern that was pleasing to the eye. Two blocks later, at the end of the street, turning the corner he was heading south and found himself about to enter the residential area of the town. Here the homes were made of wood but had a similar style to the homes found in a fairy village. At the end of the block he saw a sign hanging above the entrance of the inn, it read 'Journey's Rest'.

Webber heard the commotion even before he had entered. It was as if they were all talking at the same time.

"I tell you, it was the nymphs!" he heard one of the pixies say as he entered the door.

"We have no way of telling for sure," another replied.

The pixie at the bar banged a wooden hammer down several times to bring the assembly to order. When they all finally quieted down the pixie with the gavel spoke, "We can not jump to conclusions, we have to send for the intermediary to find out for sure if it was the nymphs. Is there anyone here that will go to Millville to get the ambassador?"

No one had seen Webber enter their midst so they were surprised when he spoke up, "I am on my way to Millville to see the ambassador!"

Webber looked around the room, and then continued, "I am delivering a message to him and I can deliver a message for you as well."

"Sire frog, you came at a most opportune time for us," the pixie behind the bar said, "Several of our children are missing and it is believed that the nymphs are behind it. The citizens of my town are ready to go to war."

"Why do you think the nymphs are responsible?" he asked.

"We have searched everywhere for the children and there is no sign of them anywhere," the pixie answered, "It is like they vanished. The nymphs have taken captives in the past although this would be the first time they have taken children."

58

"You should not act in haste. I will give your message to the ambassador and he can find out if the nymphs are behind this," Webber said, "When did this happen?"

"The children were missing last evening and we have searched through the night. With that many there would have been signs," the pixie said, "We will wait for the ambassador to check into this, but in the meantime as mayor of this town I am calling the militia to assemble just in case."

"How many children are missing?" he asked.

"Five!" the mayor said.

"With the rains that came in the afternoon they might have sought shelter somewhere," Webber said.

"We considered that. That is why we checked the mines and other places they might have gone," the mayor responded with a note of irritation in his voice at the perceived criticism.

"Were they all together?" he asked, ignoring the mayor's indignation.

"No, they were not, they were from different parts of the town," the mayor said.

"I will relay these facts to the ambassador," Webber told the mayor.

"Thank you, Sire frog. When will you be on your way?" the mayor asked.

"I stopped in your town to refresh myself and rest my mount. If I can get some bread and berry brew I will return to my travels. I have two urgent messages to deliver now," Webber said looking around for a place to sit.

"Innkeeper, see that Sire frog gets what he needs so he can be on his way," the mayor ordered the pixie standing at the end of the bar, "The rest of you go home now and the militia members will report back here with their gear."

As the citizens of the town filed out of the inn, Webber found a chair at a table not far from the door as the innkeeper, a middle-aged pixie, slender in build for a pixie, blue-black hair that hung to his shoulders and emerald green eyes, was already bringing him his bread and brew.

"Sire frog," he said hesitantly, "My name is Puck. If I might be so bold, I would like to accompany you."

"Puck, I have to deliver these messages as soon as possible. I can not be slowed down by anyone," Webber looked at him wondering why this innkeeper wanted to go along with him.

"I would not slow you down at all, I have a red bush-tail that I keep in the stable," he quickly said.

"Why do you want to ride with me?" Webber asked.

"One of the children missing is my youngest son," Puck replied, "My eldest son and my wife can take care of the inn."

"Can your red keep up with a gray?" he asked the innkeeper.

Puck responded, "The question should be can your gray keep up with my red?"

"OK," accepting Puck's company, "My name is Webber."

"Thank you, Sire Webber. If there is trouble on the road you will find that I am a better than average fighter," Puck said, wanting to make sure there was plenty of reason for Webber to have accepted his company. Now that it had been settled, he hurried to tell his wife and son what had been decided.

The idea of trouble and of having to fight had never crossed Webber's mind before this. He was a frog and a citizen of all five domains; this meant that he was never involved in that kind of situation. Puck's comment put Gribit's warning foremost in his mind now, *"Remember haste and caution, there is danger out there that is not yet fully understood."*

Webber quickly ate his bread and downed his brew. "We must leave now!" he called to Puck.

Puck had anticipated that someone would have to be sent to get the ambassador and planned to volunteer to make the trip to Millville, before Webber had spoken up, so he sent his wife to bring him his hip pack and sword for the journey.

As Webber and Puck were on their way out the door, Puck's wife handed him his gear. She looked deep into his eyes with a look that told him to be safe and to find out what had happened to their son then gave him a quick kiss good bye.

When they entered the stable Puck called to the smith, "Get Fleetfoot out for me!" he ordered.

"Right away Sire Puck," the smith said, "He's been a bit restless!"

The smith went to the stalls and led out the largest red that Webber had ever seen.

"Why he's nearly the size of a gray!" Webber said in amazement.

"Yes, he is one of a kind. It took some doing, but after many tries we finally succeeded in breeding a red and a gray. Fleetfoot is the result," Puck said with pride.

Fleetfoot stood only slightly shorter than Webber's gray and he was eager to run.

It took only a few moments for Puck and the smith to saddle Fleetfoot. Webber's gray had been made ready for his return to the stable, by the smith, as Webber had ordered.

There was determination of purpose that was evident in Puck's face as he swung up into the saddle.

"Put Sire Webber's fee on my voucher," Puck told the smith.

Webber mounted his gray, "Thank you Puck. Let us not waste any more time!" he said.

"I will learn the fate of my son, Webber! As for those that caused this ill, let their ancestors have mercy on them because I will not!" Puck said as they wheeled their mounts out of the stable and onto the road to Millville.

Northward they rode on the border road with the scrub brush of the Rolling Hills on their left and the tall marshland grasses of Lily Pond on their right. The road gradually turning toward the west as they approached Winding Creek near its mouth where it opened into Lily Pond. From here Webber could see that it ran parallel to Winding Creek due west toward Millville.

The scrub grew thicker along the creek and the hills were speckled with small clusters of sumac and low growing yew.

Following the road west, they passed the first of the mills. This was the large grain mill, its great wheel turning steadily in the side channel the Pixies cut into the southern bank to parallel Winding Creek and control the water flow.

Upstream from the mill were the rapids and a short distance above them the bridge crossing at the narrows that led to Whitewater, home of the pixies that operated the grain mill and a lumber mill on the northern bank a little further up stream.

The rest of the way was wilderness until Millville, where the pixies established the original grain and lumber mills and was now home to the brickworks as well.

As they rode, the sun moved further into the west and slowly dropped behind the western hills. Reaching the top of the rise that looked down on Millville and the wide lazy bend of Winding Creek in the valley below, they could see the ferry making its way from the northern shore, its lantern already lit in the darkness of the deep shadow cast by the hills.

◆◆◆◆◆

The sun was low in the western sky and the shadows grew deeper under the forest canopy as Fernon and Nedalia and their company neared Broadleaf. The travel had gone well, and they had made good time as they intermittently flew and walked the trade road through the forest southeast toward Broadleaf. The only thing out of the ordinary was meeting a frog messenger riding to Lone Oak to deliver a message to the Ambassador.

They had stopped only once to take refreshment at the halfway village of Raven's Roost where the treetop villagers dropped their daily chores and an impromptu festival began to honor the arrival of their King and Queen.

Though their stay was short they could hear the festival continuing long after their departure. Fernon knew that when they reached Broadleaf it would be a repeat of the festival, only on a larger scale.

Suddenly a point scout came rushing back to the column and reported to the Commander of the Guard. They talked briefly and the scout returned in the direction he had come from while the Commander approached Fernon.

"Your Majesty," he said, "The point scouts have reported that there is a large group of searchers at the pool in Bale's Hollow."

"Do you know what they are searching for?" Fernon asked.

"Two of the children from Broadleaf had gone there to swim and did not return," the Commander explained.

"How long ago?" Fernon asked apprehensively.

"They left Broadleaf in the early morning." The Commander continued, "The strange thing is that there is absolutely no sign of them at all. Even them having been there."

A pained look of concern crossed Fernon's face. Surveying the surrounding area, he looked over to Nedalia, and saw that she had lost the color in her face and stood there as if she were holding her breath. She was taking in what Fernon and the Commander were discussing, and this together with the knowledge that something had happened to bring Obrin into the picture disturbed her deeply. Her thoughts were of her own children's safety as well as the safety of the missing children of Broadleaf.

"Commander, we will continue on to Broadleaf, then you and a contingent return and assist the searchers," he ordered, "Look for signs that the villagers would not think to look for. I will want a complete report of your findings."

"Yes, Your Majesty," he said, accepting his orders, "It will be dark soon, do you want us to start during the night or wait until morning?"

"The sooner we start the better the chance of finding clues," he said, his words intensified by the stare of his eyes.

Fernon turned his gaze to Nedalia and gave her a reassuring look as they moved on again.

Because of the distance between Lone Oak and Lily Pond and the forest that lies between, Fernon wasn't aware of the previous day's warning alarm that Gribit had sounded. He also didn't know about a similar event that had taken place at the Pixie town of Limonite, so he had no reason to consider any other options for these events other than what he concluded.

Fernon did not give voice to his thoughts as the procession moved along. *First the missing scouts and now missing children. The Nymphs had never taken children captive before, but this had the appearance that they were behind the sudden disappearances. If Isalia is behind this she will pay dearly. No one harms our children!*

CHAPTER FOUR

Beyond the southern borders of the domains of the Rolling Hills and Southern Field Fairies lay the uncharted wastelands. Deep in the heart of this land and seldom thought of, live the Imps.

The Imps, unlike the Fairies and Pixies, live to mold nature to their needs through industry, while the Fairies and Pixies believe that industry can coexist with nature.

Centuries ago the Imps and their minions, toads and slithers, after trying to impose their will on the inhabitance of Lily Pond had been driven from the realm in an epic struggle that engulfed the entire realm. There had been three decisive battles won by the unified forces; the Fairies and Pixies with the aid of the Frogs. First was the battle at Slither Clearing where King Bale and King Arlen had split the Imp forces and drove them south. Next were the victories of Bale's Hollow and of Arlen's Rise, the later obtained with the loss of King Arlen. The fairy, General Zarlan, then led that eastern contingent of the forces as they re-combined with the western forces of King Bale to push the Imps completely out of the realm to the south, into what has now become the wasteland.

There were only three domains bordering Lily Pond at this time. These domains were the Forest, Fields and Rolling Hills. Some of the Pixies and Fairies commingled and the result of these unions brought about the first of the Nymphs, the offspring always female, were rejected by both the Fairies and the Pixies. Being rejected by both fairies and pixies, they sought refuge in Lily Pond itself. Soon after, struggles within the domain of the Fields led to it breaking into the two separated domains, Southern and Eastern, bringing about the five domains that exist now.

As time passed nothing had been heard from the surviving Imps while the slithers turned on the toads without the Imp control.

Now, moving through the moonless starlit night, a force of toads and slithers position themselves to attack the southern most mining town, Feldspar, of the Rolling Hills nearest the Southern Field Fairy domain.

"Remember," the Toad Commander said, "No survivors! This is to appear to be a fairy attack! Those are our orders."

"We can not eat our kill?" a slither asked in his loud whisper voice.

"Only one for each of you, no more!" he glared back, "The Lord DeMonas has given his orders."

"Yes Sir," the slither replied, fear flashing in his eyes at the mention of the Goblin King of the Imps.

"Archers, ready your bows and make sure your arrows are fairy arrows. The rest of you ready your swords," the Toad Commander spate out the orders.

Silently they encircled the sleeping town then entered the homes one by one and slew the Pixies in their sleep. As they worked their way toward the center of the town, the Pixies started to wake as the sound of cries rang out in the night. In one of the homes a young Pixie that had been wounded managed to find a hiding place where he had gone undetected by the toads and slithers.

Overhead, as the battle raged, an Imp General circled on his giant bat watching the carnage below. When it was all over he landed near the Toad Commander.

"Gather up our dead and wounded," he ordered, "Leave no evidence of us to be found."

"Yes Sir," the Commander replied, "It *will* appear the fairies made this attack."

"Make it quick! It will be daylight before long and we have to be well away from here by then," the General scowled then, reining his bat, left to report the success of the night to Lord DeMonas.

◆ ◆ ◆ ◆ ◆

Croaker woke with a start, panic trying to set in as his eyes were trying to cut through the unyielding blackness that covered them like a smothering veil. His heart pounding as the feeling of uneasiness grabbed at his very soul with a crushing pressure on his chest making every breath an effort. Long moments of struggle passed until the realization of where he was finally began to set in. Slowly calmness returned and he reached out, his hand finding the cover of the light globe at the bedside table. Opening it with a twist of his hand a blue-white light lurched out and filled the room with its moonlight glow.

The pall of something unexplained hung heavily in the air as Croaker gradually regained his composure. It had only been a short time since he had managed to finally sleep though he was tired from the trip to Granstone and the events after his arrival.

Though this uneasy feeling was so strong, the excitement at the sights and sounds of the city that he'd experienced when he first entered the gates was still with him.

As Croaker sat up he pulled the bell cord at the head of the bed. Then swinging his legs over the side, he stood and began to pace while trying to exorcise the feeling of gloom by thinking about those sights and events.

"Welcome to Granstone, Sire Ambassador," the messenger said, as Croaker looked up at the top of the entrance as they passed through the gates of the outer palisade into the bailey. There were stables to the left of the entrance and a training area to the right just beyond a smithy and forge. Ahead was the entrance to the second and taller palisade and atop, behind the battlement parapets, he could see the sentries on duty. Near the top of the second palisade entrance to either side were sculpted fairies that jutted out from the wall as if they were in flight. The one on the right was holding a bow with a quiver of arrows slung over his back while the other carried a scythe in one hand and a bundle of grasses under the other arm. Inside the second entrance, a market place stretched in either direction around the city. A fountain stood at the center of the bailey. Across the open bailey Croaker saw the entrances to the city quarters and the palace that rose above all within the walls.

Croaker turned to the door at the sound of the knock and a voice.

"You rang, Sire?"

"Yes," he responded, as he opened the door, "I would like some berry brew, if you please."

"Yes, Sire," the page replied, then seeing that Croaker looked like he was disturbed, and having been told in no uncertain terms that he was to make sure the King's guest was comfortable, added, "Is everything alright, Sire?"

"I am just having a little trouble sleeping. It must be the new surroundings," Croaker said, not wanting to make anything out of the strong feeling of apprehension that was still enveloping him.

A look of acceptance and a polite bow, the page closed the door as he left on his errand.

Croaker began to pace again and recalled the memories of the day once more to distract him from the anxiety he felt.

The messenger, beaming with pride, pointed out the stalls of the merchants from the surrounding villages as they traded their various goods.

"Over here are cloths and threads from harvested flax and from the same village, over there, the merchant's trade ink, soap, varnishes and other products from the flax seed," he pointed out by waving his arm in the direction of the vendors as they walked through the market place.

"They get all that from one plant?" Croaker asked.

"That and a lot more. There is a village that grows a variety with short fibers that is used exclusively for carpets," the messenger responded.

Croaker was surprised to see two sculptures, one flanking each side of a large entrance to the city quarters and palace. Each of the sculptures was of three individuals, a fairy, a pixie and a frog with each raising an arm to the center of the group to grasp a single torch.

Seeing the bewilderment on Croaker's face, the messenger said, "That is from a distant time when the unified armies came together to defeat a common foe."

"I did not know ... that frogs fought ...we have always been the peacemakers!" Croaker stammered, looking at the war garb of the frogs.

The messenger smiled as they ascended the stairs to the entrance. Once inside the entrance, Croaker found that he was in an expansive foyer with large staircases on either side. In the middle of the foyer floor was the seal of the Southern Field Fairy King made of inlaid jewels. Around the perimeter of the foyer and ascending with the stairs were globes and the chandelier high in the center of the foyer. All shone with a constant blue-white light that filled every nook and cranny. There were several doors around the room that led to other parts of the city but Croaker and the messenger were headed up one of the staircases that would take them to the palace above.

A knock at the door and the sound of the page's voice brought Croaker back to the moment, "I have your brew, Sire."

Croaker opened the door and motioned the page to set the brew on the bedside table, "Just put it there please."

"I took the liberty to have the cook heat it for you. When it is warm it will help you sleep, Sire," the page informed him, bowed and left the room.

After closing the door, Croaker sat on the edge of the bed and sipped the warm brew. The feeling of apprehension was almost gone now but he let his thoughts go back once more to the events of the day.

"The King will see you now," the Sergeant of the Guard announced.

Croaker and the messenger entered the King's study and gave a polite bow.

"Sire Ambassador, you are younger than I expected. Gribit must have a lot of confidence in you," Arklan said, looking up from his desk.

"Your Majesty, please call me Croaker. I just happened to be with him at the arrival of your messenger," Croaker replied.

A broad smile came across Arklan's face, "Sire Croaker it is. I see why he chose you to come." Then looking to the messenger, "You have done your job well. You can return to your post now."

"Your Majesty," Croaker interrupted, "Since I am new to this kind of position and I will need someone to guide me in your protocol, as well as your city, I would like to have your messenger continue on with me."

"Very well, Sire Croaker," Arklan agreed, then turning to the messenger, "You are assigned to Sire Croaker."

"Yes your Majesty. Sire Croaker will need to have a bush-tail available to him," the messenger pointed out.

"You can see that he gets all he needs while he is our guest," Arklan ordered, "Forgive me Sire Croaker, I have much business to attend to but will keep you informed of any new information when I receive it."

Croaker and the messenger gave a bow at the implied dismissal and exited the room.

The rest of the day was taken up with being shown his quarters, assigned a bush-tail and an instructor, then going to the training area for his first riding lesson. Later the messenger and Croaker made their way to the dining area for their evening meal.

The drain of the apprehension along with being physically worn out from the day and the heated berry brew were all working on Croaker as he sat on the edge of the bed. Swinging his legs up onto the bed he rolled over and twisted the cover to the globe closed and the blackness engulfed him, but this time no panic, and he drifted off to sleep.

CHAPTER FIVE

The first light of day hadn't shown itself yet when Webber and Puck went to the stables to ready their mounts. The Ambassador, after reading the message from Gribit and hearing what Webber and Puck had to say, told them to come back first thing in the morning for his sealed message to Gribit.

"I do not know why he would not tell us what was in the message," Puck said, irritated by his lack of knowledge.

"We will know soon enough. I am sure Gribit will understand your situation," Webber tried to console Puck.

"I am going to go to Lily Pond with you?" Puck asked, being both eager and apprehensive at the prospect of going into the nymph's domain.

"Yes, you will be under the protection of the frogs," Webber assured him.

"I will have to tell my wife when we stop at Limonite to rest our mounts and refresh ourselves," he informed Webber, excited that he would be the first pixie to enter Lily Pond in history, without being a captive!

"If nothing else, we might get an audience with Queen Isalia and you can ask her if they are involved with the disappearances," Webber suggested.

"Would she not deny their involvement even if they were?" he asked.

"I know the Queen, she *would* tell you if they were," Webber said.

"What makes you so sure of that?"

"She is a strong leader. If it was something that she felt had to be done for her citizens she would not hesitate for a moment to do it and certainly would not deny it," Webber told him, giving Puck some insight into the nature of the Nymph Queen.

"How is it that you know the Queen?" Puck asked, realizing that Webber was a messenger.

"I am with the Trade Liaison Corps. This is a special situation that I was chosen for," Webber responded, then realizing he may have said more than Gribit would want him to, "That is all that can be said for now."

Leading their bush-tails, Webber and Puck made their way from the stables through the empty streets of Millville heading back to the government quarters near the center of town. As they walked they saw a lamplighter on one of the side streets dousing the streetlights as he made his way from one to the next. Candlelight appeared in the windows as the pixies were waking, getting ready for the new day. The air was filling with delicious smells coming from the kitchens as they passed the homes along the way. From the distance came the echoing sound of an early morning cart as its wheels rolled across the paving bricks of a street as a bread vendor made his early rounds.

Reaching the inn next to the government quarters, where they had spent the night, they tied off their mounts and entered.

"Sires, I see you have returned! Are you ready for your breakfast?" the innkeeper asked as Webber and Puck came through the doorway.

"I sure am," Webber replied, remembering the smells of the morning, "I did not really know just how much until our return from the stables."

The innkeeper smiled in an understanding way as he went to the kitchen to retrieve the breakfast that his wife had prepared for the two riders.

Webber and Puck had their choice of tables in the empty dining area when they sat down but by the time they were finishing their meal the room was crowded and noisy from all the guests and a couple of mill workers that frequented the inn for their meals.

"I think that the ambassador should be ready for us by now," Webber said.

"Yes, we need to get started on our way," Puck agreed, anxious to see his wife and son again knowing that it could be some time before he might be able to see them after their stop at Limonite.

Webber motioned the innkeeper over to their table to sign the voucher so they could be on their way.

"I hope you enjoyed your stay at our establishment, sires," the innkeeper said as he handed Webber the voucher.

"It has been a thoroughly enjoyable experience," Webber replied, "and the food was excellent. Give our complements to your wife."

Pleased by the comments, the innkeeper returned to the needs of his other guests as Webber and Puck left the inn.

♦ ♦ ♦ ♦ ♦

Gribit hadn't slept well through the night. The information he received from the ambassador of Zarlan Grove had unsettled him. What he wanted to avoid had already begun in spite of his efforts to prevent it from happening. Fernon and Airlein had put their armies on alert and now he only wanted to know why. Though he knew that Airlein's actions were in response to Fernon's, he was anxious to hear from the ambassador to the forest fairies to understand why Fernon had taken his action.

The restless sleep had made him extremely irritable and his heavy steps echoed loudly as he stomped down the corridor to the dining area for his breakfast. He had decided not to inform Isalia of these events until all his ambassadors had reported back to him.

She has already put her army on alert because of the information we received from Arklan, what would she do if she thought there would be a chance for conflict between the domains? He thought; *Things could really get messy.*

♦ ♦ ♦ ♦ ♦

Fernon and Nedalia ate quietly, neither wanting to speak of the recent events. When they had arrived at Broadleaf last evening the regent had formally greeted them. There were no celebrations as there had been at Ravens Roost though that had been expected because of the search parties out looking for the missing children.

"We should be hearing from the commander before long," Fernon broke the silence.

"Do you believe that Isalia is behind this?" Nedalia asked what Fernon had been thinking.

"I am not sure, but it would appear that she is," he replied, "I did not tell you before, but the reason I called in Obrin is because three of our scouts have disappeared as well."

"Will this mean that we will be going to war?" she asked, her concern growing deeper.

"Unless I find out otherwise. I can not let this stand," he said, reluctantly accepting what appeared to be the facts.

"Should not we have the ambassador contact her first?" Nedalia asked.

"Yes, I believe we should, but the citizens will be so outraged that they will expect immediate action," he said.

"The citizens will expect carefully thought out actions," she insisted.

"I am afraid in this case they will not be thinking about that, they will just want me to act," Fernon said, shaking his head while he tried to resolve how to accomplish both action and prudence.

The two fell into silence again as they continued their meal.

Picking up the silver bell, Fernon signaled the end of the meal and the maid returned to clear the table just as the commander appeared. After acknowledging the commander, he requested his report.

"Your Majesty. There were no signs to be found anywhere," the commander informed Fernon.

"There must have been some sign," Fernon said, "some kind of trail."

"I am afraid not, Your Majesty," he said, reluctantly reaffirming his previous statement.

"*How* is that possible?" Fernon growled.

"Your Majesty. We have looked for signs that the town's citizens would not think to look for, as you ordered, and still found none," the commander answered.

"Send a messenger to General Oakon and have him move his units to the Lily Pond border and send a messenger to Lone Oak to have Obrin report here immediately," Fernon ordered, "Have the messenger request the ambassador's presence as well and have him stress the need for urgency to the ambassador."

"Yes, Your Majesty," the commander said, acknowledging the orders and with a bow was on his way.

Fernon looked to Nedalia, "I hope that things will hold until the ambassador has had a chance to speak to Isalia," he said.

"We can only hope that this does not progress further before *all* the facts are known," she agreed.

"It will take some time before Obrin can give me a report on any intelligence he may be able to gather. I should have done something about that much earlier," he said, regretting his hindsight by not having spies in the other domains before now.

Nedalia arose, walked over to her husband and put her arms around him, "You have always done what was best for your domain. We have had peace for some time and you have taken the actions necessary to insure that," she assured him then gently kissed him.

◆ ◆ ◆ ◆ ◆

Croaker had reluctantly woken from his sleep when the page knocked at his chamber. Still tired from the night before, he slowly swung his legs over the side of his bed and sat staring off into space before acknowledging he had arisen. Sluggishly rising and crossing the room, he poured cold water into the basin on the stand. Shivers ran through him as he splashed his face and he was soon awake enough to leave his chamber for the dining area and his morning breakfast.

As Croaker sat at his table in the dining area he stared across the room oblivious to the sights and sounds around him, eating slowly with mechanical movements.

"Good morning, Sire Croaker," the cheerful greeting of the messenger penetrated his trance.

"Oh, yes, good morning," he answered as if talking to someone he was not sure he knew.

"Is everything alright?" the messenger asked at Croaker's reply.

Not responding, he sat looking at the messenger for a few moments then asked, "What is your name?"

"Sire?" the messenger asked, surprised by the question.

"It is not a difficult question. My name is Croaker, what is yours?"

Stunned by the question and uncomfortable with the familiarity of it, the messenger sat at a loss for words.

"Well, is it to be a secret or am I to guess?" Croaker went on.

"No, Sire Croaker," he answered sliding his chair back on the granite floor and taking a standing position, "My name is Link," he said with a bow and a flourish of his hand.

"Well Link, I believe that we will be together for some time and while you are with me you may drop the Sire," Croaker instructed.

"Yes Sire, but why?"

"I said you may drop the Sire," Croaker reminded him, "I do not know exactly why I have come to this conclusion though I think it has something to do with last night," Croaker explained.

"What happened last night Si-, Croaker?"

"Again, I can not explain what it was but I have another question to ask you," he said.

"What is that?" Link asked, puzzled.

"Are you considered a good fighter?"

Link's amazement to the question was evident but he answered with pride, "Yes, but why do you ask?"

"I wish to *learn* the art of fighting!" Croaker informed him.

"Why?" Link asked, once more puzzled.

"It goes back to last night and yesterday when I saw the statues of the frogs in their war garb. I have a feeling that it is necessary," Croaker tried to explain.

Remembering Arklan's orders, "And so it shall be," Link accepted the responsibility.

"Thank you Link, I believe that you will make the best instructor I could have asked for," Croaker said, truly believing it.

"I will endeavor to live up to your expectations," Link said humbly.

Link motioned for a kitchen maid and ordered his breakfast. As the two ate their meal, he filled Croaker in on the schedule he had arranged for the morning and quickly figured out what needed to be done in the afternoon as a result of their conversation.

◆ ◆ ◆ ◆ ◆

Arklan looked out across the distant fields to the east from his dining area balcony as the rays of the morning sun bathed him in warmth. Below he could see the city stirring as the main gate was drawn open and the sentries at the battlement parapets were in the midst of their changing of the guard.

"Your Majesty," the page's voice broke through his thoughts.

"Yes, what is it?" he asked as he turned and acknowledged the bow of the page.

"There is a messenger from the southwest outpost to see you in your study, Your Majesty," the page informed him.

"Thank you," Arklan said as he headed for his study.

"Your Majesty," the page responded with a bow as Arklan passed by him.

When entering his study, Arklan was greeted with bows of the waiting messenger and Sergeant of the Guard.

"You have something for me?" he asked the messenger returning their bows before taking his seat.

"Your Majesty," the messenger said handing a sealed envelope to Arklan.

After reading the contents Arklan dismissed the messenger then turned to the Sergeant of the Guard, "Have someone locate Sire Croaker and have him come to my study as soon as possible."

"Yes, Your Majesty," the Sergeant of the Guard said with a bow and quickly departed the room.

Returning to his duty station, the Sergeant of the Guard called over one of his runners and sent him to search for Croaker with the message to see the King as soon as possible.

The runner found Croaker and Link in the dining area just as they were about to leave for their day's activities where, with a quick bow, the runner said, "Sires, The King requests the presence of Sire Croaker in his study as soon as possible."

"Thank you," Croaker said, then looking at Link, "There must be some new information."

When they reached the King's study Croaker entered as Link waited at the Sergeant of the Guard's duty station.

"Your Majesty," Croaker said as he bowed, "You have new information for me?"

"Yes, it would seem that early in the night the gathering of the toads and slithers just disappeared from their bivouac area. When the scouts went to investigate they found no signs of them having even been there."

"Where did they go?" Croaker asked, the feeling of uneasiness from last night returning with this information.

"The scouts were unable to determine that. It is as if they just vanished," Arklan answered.

"Is this all we have?"

"Yes. Do you wish to return with this to Gribit?" Arklan asked.

"Until we know where they went, I do not see how this can be of any help to Gribit," Croaker said, speaking his thoughts while not mentioning last night's experience.

"I agree with your analysis of the situation," Arklan said, a slight smile coming to his face at the mature thoughtfulness of this young frog.

With a bow, "If there is nothing else, Your Majesty, I must get to my riding lesson," Croaker said, his way of asking to be excused.

"Of course Sire Croaker, I will advise you of any future information when it comes in," Arklan replied, excusing him.

Croaker and Link walked down the corridor past the two sentries at the top of the spiral staircase. As they walked, Link didn't ask any questions. He knew that if Croaker wanted to tell him anything, he would. They made their way to the far end of the corridor to the large staircase that they had come up yesterday and made their way down several flights until they reached the foyer. From there they proceeded through the market area to the stables.

"I have your mount ready, Sire Croaker," the instructor said as they approached, then turned and entered the stables to retrieve Croaker's bush-tail.

"Croaker, I will have to leave you for a little while. I have some things to attend to but will join you shortly at the training area," Link informed Croaker.

Croaker nodded his understanding as he entered the stable area while Link left in the direction of the smithy.

"Thank you," Croaker said as the instructor appeared through the doorway of the stables leading Croaker's bush-tail.

It was a magnificent animal he had been given as his mount yesterday. Croaker viewed him with great pride that he should receive a mount so stately. Cloud Whisper stood tall and strong and was an eager runner, living up to his name with his coat of white and fire opal pink eyes.

"He has been waiting for you Sire," the instructor grinned, "You are the only one that he has let ride him."

With his bush-tail in tow, Croaker and the instructor left for the training area.

As Link entered the smithy, to the sounds of clinkety-clink-clinkety-clink of the smith rhythmically hammering out the steel he was working on, he could smell the fires of the forge and the steam of the hot metal being dipped in water. As his eyes adjusted to the yellow-red light he saw sparks fly as the smith hammered the metal again and again pausing only to cool the metal in the water, inspect his work, then stoke it in the fires again to hammer once more.

"Can I help you Sire?" the smith asked as he returned the metal to the anvil.

"Yes, I would like to have a sword made for a frog." He replied.

"A frog?" the smith asked with surprise.

"Yes, he has requested my training in the use of one."

The smith stood for a moment, at first stunned by the request but then thought of the statues in the market place which reminded him of something his father had told him.

"I might be able to provide you with what you require, Sire," he said, a smile appearing on his face, "It will only take a few more moments to finish what I am working on then we can go to a storage place my father told me about that lies in the depths of the city."

Link nodded his understanding as the sparks flew again when the smith resumed his hammering.

"This storage place was told to my father by his father and in turn our fathers before him since the time of the end of the unified forces. Our family was entrusted with this information if ever the frogs needed to have use of the artifacts stored there once more," the smith informed Link as he dipped the finished sickle blade in the water then putting it in oil to complete its cooling.

"What kind of artifacts?" Link asked, surprised by this new knowledge.

"I am not sure," the smith replied untying his apron and slinging it over the anvil, "I am guessing it would be that of the statues outside the great entry."

"Of course! I should have realized," Link said, as they walked out into the bright sunlit day.

Weaving through the crowd of fairies at the market place and past the statues they entered the foyer. Link could hear the echo of the smith's heavy boots on the granite floor drowning out the quiet whisper of his slippers as they approached the first door on their left.

"It is in this section of the city," the smith motioned Link to follow as he opened the door.

Following the corridor to a stairway they descended three levels to a part of the city that had not been visited. Here they found that no light globes had been placed in the corridor that lay before them.

"We will need the Fire of Elgin," the smith said, pulling out the medallion from under his tunic. Opening the face of the medallion the same familiar blue-white light of the globes of the city shone from it as the smith held it high in the air illuminating the granite corridor that led to the chamber at its very end as his father's instructions had told him where it would be.

"This is the place," he told Link as he opened the door.

Behind the ancient wooden door he found a large wall globe within easy reach and opened its cover, flooding the chamber with the bright glow of Elgin's Fire.

The dry stagnant air engulfed them as they looked across a chamber that was larger than what either of them had expected and saw row upon row of granite storage shelves, all filled with neatly wrapped linen bundles, each one its own compartment. At the most prominent space they found a scroll placed alongside the linen bundle.

"I think we should see what the scroll contains," Link suggested.

"Alright," the smith responded, gently removing it from its resting place and blowing away the covering of dust that gathered over the centuries, "It looks as though no one has been here since they have been stored."

Carefully unrolling the ancient linen scroll the light of the medallion revealed the words written upon it; *It is now the twenty-fifth year since the war with the imps and their minions. We have driven those that survived far to the south where they have not been heard from since. But now there is conflict between the Field Fairies and the offspring of the fairies and the pixies have found*

their way to Lily Pond itself, forming their own domain to seek
refuge from those that shun them. It is time for us to lay down our
arms and intermediate for peace between the domains since they
have given us citizenship in all. For us this is our greatest task to
undertake but if in the future it becomes necessary, the Southern
Field Fairies have consented to store our armaments in the event it
becomes necessary that frogs take them up again. It is with this
possibility that I leave my personal armaments to the new leader of
the frogs and may they protect him as they have me.

General Longhopper

It is now the twenty-seventh year since the war with the
imps and we have negotiated a peace between what are now the
five domains. Among the treaty conditions we have taken on the
role of trade negotiators and transporters as well as mediators. I
have had the fairies construct a special vault at the rear of this
chamber to store my personal scrolls in.

To open the vault requires three rings which I have had
specially made, each to fit its own opening in the vault door to
unlock it and allow access to the scrolls. I have given one ring to
each of the fairy leaders and have told them this is your seal and is
to represent your authority over your domain. I have further
instructed that these rings be passed down to their successor and
only when a Sage frog approaches them for the rings are they to
release them to that Sage. I have procured many of the personal
scrolls of Bale, Arlen, Zarlan and others, which are also stored

there only to the knowledge of myself and the one reading this scroll.

Sage Longhopper

Link and the smith stood looking at each other stunned by the revelations of the scroll. Here was the key to learning forgotten history.

"I think I should take this scroll to King Arklan," Link broke the silence, getting a nod of agreement from the smith.

"Let us see what the armaments look like," Link continued gently removing the linen bundle and brushing away the dust.

Carefully they unfolded the linen to reveal a helm atop a drab tunic. Along side the tunic the ivory hilt of a sword extended out of a scabbard wrapped by a broad belt. Further down the scabbard a dagger was sheathed in a secondary sheath and had an identical ivory hilt, both being carved in the fashion of a fairy. At the base of the hilts were ornate guards of polished bronze with blood red jewels embedded at the centers front and back. Anxious to examine the sword the smith withdrew it from its scabbard and as he did the sword glowed blue in the light.

"This is a quality of steel that even I can not attain," the smith said excitedly,
"The balance is perfect," he continued, swinging it through the air, "and it is as light as a feather!"

"I have never seen craftsmanship like this before," Link added, "It is worthy of a great warrior!"

"What is under the tunic?" the smith asked with child like expectation.

Link removed the tunic, noting that the years had taken their toll on the material; it was near disintegration without careful handling. Under it was a blouse of mail unlike any he had seen before. Made of threads of steel, drawn finer than fairy hair, so closely woven it would not let even a prickle pass through while still flowing like silk. The mail shone with iridescent colors, much as light passing through the facets of a diamond.

"We will need something to carry these in," Link said, "We will tell King Arklan of what we have found but no one else. He will decide what is to be done with the scroll."

"I will fetch a lidded basket if you will wait here?" the smith offered as he headed for the corridor.

"Do not be long," Link replied still marveling at the sight that lay before him on the granite floor.

While he waited for the smith to return, Link walked to the back of the storage chamber where he found another globe. He opened the globes cover and was surprised, as the light flooded across the rear wall, at glyphs that appeared depicting an epic battle. In the scene were frogs, fairies and pixies battling slithers, toads and grotesque creatures that looked something like pixies in battle armament that he surmised to be the imps mentioned in the scroll. Though he looked for the vault door he could not see it. Examining the glyphs closely he discovered an opening the shape of the Southern Field Fairy Domain Seal the size of the King's ring. Once he found the first opening it was not long before he found the other two openings as the three formed a pyramid within the glyphs.

How can this open a door? he wondered, *and where is it?*

Link hadn't realized how long it had been that he had been searching for the door until he heard the smith call to him, "Sire, I have returned."

"I am back here," he said, closing the cover to the globe before heading to the front of the chamber.

Carefully they packed the armaments and scroll in the woven basket that the smith had brought. They closed the cover of the globe and pulled the door shut behind them. With the smith leading the way, holding his medallion high, each held a handle of the basket as they continued back through the corridor to the stairs.

Entering the foyer, Link said with a slight bow, "I will take this to the King and you may return to the smithy. I will tell the King of your part in the recovery of these items. I thank you for assistance in acquiring these artifacts."

"Yes Sire," the smith said, disappointed that he was being dismissed.

"I am sure the King will want to thank you himself," Link said, sensing the disappointment of the smith, "You have served your family well with your charge."

The smith's posture changed as a look of pride showed on his face at these words, then with a slight bow he exited the foyer returning to his forge.

CHAPTER SIX

Webber and Puck had ridden hard and their bush-tails were in need of a rest when they reached the stables at Limonite.

"Sires, the mayor is waiting for your return at the inn," the smith said taking the reins of their mounts.

"Thank you, please see that they are fed and ready to go when we return," Webber instructed.

"We will be leaving soon," Puck added.

"Yes, Sires," the smith acknowledged as he led the mounts back to the stables.

There were only a few pixies out at the mid-day but each stopped with a questioning look as Webber and Puck passed by on the boardwalk.

"They are looking for answers," Puck said.

"I know, we just do not have any for them now," Webber agreed.

Entering the inn, Webber and Puck noticed the mayor having his mid-day meal as he sat at the most prominent table in the room. The mayor, looking up and seeing the two, motioned them to the table.

"You go. I am going to see my wife and son and I will bring our refreshments to the table," Puck said, motioning Webber to the mayor and leaving in the direction of the kitchen.

"What word do you bring from the ambassador, Sire frog?" the mayor asked as Webber approached the table.

"I am sorry, he has only sent a sealed message to be delivered to Sage Gribit," Webber said, taking the seat across the table from the mayor.

"He is not going to do anything himself?" the mayor asked looking surprised and angry, "He should at least make an appearance here!"

"I do not know his reasons for not coming. For that matter I do not know that he does not plan to come here," Webber said, attempting to calm the mayor, "Just give it some time."

"How much time?"

"At least two days, enough for me to see Gribit and deliver any response he may have for the ambassador."

"My citizens want action now," the mayor informed Webber.

"I understand that, but you need to keep them from acting without knowing the whole situation," Webber cautioned.

"It seems obvious who is behind this," the mayor said, showing his animosity toward the nymphs.

The mayor's attitude struck Webber like someone had rubbed their hand over the fur of a bush-tail on a dry day and touched a spark to the end of a raw nerve bringing a long forgotten lesson to the front of his mind; *We frogs are to maintain the peace, that is our main purpose in the scheme of things.*

"It is your responsibility to keep your citizens from going to war without knowing who or what is behind the disappearances," Webber admonished the mayor.

"Yes, Sire frog," the mayor winced awkwardly, sitting back in his chair, stung by Webber's response, "It will be as you say."

Puck and his wife were approaching the table with the refreshments. Hearing Webber's remarks to the mayor they stopped and stood motionless. No one had rebuked the mayor in public before.

Sensing they were behind him, Webber turned in his chair and saw the food they carried, "Thank you," he said smiling at Puck's wife, "Puck, please take your seat, if we are to make Lily Pond before nightfall we will have to leave soon."

"Puck is to accompany you, Sire?" the mayor asked with surprise.

"Yes." Webber said, "He will come to no harm. He will be under my protection and Gribit's as well."

While they ate Webber assured the mayor and Puck's wife that the answers would be found soon.

Puck thought; *Webber was obviously more than what he appeared. He had access to heads of state and had shown an authority that was unexpected.* With this thought he was gaining a great deal of respect for this young frog.

◆ ◆ ◆ ◆ ◆

The young pixie crawled from his hiding place and stumbled across the bodies of his family strewn about the house. Falling through the doorway into the bright daylight he lay for a moment before picking himself up only to stumble and fall again. As he lay there he wondered; *how long had it been since the attack? Was it hours or days?*

Burning fever from his wounds and the brightness of the sun caused all he saw to be a blur before him. A thought occurred to him; *I must tell mother and father of the dream I had. The monsters came at night.* Then reality returned and he began to sob uncontrollably until he could sob no more. Only a determination to tell of what had happened remained.

Stumbling around the city disorientated he went in one direction then another until he reached the edge of town and wandered into the hills. Clad only in his nightshirt he made himself keep moving unaware he was cutting his bare feet on the rocks that protruded from the ground. Falling over and over again he picked himself up only to tumble down a hillside and through the bramble. Aimlessly he wandered the hillsides with no direction. His mind ebbed and flowed between lucid thought and delirium until at the bottom of a hill he finally collapsed and lay near death from exhaustion and his wounds.

◆ ◆ ◆ ◆ ◆

Riding Cloud Whisper was a pure joy for Croaker. It was as if his mount knew exactly what Croaker was thinking and did what was needed almost before he directed him with the reins.

97

"You two *are* as one, Sire frog," the instructor said as Croaker brought Cloud Whisper to a halt by the corral gate.

"Yes, I believe he reads my thoughts," Croaker beamed at the bond that had formed between him and his mount.

"It is as if he was meant only for you, Sire," the instructor remarked, knowing how many others had been rejected by the white bush-tail.

"I see it did not take you long to master riding, Sire," Link smiled as he approached the corral.

"Cloud Whisper has made it very easy for me," Croaker said, gently patting his mount at the shoulder.

"We should see to our mid-day," Link said, "We have to maintain our schedule."

"Alright, Link," Croaker replied, swinging from his saddle to the ground and leading Cloud Whisper through the now open gate, following the instructor toward the stables.

After seeing that Cloud Whisper had been groomed and fed, Croaker and Link went to the dining area for their mid-day meal and to discuss the agenda for the afternoon.

"I have reserved some time at the archery range and then we can practice sword training," Link informed Croaker between bites of his honey bread.

Croaker sipped his tea as his thoughts went to his home; *I wonder what Lily and the others are thinking about my not returning? Webber would surely be surprised that I have learned to ride a bush-tail. I will bet that they are sunning themselves by the waters edge.*

"Croaker, have you heard a word of what I have been saying?" Link asked, noticing the distant look in Croaker's eyes.

"Yes, archery, then swords," Croaker responded, bringing his thoughts back to the moment, then taking another sip of his tea.

"You will have to be more focused than this when we are training," Link cautioned.

"I was wondering if my friends were worried about me," Croaker confessed, "I left without a word to them."

"I am sure Gribit would inform them," Link said.

"Yes, you are right, that is if he has had the opportunity to do so. He was after all going to meet with Isalia and that was foremost on his mind," Croaker pointed out.

"In any event, you will need to focus on your training. It will take all your effort and thought," Link stressed.

Croaker nodded his understanding as the two continued their meal in silence and Croaker's thoughts went back to Lily Pond; *Lily will sure be impressed at the new me, for that matter they all would be surprised when I ride up on Cloud Whisper. He is a magnificent animal.*

Link hadn't spoken to Croaker of what he and the smith had discovered; *if this frog is what I believe he is, then he will be worthy of the armaments of the frog Longhopper. I will have to train him hard.*

Link didn't know what the message he had delivered to Gribit contained but the reaction to it combined with Croaker's asking for training in combat made him wonder what it was all about. Adding to all of this the glyphs, he found carved in the chamber wall, and Link was forming an opinion of what might be happening.

I must have a new tunic made for Croaker, the one from the chamber would be a good pattern, Link thought.

After finishing their meal Link led the way to the archery field in the training area on the south side of the city. This was a place that frogs had not attended in the memory of the fairies that now lived, so when Croaker appeared with Link many of the trainees stopped in the middle of what they were doing to stare at this unusual sight.

"Pay them no mind," Link said as they approached their target range, "This is something new for them."

"I did not think that I would disrupt things," Croaker said with surprise to their response at seeing him.

"It will be only momentary," Link said, not being sure how the others would react.

Reaching the range, they found two bows and quivers of arrows awaiting them as Link had requested when making the arrangements.

"Our long bows are made of the finest yew imported from the Rolling Hills," Link said with pride as he began his instructions, "and our craftsmen make the truest arrows."

Then notching an arrow Link drew back the bow and let loose the arrow. Two hundred and fifty yards and moments later it struck the target near exact center.

"All right Croaker, now it's your turn," Link motioned him to take up the other bow.

Croaker mimicked Link's actions and let loose his arrow. He yelped in pain at the stinging burn of the bowstring against his arm and watched the arrow fall considerably short of the target. A collective chuckle rose around him. The others knew too well what he had just experienced.

"Was I brought here for your amusement?" Croaker snapped at Link, his arm still stinging from the string.

"No, that was your first lesson," Link smiled.

"What kind of lesson is that?" Croaker asked, still sore.

"That if you do not pay attention here, your weapon can hurt *you*."

Croaker nodded his immediate understanding, "I will not forget that lesson."

"Good, we can begin."

Croaker paid intense attention to Link as he showed him how to hold the bow, how to breathe and how to release the bowstring. Link had the target moved up to fifty yards and as Croaker released his arrows, explained how to sight for distance. After his second quiver of arrows Croaker started hitting the target, striking closer to center with each shot.

"You have done well for your first lesson," Link said.

"I was right about you being the best instructor I could ask for," Croaker returned the compliment.

"It is time to move to the sword training area," Link said.

"My arm still stings a little and my finger webbing is sore as well," Croaker said now that he was not focused on the task at hand.

"That is normal. Your hands will callus in time and your arm will heal. Let us continue on to our next task," Link said as he led the way to the next training area, "You have only begun to experience your education."

Croaker didn't like the sound of what Link considered to be normal although he was fully committed to the program. The thought of the uneasiness he experienced in his chamber the previous night was enough to make him want to continue no matter the difficulty.

As they approached the combat area they saw at least two-dozen fairies wielding broad swords in mock combat. Croaker watched as the pairs dueled, swords clanking loudly as one parried the others strike maneuvering to gain an advantage for their own attack.

"It looks as though one might get hurt. How often does that happen?" Croaker asked.

"Not often, the swords are training swords and have blunt edges. There are some bruises and an occasional broken bone," Link said, "We will begin our lessons with wooden swords."

Stopping at the training armory, Link selected the appropriate weapons for Croaker's training before proceeding to the field.

"I think this should be about right for you," Link said as he handed Croaker his sword.

"Thank you," Croaker said swinging the sword to get the feel of it in his hand.

Without a word Link swung his sword at Croaker's head stopping less than an inch away. It had happened so fast that Croaker didn't react, he just stood there, heart pounding.

"You are in combat. Be ready at all times! That means from now on," Link growled at him.

"At all times?" Croaker asked his heart still beating wildly.

"Yes, even while sleeping." Link said.

"How?"

"Do not worry about that. It will become second nature to you."

Over and over Link showed Croaker how to defend against different attacks and the proper reaction to gain the advantage to counter. Link pressed him hard and Croaker felt every blow when he made a mistake. Croaker was so intent on learning his lessons that by the end of the training session he had already advanced beyond what other trainees took weeks to learn.

I was right about this frog, he is the fastest learner I have seen, Link thought to himself.

"That was a good start," Link said, "It is time to end our lessons for the day."

Croaker ached from his head to his feet. It was good news that the lessons were over for now but he could not manage a smile. He was tired and needed nourishment for his punished body.

Link could see the fatigue in Croaker but knew from experience that this would only make him stronger as time passed. Now, food and rest were in order.

◆ ◆ ◆ ◆ ◆

Webber and Puck arrived at the south shore stables of Lily Pond as the sun was sinking behind the western hills. The clouds shone with iridescent pinks and oranges against a sky that was turning a deep cobalt blue. A slight breeze whispered across the rushes in the shallows and danced the water's surface distorting the reflections cast upon it as they brought their bush-tails to a halt near the sentry posted at the stables.

"Sire Frog, what is the meaning of bringing this pixie into our domain?" she asked.

"This pixie is under the protection of the frogs. He is to be treated as a guest," Webber told her in no uncertain terms.

"Sergeant of the Guard," the sentry called out.

Webber and Puck dismounted as the sergeant raced to the sentry's post to see what the problem was. Seeing the pixie she drew her sword and Puck reached for his. Webber quickly put his hand on Pucks before he could draw his sword from its scabbard.

"Put that away! This is my guest and we are here to see the Sage Gribit." Webber glared at the sergeant.

Stopped short she slowly sheathed her sword in complete disbelief that this was really happening, "Of course, Sire Frog."

"See to our mounts and have the canoe readied to transport us to the lifts," Webber ordered.

Reluctantly the sergeant did as Webber ordered, "I will have to have a guard accompany you," she said.

"Yes, that would be best, her presence would avoid any possible incidences like this from occurring again," he reasoned.

"I meant for *security*, Sire," she said, making her purpose clear.

"I understood that, but it will be to our benefit as well," Webber acknowledged.

Boarding the canoe, Webber, Puck and the guard took their seat. Two nymphs, one fore and one aft, dug their paddles into the water. The craft silently slid through now calm water toward the floating dock and tube lifts as the light of the day begin to slowly fade.

Puck looked amazed as they walked through the translucent tunnel dome to the main dome of Lily Pond. He had never seen a sight like this before. The city was already starting to glow in the cast green light of the phosphorus deposits. The feeling of confinement was strong with the water pressing in on the domes. He took in all the new sights as they walked through the city and only once inside the palace did he start to feel more comfortable.

They will never believe me when I tell them about this at home, Puck mused.

Gribit and Isalia were in the meeting chamber when the escort announced the arrival of Webber and Puck, "Sire Webber and companion to see Sire Gribit!"

Gribit rose from his seat anxious to learn what the Pixie Ambassador's reply was, but a look of uneasiness crossed his face when he saw Puck; *Why would Webber bring a pixie to Lily Pond?*

"Webber, what news have you for me?" He asked, his voice hiding his concern.

"A letter from the ambassador," Webber said, handing the message to Gribit.

Breaking the seal, Gribit removed the letter from its envelope and became aware of the events at Limonite and the explanation for Puck's presence. Slowly he folded the letter as he pondered the information that it contained.

Gribit turned his attention to the guard, "You may return to you duties, I will be responsible for the pixie."

The guard, looking to Isalia and seeing the Queen nod in agreement, bowed and departed.

"Sire Pixie, I take it your name is Puck?" Gribit asked as he now focused on Webber's companion.

"Yes, Sage," Puck answered proudly.

"Take Webber and his guest to the dining area," Gribit directed the escort, "I am sure they are in need of food."

The escort looked to Isalia for approval as the guard had, then bowing asked Webber and Puck to follow her.

The companions gave a courteous bow but before they could depart Gribit instructed them, "We will send for you after we have discussed this message."

It was past the normal dinner hour so the dining area was nearly empty. They took their seats at a vacant table while the escort talked to the kitchen staff then returned to her post.

Two curious kitchen maids approached the table shortly with trays of food. As they approached they could not stop staring at Puck.

"I hope this will be to your satisfaction sires," one of the maids said, "We have grilled fish, boiled cattail root, watercress, honey bread, and hot tea."

There were items on this menu that were foreign to Puck but he thought they sounded quite good, "Yes, I believe it will," he smiled.

Webber nodded in agreement and dismissed the two.

As they sat eating their meal, their arrival at Lily Pond had not gone unnoticed just as the departure of Croaker and Link had not been unnoticed. A fairy messenger had been dispatched from the western border of the Eastern Fields Domain and was hurrying to Zarlan Grove.

CHAPTER SEVEN

The dew was still heavy on the grass as the first gray light of the morning filtered through the leaves of Zarlan Grove when the messenger from the west arrived with his message. He had traveled through the night and was now on his way up the spiral stairs to the palace in the giant walnut tree to deliver his message to the Queen.

"I have an urgent message for the Queen from the western outpost," he told the sentry guarding the palace entrance.

"Wait here, the Corporal will have a page inform the Queen's handmaiden," the sentry instructed him, then called, "Corporal of the Guard, post one!"

The call was repeated from post to post as if it were an echo through the halls of the palace.

After a few moments a fairy, with a bearing of authority, appeared at the entrance, "What is the problem?" he asked.

"This messenger from the west has an urgent message for the Queen," the sentry informed him.

"Thank you, I will see she is informed immediately," he said, disappearing through the entry to dispatch a page.

Airlein opened her eyes blinking back the sleep that kept trying to pull her back to the comfort of her dreams where her mind could live out the pleasant memories of strolling through her garden without a care or worry.

"Your Majesty," the handmaiden said again, "there is an urgent message for you from the west."

"Thank you, inform the messenger to meet me at the war room, I will be there shortly. You may go now," Airlein instructed, arising from her bed and reaching for her gossamer dress.

Though her dress was sheer, it held the warmth of her body close and was enough to block the chill of the damp morning air in her chamber.

Sliding her feet into her slippers and tying her hair tight at the back of her head, leaving it to swing like a tail, she left for the war room wondering what had happened now.

I wonder if it is a message from the ambassador about his meeting with Gribit, she thought as she made her way to the hexagon room.

When she arrived the messenger was waiting for her, "Your Majesty," he said as he bowed while extending his hand with the message in it.

Taking the message and breaking the seal, her face formed a scowl as she read.

"Arlen's fate!" she cursed, "Get General Broadstem here now!"

The page assigned to the intelligence cadre jumped to his feet at a run, without taking time to bow, racing out the door to retrieve the General.

Airlein gathered herself and looked at the messenger and realized that he would be tired from traveling all night, "You are dismissed to take food and rest," she said calmly.

"Yes, Your Majesty. Thank you," he said bowing, relieved her ire was not focused on him.

Something major is happening and it appears that the other domains are all involved in it and we have been left out, she thought to herself as she studied the relief map trying to make some sense of the events she knew about.

A few minutes latter General Broadstem appeared through the doorway.

"Your Majesty," He said, giving a quick bow as she turned toward him, "You sent for me?"

"What is wrong with our intelligence?" she snapped, "There are things happening that are unheard of!"

"Your Majesty?" a puzzled look flashed across Broadstem's face, "I am not sure I understand."

"It would seem that a pixie envoy arrived at Lily Pond last evening," she said handing the message to the General, "And it appears that the frogs are involved with whatever is happening since the envoy was accompanied by a frog."

"The frogs are involved?" he questioned.

As he read the message another messenger appeared at the door.

"Your Majesty, I have an urgent message from our northwest outpost."

Taking the sealed envelope from the messenger, Airlein broke open the seal.

"I was right about something major happening. Our forest agent reports that last night Fernon had most of his forces start moving toward their southern border." She said, reporting the contents to Broadstem, "and the frog ambassador left in a hurry to Broadleaf where Fernon is at this very moment."

Airlein thought for a moment then called for paper and pen. Quickly one of the cadres brought her the requested items and she began to write.

"I have requested an immediate meeting with Gribit," she informed Broadstem as she wrote, "I will get to the bottom of this one way or another."

"I still believe that we should reinforce our borders as I said before," the General offered the suggestion again.

"Yes, call up the reserves and have them placed at strategic points along our northern and western borders," she agreed.

Then after sealing the message, "Have this delivered to the Sage Gribit in Lily Pond. It is *urgent*," she told the messenger, "then you may take food and rest before returning to your post."

"As you wish, Your Majesty."

"Has there been any word from the ambassador?" she asked Broadstem.

"No, Your Majesty," he replied, then continued, "I think that we have done all we can here for the time. We need to take our morning meal."

"Yes, I agree. I will be in my chamber if I am needed," she informed the General and the intelligence cadre.

◆ ◆ ◆ ◆ ◆

The patrol made its way along the southwestern border of the Southern Field Fairy Domain as the first of the sun's rays touched the base of the Rolling Hills. The scouts had been extra alert these past days since the original sighting of the gathering of the toads and slithers.

"What is that at the base of that hill?" the scout asked his partner.

"I do not know," he replied, "We should have a look."

"It is in the Rolling Hills Domain, do you think we should cross the border?"

"I do not see anyone to care about it one way or the other if we enter," the second scout noted.

"All right," the first scout agreed.

As they approached they saw it was the body of a young pixie. Noticing his wounds they thought him to be dead but when they had a closer look found he was still breathing; ever so faintly but still breathing.

"We better get him to our healers," the first scout said, "See if you can find branches for a stretcher frame and I will cut some grasses for its mat."

"First I will see if he will take some water in his state, he is burning with fever," the other said, "you go ahead and start cutting the grasses."

With his fingertips wetted from his canteen, he placed them on the pixie's lips and the boy automatically licked at the moisture, though still unconscious, and took in the meager amount of liquid.

The scout ripped off a strip of the pixie's nightshirt, dampened it and placed it on the pixies forehead before setting about finding suitable branches for the stretcher.

As they wove the grasses to the frame they wondered at the cause of the boy's wounds and where he had come from dressed only in a nightshirt.

"Do you think we can get him to the healers in time?"

"I do not know, but we will try."

◆ ◆ ◆ ◆ ◆

The early morning sounds of life in Broadleaf grew louder as the coach carrying the ambassador approached from Lone Oak. His carriage rolled quietly over the pine needle covered streets, the dirt packed hard as stone beneath from centuries of use, as they proceeded to the royal quarters.

"Driver, you can let me out here," he said as they arrived, "Take the coach to the stables. I will send word if you are needed."

The royal quarters, as with all the buildings of Broadleaf, were tucked in between the trees. The construction was nearly the same as any other fairy village, even the treetop villages like Raven's Roost, with the exception that the roofs and exterior walls were covered with wooden shakes instead of thatched grasses.

Though the city was dappled with the dim early morning sunlight that managed to filter down through the leaf canopy, it was still dark enough that lights shone in the windows of the homes as the fairies prepared for the new day.

The ambassador presented himself to the sentry posted at the front door of the quarters. He was then escorted to the waiting room just inside the door.

"If you will have a seat Sire Ambassador, I will announce you to the King," his escort gestured, "He has been expecting you."

The waiting room was quite comfortable. The lounge on which he sat was stuffed with cattail cotton and upholstered with richly embroidered spider-silk cloth, matching the draperies that covered the windows. The sheen of this material reflecting the light from the beeswax candles of the wall lanterns, hanging from sconces located around the room, gave it a warmth that felt comfortable after coming out of the early morning chill. The wood floor was covered with a golden colored carpet that had the feel of dry moss beneath the ambassador's webbed feet.

"The King will see you now Sire, please follow me," the escort said when he returned to the waiting room.

The ambassador followed the escort through a doorway that led to a staircase. Ascending to the second floor of the quarters they followed the corridor, passing two other rooms at either side, to a room at its end.

Fernon sat at a large oak desk while Nedalia was sitting on a lounge across the room from him when the ambassador entered.

Seeing both Fernon and Nedalia, "Your Majesties. You sent for me, Sire?" the ambassador said as he bowed near the entrance.

"Yes, Sire Ambassador, there is an urgent need for you to talk with Isalia on our behalf," Fernon said motioning the ambassador to take a seat in the chair next to the oak desk.

As the ambassador sat, Fernon explained the events that had happened and his assessment of those events.

"If we are wrong about Isalia, then we need to know," Fernon told the ambassador.

"It does not sound like her," the ambassador replied, "She would never take children."

"That is why we sent for you," Fernon said, "I do not want to commit to an action if I am wrong."

"I will talk with her but do nothing until I return to inform you of what I have learned," the ambassador cautioned.

"How much time will you need?" the King asked.

"Give me a couple of days," he said, "I will need time to travel and if I can not get an audience right away, I will need the extra time."

"All right, two days it is," Fernon agreed then added, "Have you had a chance to take your morning meal?"

"No, I just arrived," the ambassador replied.

Fernon reached behind him and pulled on the bell cord to summon the escort. The escort reappeared at the door a few moments later.

"Take our guest to the dining area and have a meal prepared for him," he instructed then addressing the ambassador, "Will you need anything else, Sire Ambassador?"

"Thank you, no, Your Majesty. That will be enough before I leave, I will nap in the coach," the ambassador said as he stood and bowed before exiting the room.

Fernon, now turning his attention to Nedalia remarked, "I must finish inspecting the warehouses and I would very much like you to accompany me again today."

A smile came to her lips as she arose from the lounge and replied in a manner that was nearly a song, "Try to keep me away,"

"It is not often we get to spend this much time together, even if it is doing official business," he said returning her smile as he stood and reached out his hand for hers.

Even though events could be trying they could find joyful pleasure in each other's company. This was one of the many reasons Fernon was glad he had chosen her to be his wife.

As they were about to leave they were interrupted by the announcement of General Oakon's arrival.

"Your Majesties," he said with a curt bow, pulling a map from under his tunic and laying it on the oak desk, "I will be brief Sire. I have deployed my units at these points along the border. Does this meet with your approval?"

"Yes," he said noting the positions Oakon pointed out, "Well done. We will not be making a move for at least two days. I have given the ambassador my word that I would wait to hear from him before any action will be taken," Fernon briefed the General, "Keep the troops on alert in case things change."

"So it will be, Your Majesty," Oakon acknowledged, giving another curt bow and leaving to return to his troops.

"I did not think that I would look forward to inspecting warehouses this much," he smiled at Nedalia.

◆ ◆ ◆ ◆ ◆

Gribit paced back and forth across his chamber as the pale green glow slowly faded and the muted light of the new day replaced it through the chamber window. He hadn't been able to get a full nights rest since receiving the news of the missing children at Limonite and the pixies preparing for war with Lily Pond. Isalia had assured him that her citizens had nothing to do with the missing children and he was welcome to inspect the breeder domes but he had no intention of doing so because he knew that Isalia was true to her word.

It has to be more than a coincidence that the children went missing at the same time a slither had been sighted on the western bank of Lily Pond, he thought. He knew this was speculation but his mind was racing for answers, he had to prevent a war from breaking out, a war he believed would be different than any they had seen in centuries.

I wonder if Croaker has any news for me? I should have heard something from him if there was anything, his thoughts going back to Arklan's message.

Leaving his chamber, Gribit walked toward the dining area still deep in thought; *If Webber and the pixie Puck are not there I will send for them.*

The dining area was alive with the sounds of conversation and kitchen preparations as he emerged from the isolation of his thoughts and the empty corridor.

The kitchen staff, noting his arrival, waited for Gribit to be seated before bringing the special meal they had prepared for the visiting dignitary.

Surveying the room for Webber and his companion, he finally located them on the far side at a corner table.

Maneuvering his way through the maze of nymphs and tables he caught the attention of the two companions.

"Good morning," he said as he approached.

"Good morning Gribit," Webber responded, "Will you join us?"

"Good morning Sage," Puck said respectfully standing while Gribit took his chair.

"Thank you, I would be happy to," Gribit graciously accepted.

Puck wanted to know what Gribit and Isalia had said about his son and the other missing children but patiently waited for Gribit to start the conversation.

"I hope this is to your satisfaction Sire," a kitchen nymph said as she placed a tray containing a bowl of oat porridge, hot tea, bread and honey on the table, "The oats are imported from the Southern Fields!"

"Thank you," Gribit smiled back at her, knowing that she wanted him to understand that this was a special treat prepared for him, "This will do just fine. That will be all."

As the kitchen nymph returned to her normal duties, Gribit turned to Webber, "Isalia and I had a discussion after reading the message from the pixie ambassador. She informed me that she would not condone the taking of children."

"Then what do you think happened to the children?" Puck asked abruptly.

"I can only speculate at this time," Gribit said, seeing the concern in Puck's expression, and then turning his attention back to Webber, "Lily and Lotus reported a slither in that general area if you recall."

"But there were five children missing at the same time. A single slither could not be responsible for all of them," Webber pointed out, grasping Gribit's implication.

"I said it was only speculation, but I have my reasons to consider it a possibility," Gribit said.

Though events of the past two days had made the decision for him, Gribit sat re-evaluating the situation and wondering if this was the right time to make the message from Arklan known to others. Though his heart was telling him the timing might not be right, his intellect prevailed and the message could be kept secret no longer.

Webber thought for a moment then seeing the questioning look on Puck's face, "Are you alright with this, or would you like to hear it from Isalia herself?"

"If the *Sage* accepts her word on it then that is good enough for me," Puck replied, though maintaining a look of questioning in his eyes.

"What of us now, Gribit?" Webber asked the Sage.

"I will be sending you back to the pixie ambassador with a message to have him come to Lily Pond for a summit," Gribit instructed, "I will be sending for the other ambassadors as well except Zarlan Grove's, he is already here."

Gribit's warning, when he had sent him on this task, came back into Webber's thoughts, "Is there something happening that we are not aware of?" Webber asked.

Gribit stared at them for a long moment before replying, "Yes, I received a message from King Arklan while Croaker was at my pad. The message was about a sighting of toads and slithers along the southwestern border of the Southern Fields."

Astonished by this revelation, Webber asked, "How can that be?"

"In history long forgotten by most, the toads and slithers were minions of the race known as imps. This history has been passed down from sage to sage so it would not be lost to time. I fear that this threat has returned to Lily Pond," Gribit informed them.

Puck's face paled and a look of sorrow engulfed his whole demeanor as he realized the fate of his son and the other children.

"Are you sure?" Puck asked hoping that this could not be the case.

"Yes, that is why I sent Croaker to Granstone as my liaison. He is to report any new information to me that Arklan's scouts learn," Gribit informed them, "Puck, there is something I wish you to do."

"And what would that be?" Puck asked.

"Speak to your citizens and keep them from taking any action until I learn more. *You* have to make them understand that action can wait for information," Gribit said in a tone that stressed the import of his words.

Puck nodded his head, "Yes Sage."

◆ ◆ ◆ ◆ ◆

"Since you have done so well with your riding lessons I think we should go to mounted weapons training after the mid-day," Link said, sipping his hot tea.

The dining area was alive with the sounds of kitchen staff at work and the conversations of fairies conversing as they ate their morning meal.

Across the table, Croaker looked up with surprise, "You think I am ready for that?

"Yes. The bond between you and Cloud Whisper is quite apparent. When you ride him it is as if the two of you are one," Link said, a slight smile forming at the corners of his mouth.

"I would not have guessed that it would feel so natural. He seems a part of me," Croaker said, elation flooding over him at the thought of riding Cloud Whisper.

"While you are riding this morning, I have some maters to attend to. I will meet you at the stables when I finish them," Link said, swallowing the last of his tea and grabbing the last piece of honey bread from his plate.

"By your leave Croaker, I have to go to my quarters," he said as he stood, leaving Croaker to finish his meal.

Entering his quarters, Link heard the latch fall into place as he pulled the door closed behind him. His eyes traveled to the storage area at the foot of his bed where he had placed the artifacts for safekeeping. Opening the storage space he thought to himself; *I will take only the scroll to the King. The weapons and armor are for Croaker, I am sure he is the leader Longhopper meant to leave them to.*

Carefully retrieving the scroll to present to the King, he closed the storage area once again.

Link thought of yesterday as his footsteps fell like whispers along the corridor to the stairs that led to the King's study; *The Sergeant of the Guard had told him to come back the next day*

122

because the King had urgent business to attend to and could not be disturbed at that time.

"Is the King in his study?" he asked the Sergeant of the Guard as he approached his station.

"Yes, I will announce you," the Sergeant said, rising to his feet from the chair behind his desk.

"Your Majesty, the messenger assigned to the frog wishes to see you," he informed Arklan.

"Thank you, send him in," Arklan said as he turned from the window he had been looking out. He hadn't really been looking at anything in particular; his thoughts were on the situation in the southwest.

With a quick bow and a turn through the doorway, "The King will see you now," the Sergeant said, returning to his chair.

"Your Majesty," Link said with a bow while holding out the scroll, "With the aid of the smith I have made a discovery that you should know about."

Arklan listened intently as Link described the events of yesterday.

"The smith mentioned a charge their family had been given. He recalled that his father had passed down to him information about a storage chamber that lies within the city. For generations the storage and location of the frog artifacts had been entrusted to his family." Link said.

"A chamber. Here in the city?"

"Yes, Sire," Link continued, "Among the artifacts we found this scroll belonging to a General Longhopper. I knew it would be important to you."

"Sire, on the back wall of the chamber there were glyphs depicting a great battle. I located the three openings mentioned in the scroll for the rings that would open the concealed door," he said.

Link's excitement grew as he watched Arklan read Longhopper's words from the scroll and the long forgotten history being revealed to the King.

"Sire, it is my belief that the armaments of General Longhopper should go to Sire Croaker," Link said.

"Why?" Arklan asked, surprised by the suggestion.

"Sire Croaker requested that I should train him in the use of weapons," Link informed him, "That is why I went to the smith and what led to finding these things."

"A frog asked you to train him?" Arklan asked, puzzled about the possible motive of Croaker.

"Yes Sire. He gave no reason other than he had a feeling that it was necessary."

◆◆◆◆◆

The mid-day sun filtered down to the depths of Lily Pond as the tranquility of the city belied the turmoil of the world above.

"Your Majesty," a nymph messenger interrupted Isalia's thoughts.

Isalia, gazing out her window at the dome, snapped her head around in the direction of the voice, her ebony hair fanning in a swirl, "Yes, what is it?"

"Reports from our scouts, Your Majesty," the messenger said as she straightened from her bow, "The Forest Fairies have moved troops up to our northern border and the Lone Oak Ambassador approaches the southern stables."

"Gribit just sent for him this morning!" Isalia spoke her thoughts aloud.

"The frog messenger returns with the ambassador, Your Majesty," the messenger answered, "He must have met him on the way."

"Thank you," Isalia said. Sitting at her desk she wrote out orders and handed them to the messenger, "Inform the commanders that our troops are not to take any action unless it is defensive."

"Yes, Your Majesty. I also want to report that a message from Queen Airlein just arrived for the Sage. It was delivered as *urgent*," the messenger said, bowing then departing to deliver the Queen's orders.

Standing from her chair, Isalia began to pace around her study trying to sort out the facts she had; *Clearly all the domains are involved in what is happening. Gribit must be right about the toads and slithers. They are obviously doing something to cause the domains to take provocative actions that appear to be directed at Lily Pond. The missing children of the Rolling Hills is the pixie*

125

motivation, so I must assume that something similar has happened in the other domains as well. I think that it is time to call the leaders of all the domains together to assess what is really happening.

Moving to the bell cord near her desk, Isalia went to summon a page.

"What can I do for you, Your Majesty?" the young page asked as she came through the door and bowed.

"Ask the Sage and his ambassadors to meet me in the meeting chamber as soon as the one from Lone Oak arrives. You can inform me when they are ready," she instructed.

♦ ♦ ♦ ♦ ♦

Webber and Puck had left Lily Pond with the messengers that Gribit sent to Granstone and Lone Oak. They were to escort the ambassadors from those domains to the summit at Lily Pond, as was Webber to escort the Rolling Hills ambassador.

It had been a hard morning's ride to reach Limonite. With the sun now directly overhead and beating down on them like a dry fire, both riders and mounts were being sapped of their fluids from its intensity and the sight of the town meant that relief would be coming soon.

"It has been getting hotter and dryer every day since the rain," Puck said as they turned off the border road onto the street leading to the stables.

Webber nodded in agreement. All he wanted at the moment was to get to the inn and quench his thirst and find shelter from the sun.

As Webber and Puck brought the gray and Fleetfoot to a halt at the stables and dismounted, the smith emerged from the entrance.

"Walk them out and groom them before you water and feed them," Puck told the smith, "They have earned special care this morning."

Nodding his head, the smith took the reins of both mounts to lead them to the paddock at the back of the stables, "The ambassador from Millville arrived this morning Sire Puck. He is meeting with the mayor in the town hall," he said, before disappearing from view.

"This is better than I hoped," Webber said, relieved he would not have to make the ride to Millville again.

"You can be back in Lily Pond before sun comes up tomorrow," Puck grinned, a mischievous sparkle appearing in his eyes.

"And you think you will not?" Webber smiled back.

Webber and Puck crossed the street on their way to the town hall as a dust devil swirled past them making an erratic path on its way east toward the border road they had just traveled. Webber turned his face trying to cover it when the devil threw up a cloud of dust next to him. Brushing away the dust that clung to him, he noticed a few of the town's pixies were milling about the front of the general store. They had fallen silent as they watched the companions make their way to the town hall.

"Sire Puck. Sire Webber," the mayor said, almost running into them as he and the ambassador stepped through the door, "You are back in town!"

"Yes, we just arrived," Puck, said stepping back out of the way.

"We were on our way to your inn for our mid-day. Will you join us?" the mayor asked.

"Yes. I was going to go straight there but the smith informed us that you and the ambassador were meeting here."

"What news from Lily Pond?" the mayor continued questioning as the four headed down the street toward the corner to the inn.

"Gribit sent us to inform the ambassador that he was to attend a summit in Lily Pond," Webber said while looking at the ambassador.

"A summit!" the ambassador said with surprise.

"Yes Sire. The three of us can be there before the morning light," Webber, continued, "We need to let our mounts rest before returning. If not for that we could leave as soon as we have taken nourishment."

"Why does the pixie have to return with us?" the ambassador asked.

"Because Gribit has requested his return," Webber explained.

"I did not know this!" Puck swung his head around to view Webber, tripping on the boardwalk as he did, "I thought you were joking at the stables. When did you learn of his request?"

"Just before we left," Webber said, sorry that he hadn't said anything to Puck sooner, "I was to stop and get you on the return trip."

"Why does he want me to return with you?"

"He did not say. He just said that it was important that you did," Webber confessed that he too was in the dark about Gribit's motive.

Entering the inn, Puck excused himself from the others as they sought out an unoccupied table. "I must speak to my wife and son," he said, the muscles in his throat tightening at the thought of what he had to tell them.

Puck's eldest son had been taking care of the dining area and bar when his father returned with the mayor, ambassador and Webber. Seeing his father, he left his chores to greet him. "You have returned quickly. What news have you brought us?" he asked, noting the stress on his father's face.

"Come. We will talk in your mother's presence," Puck said, leading him through the door to the kitchen. This was the moment he had been dreading since Gribit informed him of the probable fate of their son and the other children.

It wasn't long before the citizens of the town learned of Puck and Webber's return and the dining area of the inn became so crowded that many had to stand outside the door.

"Are we going to do anything about our children?" one of the pixies shouted.

Soon there was only a loud commotion with the mayor waving his arms, trying to calm the unruly crowd, "Quiet …Quiet …Quiet!"

Puck quickly emerged from the kitchen and went behind the bar and grabbed the wooden mallet from the shelf, slamming it down hard on the bar-top several times, demanding the crowd's attention.

"I have spoken to the Sage!" he bellowed out, the room now falling silent.

"And what did he have to say?" one of the pixies asked after a long quiet moment.

"He has assured me that the nymphs are not responsible. He has asked that we do not act without knowing the true facts," Puck spoke in an assuring tone, "As the father of one of the children, I intended to follow his instructions."

"What are those true facts?" another pixie asked.

"That is still to be determined, but I am not willing to go to war with the wrong community," he said sternly, "I want to punish those that are truly responsible."

"Does the Sage have any idea who is responsible?" the question asked by a pixie near the entrance.

"Yes, but verification is needed. I will be returning to Lily Pond this evening and as soon as I learn the truth I will return and inform you. Please continue with your normal life until then," Puck said, a sincere plea in his voice.

Slowly the crowd dissipated, talking amongst themselves, reluctantly accepting what Puck had told them.

CHAPTER EIGHT

The morning riding lessons over and the mid-day meal behind him, Croaker groomed Cloud Whisper as they waited for Link to arrive at the training area.

"Are you ready to begin?" Croaker heard Link call out as he approached.

"I was wondering when you would get here," Croaker said, still brushing the white mount as he turned to watch Link riding a charcoal gray bush-tail.

"Put this on," Link instructed, reaching behind him and retrieving a belted sheath with a wooden training sword similar to the one he had discovered in the chamber.

"The object of this training session is for you and Cloud Whisper to react as one in a combat situation," Link continued.

Croaker belted his training sword and withdrew it from the sheath. "This is different from the other swords. It feels better in my hand," he remarked as he looked up at Link.

"I had it made for you this morning. I thought it would be better if you had one that was specially prepared for your hand," Link said, not wanting to make anything more of it, "If you are through playing with that we can get started."

Croaker sheathed the sword and swung up onto Cloud Whisper, "I am ready."

Throughout the afternoon Link would explain a maneuver and walk through it, increasing the speed each time they performed it, until they were able to execute it at the full speed of a real combat situation. Rider and mount in unison.

◆ ◆ ◆ ◆ ◆

Arklan broke the seal on the message that just arrived from the southwestern outpost. After reading it, he called out "Sergeant of the Guard".

Turning his attention to the messenger; "You can rest here tonight and return to your post tomorrow. You have done well in the haste of delivery."

"Yes, Your Majesty," the sergeant said as he appeared through the entrance to the study.

"Send someone to bring Sire Croaker to my study and the messenger assigned to him as well. Also, see to it this man is given quarters for the evening."

"Yes, Your Majesty. I will see to it at once," the sergeant said, giving a bow and motioning the messenger to follow him.

The sergeant called one of his runners over to him and sent him in search of Croaker and Link, then proceeded on with the messenger to the guards stationed at the spiral stairs.

When the runner found Croaker and Link, they were leaving the stables after having put up Cloud Whisper and the charcoal gray for the evening.

"Sires, the King wishes your presence in his study at once," he informed them.

Hurrying through the market place, the three made their way to the main foyer, up the staircase and down the corridor to the King's study.

"Your Majesty, Sire Croaker and his companion have arrived," the Sergeant of the Guard announced.

"Thank you. Send them in."

"Your Majesty," Croaker said as he and Link entered with a bow.

"I have received a message from the southwest. A young pixie was discovered at the border. He was near death, though our healers were able to save him," Arklan said, deep concern showing in his features, "They were able to discern, from his fevered ranting, that an attack took place in the mining town of Feldspar. He spoke of monsters killing all."

Croaker and Link looked at each other in disbelief before Croaker spoke, "Your Majesty, do you suppose it has to do with the sightings?" the apprehension he had felt two nights before washing over him again.

"We have no way of knowing, that is why I sent for you. I would like you to lead a column to Feldspar to investigate," Arklan informed Croaker.

"Why would you need me to lead a column?" Croaker asked.

"What I *need* to have is the presence of a frog to prevent any misunderstanding of the column. What I *do not need* is an incident that will start a conflict," the King informed him.

"When would you like us to leave, Sire?" Croaker asked.

"You will leave for the southwest outpost immediately. Your messenger friend will be taking a message to the Sage in Lily Pond," Arklan said, turning his gaze toward Link, "You must deliver this message to the Sage even if it means going to the nymph city itself!"

"Yes, Your Majesty," Link said, with a slight hesitation, knowing the ramifications of what Arklan was asking him to do.

"I will have the ambassador write you a letter of protection. I hope it will help you if needed," Arklan said, trying to give Link some ease of mind.

"Your Majesty, may I give the artifacts to Croaker before we leave?" Link asked.

"If you feel you should," Arklan agreed.

Croaker looked at them with surprise as he blurted out, "What artifacts?"

"If you will come with me to my quarters you will see. It is a legacy from a General Longhopper from an ancient time," Link informed him, "I will tell you more on the way."

"Both of you report back here as soon as that is done. I should have your letter ready for you then," Arklan commanded Link, then turning his attention back to Croaker, "I will have orders for you to carry to the outpost commander."

After leaving the King's study, Link began to tell Croaker of how he had gone to the smith to have a sword made for him and how that led to the discovery of the artifacts in the forgotten chamber. Croaker listened, transfixed by the telling of the contents of the scroll left by General Longhopper.

"You said that he was leaving his armaments to the next frog leader. Why are you giving them to me?" he asked Link.

"Because I believe you are that leader, as does King Arklan," Link stopped in the middle of the corridor to look Croaker in the eye, "The fact that you asked for training *shows* that is the case."

Trying to accept what Link had just said, Croaker thought; *I just had this feeling of uneasiness, I do not feel like I am a leader. Gribit is the frog leader.*

"Now let us go. We have to make one other stop before we go to my quarters," Link said, continuing down the corridor.

"Where is that?" Croaker asked, following beside Link.

"We must stop by the seamstress. I have requested a new tunic be made for you."

"A tunic?"

"Yes. I gave her the one belonging to General Longhopper as a pattern since that one was about to disintegrate from age. It should look like the ones worn by the frog statues near the entrance," Link said as they descended the stairs to the ground level of the city.

"Sire Link. I see you brought your frog friend along this time," the seamstress said, looking up from her sewing as the two entered the shop, "I have the finished tunic and we can try it on him."

"Good, we will need it immediately. The King has given us orders and we must leave right away," Link said, watching her as she stood and walked across the room to a folded bundle lying on a table.

"Come here, Sire Frog," she commanded as she flapped the garment with both hands, shaking out the folds.

Made of spider silk material, the tunic she held in her hands glistened like a dragonfly in the sun's rays that poured through the shop window. Snow white, the tunic contained a crest showing a white water lily atop an emerald green lily pad in the center of the chest. Broad accent bands of blue ran up either side to the armpits and around the collar and sleeve cuffs.

"*What* is this?" Link asked as it unfurled in front of his eyes, "It should be drab and of earth tones!"

"It is not every day that I am asked to make a tunic for a frog. I believed it had to be distinctive and should have the elegance merited of someone special," she defended herself.

It was a strange feeling as Croaker tried it on. It was softer than the slicker he had tried on at the inn in Weavertown but this material felt much more agreeable against his skin.

"Do you have a drab cloak he can wear over it?" Link asked.

"Yes, Sire," she said sheepishly and went to retrieve it.

Link regarded the tunic with mixed emotions; *on one hand it was battle garb and Croaker did not need to stand out as a target. On the other hand, she was right, Croaker was a special frog and the tunic was worthy of his station.*

"You have done an ideal job and with the cloak . . . all will be well," Link said, bringing a smile to her face.

Giving Croaker no time to admire the tunic, Link took the cloak from the seamstress, "Thank you."

"We must leave for my quarters now," Link said calling to Croaker, motioning him to follow.

Removing the tunic, Croaker quickly folded it as he hurried after Link who was already nearing the foyer.

"Have one of your runners go to the stables to have Sire Croaker's mount readied. He will be returning in a few minutes," Link told one of the sentries posted at the main entrance of the foyer.

"Yes, Sire. His mount will be waiting."

Thanking the sentry, Link turned to Croaker, "You will be leaving by the southern gate."

Croaker and Link hurried up the staircase to the next level. The sounds coming from the dining area mingled with the aroma of the evening meal as they passed by its entrance on their way to Link's quarters. Each knew that they would be eating from their tack as they traveled their separate ways; *there would be no hot meals in their immediate future.*

Entering his quarters, Link went to the storage area as Croaker, pulling the door closed behind them, nervously anticipated of what Link was about to give him.

"Put this on," Link said, handing Croaker the mail.

Croaker's eyes widened at the sight of the shimmering garment. Marveling at the lightness of it Croaker slid his arms through the sleeves and pulled it over his head to have it rest on his shoulders, "What sort of blouse is this?" he asked.

"This is mail. It is to protect you from weapons piercing through to you," Link said as he turned to retrieve the sword and scabbard from the storage area, "Put the tunic on over it."

When Croaker's head appeared through the collar of his tunic he saw the belted sword that Link was holding out for him, "This armament is beyond anything I could have imagined!" Croaked said, unable to restrain the excitement he felt as he belted the scabbard over his tunic.

"Yes, now you look the leader I know you are," pleased by what he saw, Link then reached for the helm and presented it to Croaker, "Now drape your cloak and all we have left to do is stop at your chamber and get your hip pack."

As Link grabbed his own hip pack, Croaker could not resist taking his new sword from its scabbard to feel it in his hand.

"You will have plenty of time for that when you get to the outpost," Link smiled then turning somber again, "We are losing daylight, you will have to ride hard."

Walking taller, Croaker had a little more bounce to his step as he and Link hurried to his chamber. He felt regal, dressed in his new garb, and looked regal as well.

"I only hope I am worthy of the battle armaments," he told Link, holding the helm tightly under his arm as they hurried along.

"I have no doubt that you will apply yourself honorably," Link said when they stopped at Croaker's chamber door.

Croaker stepped into his chamber and a moment later reappeared with the belted hip pack, containing his slicker and tack, slung over his shoulder. Hastily they climbed the stairs. Walking briskly though the corridor, the sight of Croaker drew the attention of the sentries stationed at the spiral stairs, their eyes following them, toward the Sergeant of the Guard's duty station.

The Sergeant stared at Croaker for a long moment without saying a word, giving Croaker time to belt his hip pack on the opposite side from his sword.

"The King wants you to go right in," the Sergeant finally said, still staring at Croaker then suddenly standing and giving a bow, "Excuse me Sire. Forgive my manners."

Croaker acknowledged his bow and the Sergeant stepped through the door and announced them to the King.

Arklan was pleasantly surprised to see the transformation in Croaker's appearance as he returned their bow, "Sire Croaker. Here are the orders that I would like you to deliver to the commander of the outpost."

Handing the sealed envelope to Croaker, Arklan turned to Link, "This is the message for the Sage and this is the letter of protection from the frog ambassador."

"Sire Croaker," Arklan continued, his smile broadening, "Your companion has very good instincts I believe. May both of your journeys be swift and safe!"

"Thank you, Your Majesty," Croaker said as they bowed and then exited into the corridor to retrace their steps to the foyer.

As they approached the sentries at the foyer entrance, they snapped to attention at the sight of Croaker.

"Sire, your mount is ready and waiting for you," one of them announced.

"Thank you," Croaker said, wondering why they were at attention.

"Stand at ease," Link smiled, then turning to Croaker, "They have never seen a frog warrior before, other than the statues beyond this entry," he explained.

"Give my apologies to Gribit," Croaker said as he swung up on Cloud Whisper, "Your companionship has meant a lot to me."

"As yours for me. And, yes, I will give the Sage your apologies."

The bailey was nearly in complete shadow as the sun settled lower in the sky, the high walls of the palisade and the city palace blocking it from view. Croaker wheeled Cloud Whisper in the direction of the southern gate, beginning his journey to the outpost, as Link left for the northern gate and the road to Lily Pond. It was going to be a long evening for both of them.

CHAPTER NINE

There had been a passage of two days since the attack on Feldspar and now the inky black of the moonless night had settled upon the land once more. A goblin imp went unseen, dressed in his charcoal tunic and riding his giant black bat, as he emerged from the abandoned pixie mine northeast of Millville beyond the Winding Creek.

Down along the hillsides and into the Endless Forest they flew, darting among the trees, to rendezvous with the slithers that had been dispatched a week earlier from the wastelands. Reining his bat to a halt, they silently landed in a small clearing. As the imp stepped to the ground the slithers appeared through the undergrowth and gathered around him.

"What do you have to report?" he asked in a soft whisper.

One by one they gave him the details of their actions since they had been dispatched. They spoke, each in turn, with elation in their hissing-whisper voices at how each had made a meal of the Forest Fairy scouts they had encountered and the children of the pixie town and at Bale's Hollow. They recounted with pride at not leaving any visible sign of their presence, not wanting to tell of their one mistake. The fear they had of the Lord DeMonas kept them from revealing the alarm that had been sounded from Lily Pond when one of them had been sighted near its shore.

"Are the results as we had hoped?" the imp asked.

"Yes, Lord," the leader of the slithers reported, "The Forest Fairies have moved their troops to the border of Lily Pond and the Eastern Field Fairies have responded by moving troops to their borders as well."

"And what of the pixies?" the imp asked, "I have not seen any action being taken by them."

"They have assembled their militia yet they have not moved against the nymphs. I do not know why Lord," the slither replied.

The imp stood in thought for a few moments then spoke, "They must be waiting for the other towns to join them," then added, "Continue to monitor the actions of the domains. We will meet here again in four nights. I am returning to Lord DeMonas to let him know the plan is working as he had hoped it would."

As the slithers disappeared into the undergrowth, the imp mounted his bat and reined him into the night sky. After clearing the forest they gained altitude and made their way south like a ghostly shadow blinking out the stars above as they passed under them.

In the distance the imp could see the dim lights from the windows of the fairy village of Weavertown as the night breeze wafted the damp air from Lily Pond and filled his nostrils. Veering southwestward he steered his mount toward the caves that awaited him west of Feldspar. He should reach the caves just before the first gray light of day, then he would eat and rest there before changing his mount and heading south into the wastelands.

Nearing Hillside he could see the occasional light from the pixie town as he gazed down to his right. Watching the town lights fall away behind him, they made their way over the Rolling Hills. Wildly grinning, exposing needle sharp canines to the night sky, he reveled in the knowledge that he would see no lights from Feldspar.

On they flew until the first dim gray light of the new day began to appear beyond the eastern horizon. Circling over the black gaping mouth of the caves, overlooking the wastelands to the south, they flew down into the darkness toward the faint yellow-red flickering glow of the watch fires deep within to those that awaited his arrival.

In and out they wove their way through the stalactites until they landed near the fires. In the large cavern the sound of water droplets dripping into pools, which had formed through the centuries, could be heard; their echoes blending with the voices of the toads that gathered in groups around the fires.

As the imp dismounted his bat a large toad approached, "Lord Noma. The general awaits you. I will see to your bat."

"Unbridle him and release him to the dark cavern where he can sleep with his brothers and sisters," Lord Noma instructed the toad, "I will be leaving as soon as I have taken nourishment and have spoken to the general. Have a raven ready for the remainder of my journey when I return."

"It will be as you ask Lord."

The imp unhooked his canteen and saddlebags and walked to the rear of the cavern where General O'Dias was seated at a table on which there was a map spread out.

O'Dias saw Lord Noma approach and stood while bowing his head slightly, "Lord Noma, have a seat," he gestured to a chair across from him.

"Is everything on schedule?" Noma asked.

"Yes Lord," the general replied as he took his seat again, "You can apprise your brother that we will be in position when the time is right."

"Lord DeMonas will be glad to hear that!" Noma said, a grin spreading across his face pushing up wrinkles in his avocado skin as his gold cat eyes reflected the firelight.

"When you see your brother inform him that the pixies have not made the discovery at Feldspar yet," O'Dias said.

"No one has approached the town?" Noma flashed a sneer in the direction of General O'Dias.

"I believed that there would have been travelers by now. We will just have to wait longer," the General surmised, ignoring the look from Lord Noma.

"Send a messenger when the pixies discover the attack on the town. We can not initiate our other plans until they believe the fairies attacked them," Noma reminded the General.

"Yesterday I stationed toads at points that overlook Feldspar. They will report any activity to me as soon as it happens," O'Dias assured Noma.

Two toads approached the goblin imps. One carried a large wooden bowl of fresh picked berries and plums while the other brought two mugs of hot brew.

"Lord, your raven is ready for you," the toad carrying the bowl of fruit said as he placed it on the table, "Will there be anything else Lord?"

Noma grabbed a plump plum and bit into it while waving the toads away as the juice trickled from the corners of his mouth. The two goblins ate like that until the last berry had been devoured and then they guzzled down the still hot brew.

"I am on my way to my brother now. Do not let this take any longer than need be!" Lord Noma said, wiping his blouse sleeve across his mouth.

General O'Dias resisted his impulse to snap back, he did not want to get on the wrong side of the King's brother, "Yes, Lord."

❖ ❖ ❖ ❖ ❖

Croaker woke with a start when the runner entered his tent calling for him to rise.

"Sire frog, the commander wants you to report to him in the command tent," the runner announced.

"Yes. Tell him I will be right there," Croaker said, slowly swinging his legs over the side of the cot and rubbing the sleep from his eyes, "What time of day is it?"

"It is soon to be sunrise Sire," the runner said as he turned to leave the tent and report back to the commander.

Croaker sat for a moment. It had only been about four hours since he had arrived at the outpost and had given the commander the sealed orders from King Arklan.

A smile began to spread across his face as he recalled the stunned look on the faces of the fairies when he arrived; *they did not know what to say or do when they saw me. It must have been a shock for them to see a frog in battle armament arriving in the dark of night.*

Croaker shook his head trying to get his thoughts back on track, then rising to his feet he awkwardly made his way to the basin on the other side of his tent. Dipping his hands into the cold water, he splashed his face several times to drive out the last remnants of sleep that still tugged at him.

Taking up the towel beside the basin, he surveyed the tent as he patted his face dry to see where he had left his gear. He found it on a locker at the foot of his cot stacked in a neat pile where he had placed it before going to sleep.

Pulling his mail over his head and then his tunic, he quickly belted his sword and hip pack. Grabbing up his helm on his way out the entrance of his tent, he ducked through and headed in the direction of the command tent.

"Sire Croaker," the commander said as Croaker appeared through the entrance of the command tent, "I hope you got enough rest?"

"It will have to do," Croaker replied as he scanned the room.

"Have a seat at the table," the commander pointed to a vacant chair at a small table near the corner of the tent.

Croaker saw the table was set for three and a young fairy was sitting in the chair across from the one the commander had pointed out to him.

"This is my exec, he will be in command of the outpost when we leave," the commander informed him.

The young fairy stood and gave Croaker a polite bow, "It is a pleasure to meet you, Sire Croaker."

Croaker acknowledged the bow and found a place near the entrance to set his helm before taking his seat.

Outside the bird songs mixed with the buzz of the outpost coming to life, as the dim gray light of the new day grew brighter. The air was calm and cool with the damp smell of dew as three fairies made their way to the command tent from the mess with the morning meals for the commander, his exec and Croaker.

◆ ◆ ◆ ◆ ◆

The morning sky was beginning to turn yellow-orange from the cool gray of the pre-dawn as the sun's first rays peeked over the eastern horizon. In the calm of the morning air the tall grasses muffled the humming of fairy wings when Link, still tired after his brief nap at the Weavertown outpost, broke free of the tall grasses and reeds as he flew over the open water.

Link hadn't noticed the crew of nymphs in the shallows to the east that were about to begin harvesting the cattail only a short distance from where he had emerged. As they watched him fly further out, on his way to Gribit's pad, they sent one of the crew to report his intrusion into their domain.

Approaching Gribit's pad he saw no sign of the Sage; *I was afraid of this. It looks like Gribit is still in the nymph city. I guess I have no choice but to go there.*

When Link landed at Gribit's pad to rest for a moment he heard the drone of dragonfly wings as a small patrol of nymphs soon encircled him. With swords in hand, they landed and the leader dismounted her dragonfly.

"Why would a fairy enter our domain?" she asked with hostility.

"I am here to see the Sage, Gribit," Link answered.

"And what business would a fairy have with the Sage?" the nymph demanded.

"I have an urgent message for him."

"Well that is too bad. Take him prisoner," she ordered.

"Wait a moment. You must take me to see the Sage and your Queen!"

"And what makes you think that I would even consider that?" she asked, the sarcasm to his demand evident.

"I have a letter of protection from the frogs," Link said, pulling it from his hip pack to hand to her.

"And how am I to know this is really from the frogs?"

"Take me to the Sage and he will verify it. The message I have for him is too important to not be delivered. King Arklan sent me himself," he implored her.

"Very well. If this is a ruse we will still be able to hold you," she finally agreed, and then ordered, "Take his weapons."

As one of the nymphs tried to take Link's hip pack, he recoiled and snapped, "I am the one entrusted to deliver this. No one else!"

A long moment passed as the tension shown in all their faces before the leader of the patrol said, "Let us inspect your pack for weapons. If there are none than you may carry it yourself." She had gained an instant respect for this fairy. He had great courage.

Link removed his hand from the hilt of his sword and unbelted it to hand it over to her, "Agreed!"

"There is only his tack, a slicker and a sealed message," a patrol nymph reported to the leader.

"Very well. He may carry it," the leader said.

As they flew east, toward the floating dock, Link noticed the crew of nymphs harvesting the cattail stop and watch them pass; *so that is how they knew of my presence.*

"Corporal, take my mount to the stables. When that is done, you can take the patrol to the northern shore and get the scout reports. I will take this fairy to the Sage and find out if his story is true," the leader instructed her second in command when they had landed on the floating dock.

"As you wish Sergeant!"

Link felt as though there were a weight pressing in on him as they slowly descended in the lift. He had never been this confined before and the feeling of the floor dropping away was unnerving. Though it was only a moment, when the lift finally stopped, it felt to him an eternity until the lift door was opened and he was able to be free of the confinement.

"Straight ahead," she said, nudging Link toward the doorway ahead.

When they entered the tunnel dome the feeling of pressure returned to Link as he saw the water being kept out by the dome. Seeing fish swimming, in and out of the cover of vegetation and rocks outside the dome, soon distracted him enough to forget about the apprehension he had been feeling as they entered the main dome of the city.

"Your city is in many ways as grand as is mine," Link said, bringing up a smile of pride on the sergeant's face as they made their way through the ring streets to the palace entrance.

The sentries at the entrance snapped to attention and thrust out their staffs in salute at the approach of the sergeant and also blocking the way to the entry.

"I am taking this fairy to see the Sage. He is carrying a letter of protection from the frogs," she informed them.

The sentries drew back their staffs, allowing them to pass, as the sergeant and Link proceeded to the orderly's desk at the back of the entry hall.

"Where can we find the Sage?" the sergeant asked.

"He should have risen. He would probably be in the dining area by now," the orderly responded, not seeming to be surprised that the sergeant was escorting a fairy.

"Thank you," then turning to Link and pointing at a staircase, "That way!"

Link nodded and the two departed the orderly's desk to ascend the stairs.

Walking along the second floor corridor, they passed the palace guest chambers on their way to the dining area. Link gazed around the large room as they entered and saw Gribit seated at two tables placed together. Seated with Gribit were three ambassadors and at the adjoining table sat a young frog and a pixie.

The dining area fell quiet as the sergeant and Link approached the Sage.

"Excuse me Sire. I do not mean to interrupt, but this fairy claims to be carrying a letter of protection from the frogs," the sergeant said as she handed the letter to Gribit, then continued, "He also claims he has an urgent message for you."

"This is as he says. It is from the ambassador at Granstone. I will be expecting him to arrive here either this evening or tomorrow," Gribit informed the sergeant, "The fairy will be my guest."

"Yes Sire," the sergeant acknowledged all the while wondering what could be happening that a fairy and a pixie should be guests of the palace.

"May I see this urgent message you have brought me," Gribit asked Link as the sergeant returned to her duties.

"Yes Sire," Link said reaching into his hip pack.

"Why is Croaker not the one to bring me this?" Gribit asked as he opened the sealed message.

"The message will explain all, Sire," Link said, "As for Croaker, he asked me to extend his apologies to you."

"How is Croaker?" Webber suddenly asked at hearing his name.

"He is well, Sire frog."

"Please, take a seat," Webber said, motioning to a kitchen nymph to bring another chair to their table, "My name is Webber and my companion's name is Puck."

"The food is somewhat different here, though pleasing to the palate," Puck informed Link.

"Thank you. My name is Link," he informed them as he moved to the open space they made available to him.

"I am afraid my suspicions may be a reality," Gribit said to the ambassadors as he looked up from the message, "We will need to speak to Isalia."

◆◆◆◆◆

The trade caravan from Hillside appeared over the crest of the last hill before reaching Feldspar as the yellow glow of the morning sky was beginning to turn azure blue when a sentinel toad hurried on his way to the caves and General O'Dias.

"Good," O'Dias said when the toad reported to him, "Have the messenger that is standing by report to me immediately."

Moments later an imp came running, "Sir, you sent for me?"

"Yes. Take this message to Lord DeMonas as fast as you are able."

"My raven is waiting at the entrance as we speak Sir."

As the messenger scurried off to the entrance, a sly smile drew across O'Dias' lips as he thought about the next part of their plan; *all is working as hoped.*

CHAPTER TEN

There were no smiles on the faces of the pixies and frogs in the caravan that arrived in Feldspar. The air was filled with the stench of death and there was only the look of disbelief at what they saw as they made their way deeper into the town. Only the creaking of the cartwheels and the buzzing of flies could be heard as they sat silently, not knowing whether to scream out or just cry at what they saw.

A pixie suddenly jumped to the ground from one of the carts yelling, "No. Oh no," then dropping down beside the bodies of a pixie couple; the husband's body shielding his wife's body to no avail, lying just outside one of the houses. "My brother. Why have they done this to you?" he sobbed as he sat on the blood stained ground cradling his brother's head.

The caravan master, the frog in charge, halted the caravan allowing several other pixies to search for their families.

Everywhere, they found signs that fairies had attacked the town and that it had happened at night since the dead were wearing nightclothes.

"They had been taken by surprise. There are families in the houses at the edge of town, some still in their beds," a young trade frog reported to the caravan master.

"I have never seen anything like this ever," the look on the frog's face reflecting the look of the pixies, "Take a bush-tail and return to Hillside. Inform them of what has happened here and then go to Lily Pond and inform the Sage," the caravan master instructed, "It appears that we have a war on our hands though I have never known the fairies to do something like this."

"Yes Sire," the young frog said, accepting his task.

The caravan master called the pixies and frogs that were still with the carts over to him, "The dead should be buried," he said somberly as he surveyed the surrounding area, determining the task that must be performed, "Inform the others searching for their families."

◆ ◆ ◆ ◆ ◆

The morning sun glared brightly as a toad cupped his hands to shield his eyes. In the distance, to the east, he could see a line of troops approaching Feldspar. Peering at the column from his vantage point in the hills to the west that rise above Feldspar, as the formation neared the mining town, he could make out that it was a column of fairies.

Wasting no time, knowing that the column would reach Feldspar in the time it would take him to reach the caves, the toad left his post to report to General O'Dias of this new development.

◆ ◆ ◆ ◆ ◆

As the column approached Feldspar, Croaker caught the faint odor of death carried on the light breeze drifting down the hillside from the mining town. As they got closer, the sound of metal scrapping against stone could be heard echoing through the strange quiet of the town.

"Someone is digging on the far side of the town," the commander said.

"Wait here," Croaker replied, "I will go ahead to see who."

"Take a couple of my troops. In case there is a problem," the commander cautioned.

"Alright, but this is an investigation and we do not want to provoke an incident," Croaker accepted the commander's suggestion, "If all is well I will send one of them back for you."

"Yes, Sire," the commander, agreed.

Croaker and the two fairies entered the east side of town and were making their way through the streets when two pixies emerged from a doorway carrying the body of one of the slain pixies.

"Fairies!" one of the pixies cried out when he saw Croaker in his battle garb and the two fairies with him.

The sound of metal scrapping against stone ceased; only to be followed by the sound of heavy footsteps as pixies and frogs came running around the street corner. With shovels and other tools in their hands, they came to a sudden stop at the sight of Croaker and Cloud Whisper.

The shout had also reached the commander's ears and he quickly brought up his troops behind Croaker.

"You will not take us so easily!" a pixie snarled.

"Wait!" the caravan master barked, and then turning his gaze back at Croaker, "Who are you?"

"I am Croaker, liaison to the Sage," he answered, and then pointing at the pixie that spoke, "What does he mean?"

"Why is a frog dressed in such a manner?" the caravan master asked, ignoring Croaker's question.

"I will explain later. What does he mean?" Croaker repeated, demanding an answer.

"We have seen your handy work," the frog said, stretching out his arm and moving it in an arc toward the buildings of the town around him. "Why have you returned?"

"This was not of our doing," Croaker responded, "A young pixie was found near the border near death. In his fevered ranting he spoke of monsters killing all in this town. I am here at the request of King Arklan to investigate what has happened."

"Do you mean to tell me that you and your fairies did not attack this town?"

"That is exactly what I am saying. Why would you believe it was the fairies that attacked?" Croaker asked, puzzled by the accusation.

"There is only fairy sign to be found," the caravan master said, "If it was not you then who?"

Croaker decided that he must inform them of what had been happening and what suspicions had been aroused, "There has been a sighting of toads and slithers together and we believe that when they disappeared that this is where they went."

"Toads and slithers together! Do you really expect us to believe something that outrageous?" the frog asked in amazement.

"If we were here to do you harm we would have done so by now," Croaker said, annoyed that they were not willing to listen to what he had to say, "As long as we are here, can we assist in your task? What do you require?"

As Croaker swung down from his mount the caravan master was at a loss for words, "Well, how can we help?" he asked again.

Croaker's actions and manner completely disarmed the pixies and frogs and they slowly lowered their makeshift weapons.

"We need help burying the dead," the master finally said.

"Commander. Have your troops assist with the dead and the digging," Croaker ordered.

"Yes, Sire," the commander agreed, amazed at how quickly Croaker had changed the tone of events.

"Sire Croaker. Will you answer my question now?" The master asked.

Croaker explained how he had been at Gribit's pad when Link had arrived and how he had woken with apprehension the night of his arrival in Granstone, the same night the gathering of toads and slithers had vanished. He told of how he had asked Link to train him after seeing the statues in the courtyard and how that led to the discovery of the forgotten chamber.

"When Link found the artifacts, left by General Longhopper, he and King Arklan said that I should be the one to have them," Croaker said.

"Frogs were warriors!" the master said with amazement.

"Yes, at one time long ago," Croaker said as he put out his arm and laid his hand on the frog's shoulder.

"Sire. We have sent word to Hillside that fairies had attacked the town," the master said, suddenly realizing the mistake they had made.

"Then we must send another messenger to correct that," Croaker said, "We do not want a war to start between the domains. It is obvious that is what the toads and slithers had in mind by attacking this town."

"I will send one of the pixies, Sire. He can take one of the caravan's bush-tails."

◆ ◆ ◆ ◆ ◆

Though the sun was bright in the sky now, the caverns maintained their perpetual darkness. Fires had to be constantly fed to light the area and stave off the damp coolness that engulfed the toads and slithers as they waited for the General to give orders that would take them out into the sunlight.

General O'Dias intently studied the map that lay before him, devising a plan to overcome this new development the toad sentry reported.

"Have the commanders for columns one and two report to me immediately," O'Dias barked out orders to the toad.

"Yes Sir," the toad said, jumping back a step, then leaped off into the cavern toward the fires.

As O'Dias bent over the map he thought; *why has a column of fairies entered the pixie domain? No matter, we can make this work to our advantage.*

"Sir. You sent for us?" one of the commanders said as they reached the table.

"Yes, a column of fairies arrived at Feldspar. I will need column one to go to this point on the road to Hillside. You will set an ambush for any pixies or frogs that try to take this road. We must stop them from making a report to the pixies. I will lead the second column to this point and set up an ambush. We will attack the fairies when they return to their domain," the General instructed, pointing a clawed finger to the positions on the map.

"Sir. Do we know that there has not been conflict between the pixies and the fairies that arrived?" the commander asked.

"No. But if there had been, one of the toads would have been here to report it by now," O'Dias surmised, "Once we kill the fairies, we will place their bodies around the town. That will be the proof that they were the attackers," he grinned.

"Yes Sir," the commander replied, "Will there be anything else?"

"Yes. Send a couple of imp archers on ravens to the Hillside road."

"Sir?"

"In case another messenger is sent. We can not let the pixies know the true facts," then stopping to consider if he had thought of the different contingencies, O'Dias continued with additional orders, "We will have to move fast so I will want the Rat Riders. Tell the toad commander that I want him and his troops ready to move out immediately. The slithers can catch up as our reserves. Have my bat prepared for combat!"

As soon as the slithers received their orders they hurried out of the caverns to get the warmth of the sun. The Rat Riders formed up at the entrance of the cave awaiting the general and their march to the designated ambush areas.

A large toad led a giant black bat, with black chain mail headdress and a thick black leather saddle that armored the bat's body, to General O'Dias. The General had attired himself in black chain mail as well and his yellow cat eyes shined from deep within the openings of his helm as they reflected the flickering firelight. He wore a battle axe at his side and a dagger sheathed in the side of his boot. An avocado skinned hand reach out from under his black cloak and the clawed fingers grasped the saddle horn as he swung up into his saddle. He and his bat were a sight to instill fear into any who had to face them.

Making his way to the front of the column, he commanded, "Forward!"

◆ ◆ ◆ ◆ ◆

163

Gribit, the ambassadors, Link, Webber and Puck entered the meeting chamber and found Isalia already present and waiting for them.

"Your Majesty," Gribit said giving a bow as he entered, the others following his lead, "We have received a message from Arklan that indicates the possibility of the scenario we discussed when I first arrived."

"That would explain the recent events with the fairies of the forest and the eastern fields," Isalia said, motioning the group to be seated in the waiting chairs along the interior walls.

"The ambassador from Lone Oak has told me of Fernon's actions and why he took them and Airlein has requested a meeting with me. Is there something she has done besides that?" Gribit asked.

"She has moved troops to her borders as well. It would not take much to set things off with tensions running high," she relayed the information she had obtained, then looking to Puck and the ambassador from Millville, "and you have told me of the incident in the rolling hills."

Puck and the ambassador nodded their acknowledgement and Puck added, "Your Majesty. My citizens are looking for someone to take their anger out on. It has been an effort to keep them from acting without knowing the facts and most still believe that you are to blame for the missing children."

"These are the reasons that I want to have a summit of the leaders of the domains," Isalia said as she turned and walked to the opening overlooking the city.

Before Gribit could respond she turned back to the group, "I do not quite know how to deal with the pixies. They have no one leader."

Gribit stood, "That is why Puck is here! I have chosen him to be the pixie representative. I hope that this will meet with your approval. I have other plans for him as well."

Puck sat stunned at this revelation as the ambassador from Millville spoke up, "Your Majesty. The Sage and I have spoken of this matter since my arrival and I am in full agreement. Puck has shown that he is worthy of this station."

"What will his citizens say about this?" Isalia questioned.

"The Sage and I will make it clear that this is the way it should be!" the ambassador replied, "It is in their best interest."

"Not everyone acts in his or her own best interest," Isalia pointed out.

"If Puck is willing, I am sure he will convince them that he is right for the position," Gribit said calmly, "I have listened to Webber's accounts of Puck's actions and that along with what the ambassador has told me how he handled himself in Limonite, speaking to the citizens, reinforces my decision."

"Then the question is, are you willing to take this responsibility?" Isalia asked, looking directly at Puck.

Puck gave a single nod of his head, "Yes, Your Majesty. If the Sage and the ambassador believe that I am right for the task, then I must."

"So be it. Send the ambassadors to the other domains to have their leaders attend this summit. We will schedule it for three days from now."

"Link. I want you to take this message back to King Arklan. Look for the ambassador on your way and inform him of what has been decided here. He can return to Granstone with you," Gribit instructed, then turning to bow, "By your leave Your Majesty."

"I will have letters of safe passage written for the ambassadors to take to their leaders," Isalia said before returning his bow, then dismissing the group.

◆ ◆ ◆ ◆ ◆

The clouds were beginning to build in the sky over Feldspar as a pixie swung up on a bush-tail, preparing to ride to Hillside.

"Make sure they understand that the fairies were not the attackers!" the caravan commander stressed.

"Yes, Sire frog," he replied as he reined his bush-tail onto the road northward to Hillside.

In the distance, two ravens swept down from the gathering clouds into a small grove that lie just beyond the last rise to Feldspar on the Hillside road.

As the rider approached the grove, his bush-tail in full run, he didn't hear the arrows slicing through the air from the cover of the grove. With a dull thud, each had struck their mark and the bush-tail collapsed rolling headfirst down the road as the pixie flew off its back and landed motionless on the road just beyond the dead bush-tail.

"O'Dias was right," one of the imp archers said as they walked out onto the road.

"That is why he is a general. We have to get these bodies off the road," the other responded.

"When the slithers arrive, they will have a treat," the first imp laughed.

"Give me a hand with this bush-tail. He is a heavy one."

"What about the pixie? Is he dead?"

Rolling the pixie over with his foot, "Yes. Got him right through the heart!" he replied.

◆ ◆ ◆ ◆ ◆

Noma had led his mount through the caverns to the mouth of the caves before he swung up into the saddle. Spurring the raven in its side with his heel, they were soon in the air leaving the lush green lands of the domains, soaring above the parched and barren landscape of the wastelands. As they flew deeper into the realm of the imps they encountered a growing haze shrouding the land. The air was acrid with the putrid smell of decay rising from the distant swamps and Noma felt the reassuring familiarity.

As he flew, Noma recalled the stories of how the wastelands had once been as fertile and fresh as the realm of Lily Pond centuries ago. The effect of the way the imps lived with lack of regard for the land had taken its toll through the years. Nomadic in their nature, the imps had scourged the land as they moved from place to place depleting the resources setting up industries where the toads were forced to labor endlessly to produce the goods they required.

The closer he came to the cave palace of his brother the dimmer the sun grew in the thickening haze and he thought of the need for new land; *the highlands forests had been cut to the ground as material and fuel for the factories. The waste from the factories was dumped into the river killing the plant life that kept the water pure. Eventually the waters dried up until only a trickle remained where once the flowing waters had cast great clouds of mist from the thundering falls where Lord DeMonas' cave palace sits high in the bluffs to the highlands plateau. The orchards that are still standing at the periphery of their lands no longer bear the required amount of fruits they relish.*

As Noma approached the bluffs and the cave palace he saw below, where there had once been a clear blue lake, the endless swamp that stretches for miles in all directions from the base of the falls; *He was home.*

Landing his raven near the entrance to the cave palace, Noma swung off his mount and slapped the reins into the hands of the toad that had hurried over to him.

"Feed him. We have just traveled half a day," he growled without looking at the toad as he walked toward the entrance.

"My Lord, the King awaits you in his chamber," an imp sentry informed him as he trudged past.

"Very well, have some fruit sent to the chamber. I will eat while my brother and I talk," Noma instructed, pausing only for that moment.

The main cavern walls shimmered in the flickering light of the oil lamps around the large expanse as the quartz deposits in the walls and ceiling bent and reflected the rays that touched them. The air was cool and Noma could taste the dampness while the odor of soot from the burning lamps permeated the cavern as his footsteps echoed off the walls as quietly as whispers.

A sentry opened a large, heavy, wooden door to the entrance of the Kings chamber and Noma entered.

Hearing the door to his chamber open, DeMonas watched to see who would be entering. Always on guard because he did not know whom he could trust, he never trusted anyone, especially his family for they were a true threat to his throne.

"Brother! Do you have a report for me?" DeMonas said, recognizing his younger brother entering the chamber.

"Yes, the slithers have been doing as they were told, with the desired results. As for Feldspar, there has not been anything yet," Noma reported, crossing the chamber while his multiple shadows were flitting like bats in the night from the flickering oil lamps around the chamber and the wood fire, crackling and

169

popping, in the fire place hewn into the chamber wall across from his brother's lounge chair.

"Why?" the King snapped, the fire of anger flashing in his eyes, matching the red-hot cinders in the fireplace, as he sprang from his knurly root chair, the word coming out of his mouth like a curse.

"The pixies have not been to the town yet. O'Dias will send word when it happens!" Noma growled back, not wanting to give his brother a hint of the fear he had of him, while taking a seat at the rough-hewn table with legs matching the lounge chair.

"It has been more than two days now," DeMonas spat out the words and began to pace, never taking his eyes off his brother.

"Patience brother, things will develop as you have planned. Come join me, I have ordered fruit sent to your chamber so we may eat as we discuss your plans," Noma said, trying to reassure DeMonas and quell the King's anger in the same breath.

DeMonas gave thought to his brother's words and slowly the anger in his eyes dimmed, "Yes, of course you are right. We can use the extra time to insure our troops are ready."

"Will you have any new orders for the slithers when I return to the Endless Forest?" Noma asked.

"No, the orders remain the same."

The large wooden door opened and a toad with a large bowl of fruit entered, "Lord, will there be anything else?" he asked nervously, his eyes darting back and forth between the brothers.

"Yes, I have a desire for some of that berry brew that was pillaged from Feldspar and some juicy fat grubs," DeMonas ordered.

"Yes Lord," the toad acknowledged the order and left the chamber as quickly as he could.

"When we know the Lily Pond factions are at war with each other then we will move our troops to the southern borders of the field fairies without notice," DeMonas said, taking his seat at the head of the table.

"Granstone will be lightly defended then with their troops moving to the north and west. If everything works as it should, then they would have to look to the east as well," Noma said, grinning broadly, exposing his deadly canines.

"Yes, Granstone is the key but it will not be taken by force . . . it can be defended by only a few and our losses would be high. We will take it by cutting off all supplies to it and time will be our ally. While we are waiting, we will pillage all the towns and villages in the domains," DeMonas said, the glint in his eyes accentuating the rise of his right eyebrow.

The conversation was interrupted by a knock at the large chamber door. The door swung open as the sentry allowed the imp messenger to enter.

"Lord, I have a message from General O'Dias," the messenger informed DeMonas, while standing in the opening silhouetted against the dark cavern behind him.

"Bring it here!" DeMonas commanded.

Breaking the seal, the goblin king read and a broad grin appeared across his face, "It has begun. The pixies have discovered what happened in Feldspar."

CHAPTER ELEVEN

High up in the canopy of her palace tree Airlein stands watching from her balcony as the clouds slowly build in the southwest over the Rolling Hills. The warm sun floods over her as its rays trickle down through the leaves speckling the garden below with gems of light.

"Your Majesty," General Broadstem said, breaking her concentration.

"Yes, what is it?" Airlein asked, surprised by his voice, turning quickly in the General's direction.

"We are receiving more reports from the west. There has been a lot of activity at Lily Pond," he informed her as he held out the latest message.

"I hope to hear from the Sage soon," she said, and then turning her attention back to the southwest, "Those clouds that are building are not rain clouds, yet I feel a storm is brewing."

The young Queen's apprehension flooded over her as the sight brought back the memories of the day she had lost her parents. They had been taking a trip throughout their domain, two years prior, when someone had attacked their column and all had been slain. None of the domains had taken responsibility for the attack and there were no signs as to who it could have been.

"Something is happening for sure. The frog and pixie returned last night with the Rolling Hills ambassador and shortly before them the ambassador from the Forest Fairies arrived. Now this morning the fairy from Granstone was seen being escorted to Lily Pond by several patrol nymphs," Broadstem relayed, his gaze also drawn to the gathering clouds off in the distance.

"General, I need more than vague feelings to determine what actions are needed. Can you get me information from Granstone?" Airlein asked.

"I will see to it, Your Majesty."

Making his way from the balcony to the staircase, Broadstem headed to the war room to issue orders for agents to go to Granstone as Airlein ordered; *If it were up to me I would be sending a column into the southern fields. This all started with the arrival of the fairy from Granstone and if there is trouble then that is where it will come from. Airlein is indecisive and that will be our downfall*, he thought as he walked.

Entering the war room, Broadstem was immediately approached by one of the cadre.

"Sir, we have just received another message. It is from a sleeper agent in Granstone!"

The General's eyebrows arched at the statement and he took the message in hand; *A frog arrived in Granstone with one of Arklan's messengers. Next morning the frog began training with fairies. First riding lessons and then weapons training performed by the messenger. Last evening the frog left Granstone to the south in full battle gear riding a white mount while the messenger returned to the north.*

"Arlen's fate, I knew that something was going on in the Southern Fields," Broadstem cursed, and without hesitation snapped out orders, "I want a battalion formed at Loamis and ready to move on my command!"

If Airlein will not act, then I must. But what is a frog doing in battle gear? Are they taking sides now? These thoughts and questions consumed him as he stared down at the relief map of the domains.

◆ ◆ ◆ ◆ ◆

The young frog from the caravan had pushed his bush-tail hard, so hard that it was near collapse when they reached Hillside. They had made good time with daylight left to spare when they stopped in front of the town hall.

Leaping down from his mount the young frog bolted through the doorway.

"I must to speak to the mayor immediately!" he blurted out to the pixie at the main desk.

"He is in his office,' she informed him, "May I help you?"

"No. I must speak to the mayor at once," he said sternly.

"I will see if he is available," she said as she stood and made her way to his door.

"The message is urgent. He *has* to be available now!"

"Sire, there is a frog that insists that he has an urgent message for you," she said, as she poked her head into the now open doorway.

"Send him in," the mayor replied, looking away from the paper he had been writing on.

"The mayor will see you Sire," she said, motioning the young frog to enter the mayor's office.

"Have someone take care of my bush-tail and see that another one is ready for me as soon as possible," he instructed the pixie as he rushed by her.

The pixie stared at the mayor to see if she should comply with the frog's instructions. The mayor, seeing that the frog had a determined sense of urgency responded, "See to Sire Frog's needs," waving her away to perform the task.

The mayor sat struggling to maintain his composure, as the young frog left the office to continue his journey to Lily Pond, after hearing the gruesome news about Feldspar. Although he wanted to run to sound the assembly horn, calling all the town's citizens, his position dictated that he be calm and rational. He knew that how he handled this situation would make the difference of organizing a militia or having a mob on his hands.

Resolving to control his emotions he quickly left the town hall heading directly to the town square, where the horn was located near the banner, ordering the pixie on duty to sound assembly.

The deep hollow sound vibrated throughout the city resonating into the surrounding hills and all activity ceased for a moment as the citizens reacted to the call of the horn. Within moments the Hillside residents were hurrying to the center of town as warehouse workers stopped loading the caravan carts, bakers threw off their aprons and women gathered up small children. Bush-tails drew private carts from the outskirts of town carrying families and pixies that had been working in the surrounding hills spurred on their bush-tails.

It had been a while since the last time the assembly horn had been blown but within minutes the citizens filled the town square. A low hum hung in the air as they mumbled questions to each other to see if anyone knew what was happening.

"Citizens! Citizens! Quiet please," The mayor bellowed out and the hum faded to a quiet where the only thing heard was the whisper of the breeze through leaves of the bushes that lined the streets.

The afternoon sun, muted by the clouds overhead, bathed the crowd with warmth that almost felt cool as they waited for the mayor to speak.

"I have … I have just received … received a message sent by the caravan leader that was sent to Feldspar," the mayor struggled to say, his emotions about to overwhelm him.

"I just learned that fairies attacked Feldspar," he continued after a few moments, regaining his composure, "All in the town are lost."

A collective gasp sounded at the disbelief of the words they just heard.

"I will need riders to carry the message to the other towns," the mayor continued, "I will also need the militia to form and await the other towns to join us. We are at a state of war as of now."

Cries and curses filled the air as hurt and anger showed itself throughout the crowd. Many had relatives in Feldspar.

"We need to stay calm!" the mayor shouted, "If we act rationally, then the fairies will pay for their treachery. We must not do that as an angry mob. Go home now and prepare for the next call."

The mayor's words had the effect he had hoped for. The crowd quieted down and began to disperse for their homes so the militia could retrieve their weapons and report back at the next call.

"We are ready to take your message to the other towns, Sire," a pixie said as he and several others approached the mayor.

"Yes. Come with me and I will write the message out for each of you to carry," the mayor said, motioning them to follow him back to the town hall.

◆◆◆◆◆

"Sire Fairy. The Queen awaits your presence," the words and knocking at the chamber door grew louder as Link pushed back the sleepiness, "Sire Fairy, The Queen..."

"Yes, yes," Link mumbled out a response, still partially suspended in the sleep state, "I will be with you presently."

He had not had a chance to get the rest he needed before now, the brief nap at Weavertown the night before had been enough to get him to Lily Pond. The short rest he had been pulled from would have to be enough until his return to Granstone.

Rolling out of the bed and walking to the basin, Link splashed the cold water on his face to bring himself back to a full state of awareness.

"Follow me, Sire," the nymph said as Link exited his chamber.

"Have the others left yet?" he asked, belting his tunic as they hurriedly walked the hallway to the meeting chamber then realizing he had not taken his hip pack or his canteen.

"No, Sire. They are with the Queen now," she replied.

"How much daylight have I lost?" he asked, concerned that he had slept longer than he thought he should.

"It is just past the mid-day, Sire."

Relief washed over his face that he would not have to make the trip almost completely in the dark of night and that he would not miss the ambassador along the way.

I hope that he will not slow us down on the return to Granstone! He worried.

"Your Majesty, Sire Link," the nymph announced with a bow as they entered the meeting chamber.

"Your Majesty," Link said, following the nymph's lead with a bow.

179

"You may approach. I have already given the others their letters. Here is the one for Arklan," she said, extending the envelope towards Link.

"Your Majesty, Puck, the Ambassador and I must leave now. We must not delay any longer," Webber said, as Link accepted the letter from Isalia.

"Yes, I know. May your journey be swift and safe," Isalia said with a nod.

Huddled in the corner of the room near the entrance, Gribit and the ambassadors from Lone Oak and Zarlan Grove were engaged in conversation as Webber, Puck and the ambassador from Millville were exiting.

"Make them understand about Puck!" Gribit said, turning away from his conversation to address Webber and the ambassador.

"We will," Webber assured him, nodding as he replied while the trio continued on their way.

"Your Majesty, The ambassadors to Lone Oak and Zarlan Grove should leave now as well," Gribit said, asking for her permission to excuse them.

Isalia nodded her approval, then looking at Link, "I am sure that you need to be on your way as well."

"Yes, Your Majesty, though I will need to return to the sleeping chamber and retrieve my gear first," Link explained.

"I have ordered your tack be replenished and fresh water for you canteen. Is there anything else you will need?" she asked.

"Thank you, Your Majesty, but what you have done already is sufficient and I really must be on my way now," Link said, acknowledging her thoughtfulness with a bow.

"Then I wish you a swift and safe journey, Sire Link," she replied, returning his bow.

Upon returning to the sleep chamber, he found that the nymphs had complied with the Queen's bidding and had laid out his gear for him. After securing his hip pack and canteen to his belt, Link placed the letter in his pack as he exited the room. Feeling the cool limestone through his slippers, he descended the stairs.

Emerging from the palace doors and seeing the dome above him, the feeling of pressure rushed over him again.

I wonder if I could ever accept this as normal? No, I will be glad to see the sky above me once again; he thought, slowing his pace a bit as he continued on to the tunnel dome and the lifts.

Reaching the surface and stepping out onto the dock, Link felt the cool air as a breeze off the water washed over his body. It wasn't until then that he became aware of the rhythmic drumming, like a heartbeat, that he had felt more than heard in the city below. Savoring the feeling of being back in his own element he looked to the sky as the light clouds drifted in from the rolling hills, dimming the sun as each puff passed between it and where he stood.

At the surface, the nymph on duty was still trying to accept the strange happenings of late, with pixies and frogs coming and going, and now an unescorted fairy was standing on her dock.

"Sire Fairy, is everything all right?" she asked as Link stood and watched the sky.

"Oh! Yes, of course. I must be on my way," Link replied, remembering the urgency of his new mission, then taking flight over the water in the direction of Weavertown.

◆ ◆ ◆ ◆ ◆

Croaker and the fairy column descended to the valley below Feldspar on their return to the southwest outpost in the Southern Field Fairy domain as the sun, its light muted gray by the obscuring clouds, began to dip below the hills behind them. Approaching the wide and deep gully they had traversed on their way to the pixie town, Cloud Whisper's head turned quickly to the side where a stand of trees lined the far side of the gully.

Croaker reined his mount to a halt and cast his gaze in the direction of the tree stand, "What is it?" he whispered to the bush-tail.

"Sire Croaker, why have you stopped?" the commander asked as he drew up next to him.

"Cloud Whisper reacted to something in that direction," he answered pointing at the stand.

"There is nothing there, my point scouts would have seen anything if there were," the commander assured Croaker.

"I guess that I am just upset after seeing what happened in that town. I am probably jumping at shadows," Croaker admitted, reining Cloud Whisper on his way again.

Ascending the far bank, Croaker suddenly twisted to his left nearly falling off his mount; Cloud Whisper lurched backwards in response, his body twisting and landing on its feet at the bottom of the gully. The arrow that had struck Croaker in the chest fell harmlessly to the ground. Now, the sound of battle raged all around him as he regained his breath and the realization that they were under attack struck him as quick and sudden as the arrow his mail had thwarted. Rat riders swarmed over the rim of the gully and archers were firing from above.

Croaker felt the sword in his hand before he had given thought to unsheathing it as Cloud Whisper maneuvered to intercept a rat rider. A swift blow and the rider fell, then another and yet another. With a quick lurch, Cloud Whisper was atop the rim and toad archers broke into a run for cover as Croaker sliced his way through them.

High above O'Dias watched the tide of battle turning as this white warrior and his mount charged into his troops.

"At last! A worthy opponent!" O'Dias said, eyes glinting with an unseen sinister smile crossing his face. Reining his bat, he swept down to engage this unexpected foe.

Cloud Whisper suddenly twisted away and Croaker heard the rush of air as the ominous black shadow was upon them. Catching the glint of an axe blade in the corner of his eye, Croaker ducked his head narrowly avoiding the blow. Swirling around, Cloud Whisper turned to meet the challenge only to be forced to leap far to the side as the shadow swooped at them again.

"We need high ground!" Croaker called out to his mount.

With this command Cloud Whisper made for the trees with Croaker clinging tightly to him. They scurried up the largest tree in the stand, circling it as they made their way to the top, avoiding several attacks from O'Dias.

Reaching the heights of the tree, Croaker and his mount were set for the next attack. O'Dias swooped down on them again, swinging his battle axe. As the axe came down on them Croaker was able to parry it away and in the same instant bring his blade down on his attacker's gauntlet. The axe fell to the ground far below and O'Dias reined his bat after it. Cloud Whisper followed them down and Croaker landed another blow as they leaped away from the tree into mid air. Croaker's strike cut through the bat's neck mail and severed its head causing O'Dias, along with his beheaded mount, to twist in spiral circles to the ground.

Croaker and Cloud Whisper landed near the fallen foe but O'Dias was not through yet. Pulling his dagger from his boot, the General lunged at Croaker knocking him off his mount and sending the ivory handled sword flying away from him. As they wrestled, Croaker's hand found the hilt of his dagger and, as O'Dias was about to strike, lunged it toward the eye opening of the General's helm.

The dagger found its mark and O'Dias snapped backwards without a sound and lay motionless on the ground.

Seeing their leader slain, the imp troops and their minions broke and ran as the fairies chased them down and slew them to the last.

"Thank you, friend," Croaker said as he cupped his arms around Cloud Whisper's neck, "You have saved me several times this day!"

Long moments passed before Croaker made his way to retrieve his sword then over to the slain imp. As Croaker studied his fallen foe he thought; *I must thank Link for his instructions. He prepared me well.*

Withdrawing his dagger from the General's helm, Croaker took the bush-tail's reins in hand, leading him to the large tree where Croaker sat with his back propped against it. His entire body aching, he now felt overwhelmingly tired.

As he sat, the commander of the column approached, "Sire Croaker, all will recount what you have done this day."

Croaker looked up with a puzzled look and saw the rest of the fairies falling in behind their commander.

The commander placed the tip of his sword on the ground and knelt down, "You have my allegiance from this day on," he said, as the others did the same.

◆ ◆ ◆ ◆ ◆

The trade caravan had left Feldspar shortly after the fairies departed and was now approaching the grove, where the pixie messenger had been ambushed, on the way to Hillside. They moved slowly along the road, the cartwheels groaning from the weight of the goods they had brought to Feldspar now being returned to Hillside.

"We may need the lanterns before we reach Hillside," the frog commander said, as he glanced at the sky.

Upon entering the grove the noise of the world was muffled leaving the rhythmic creaking of the cartwheels when a loud swoosh filled the air.

Like a sudden hailstorm arrows struck the caravan. Those that were not hit were soon under attack by the column of the imps and their minions. The slaughter was quick and in a matter of moments all in the caravan were dead.

"The General chose this place well," the imp commander said, elated by how quickly they had decimated the caravan.

"Take what we can use. Burn all the rest," he ordered.

The commander, making sure that they only left fairy sign, felt a thrill of anticipation as he thought how the General would respond to his efforts; *O'Dias should be pleased when he receives my report.*

CHAPTER TWELVE

The puffs of clouds were now a blanket overhead that glowed iridescent yellows, oranges and reds above the hills to the west as Link arrived at the Weavertown outpost. He hadn't encountered the ambassador along the road from Lily Pond so he was able to make good time to this point.

"Has the ambassador from Granstone arrived at this checkpoint," He asked, stopping to check with the fairy on duty.

"No, Sire. Is he expected?"

"He was sent for, but I am to intercept him and have him return with me to Granstone," Link answered.

"If you should miss him, Sire, I will inform him that he is to return to Granstone," the fairy promised.

"It will be more than likely I will encounter him on the way, but thank you," Link replied, and then continued on toward Weavertown.

Walking along the granite cobblestone street, Link saw the familiar bush-tail drawn carriage of the ambassador outside the inn he and Croaker had stayed at.

"Sire, it is nice to see you have returned. Is your companion with you as well?" the innkeeper asked with a smile from behind the bar, "And will you be staying with us again?"

"I am sorry to say no. I am here for the ambassador," Link smiled back as his eyes searched the room finding the ambassador and his driver sitting at the table next to the unlit fireplace.

The ambassador's chair creaked on the wood plank floor as he turned to see who had mentioned him by title, setting his mug of berry brew on the table as he did so.

"Sire Fairy, what can I do for you?" the ambassador asked as Link approached his table.

"Excuse me Sire Ambassador. I would not interrupt your respite except that we have urgent matters to attend to in Granstone. Gribit asked me to intercept you along the way. I will explain as we travel," Link said, apologetic for having disturbed him.

"You were in Lily Pond?" the ambassador blurted out, stunned that a fairy had been to the palace of Isalia and was free to return to the Southern Fields.

With the surprised outburst of the ambassador a hush fell over the inn that soon turned to whispers of speculation by the innkeeper and his patrons.

"My wife and I knew there was something going on when he and that young frog stayed here the other night," the innkeeper whispered, loud enough for Link to hear, to the field hand sitting on the stool at the end of the bar.

"I thought he called that frog *Ambassador* as well," the field hand whispered back, remembering Link's comment to Croaker about eating.

"Sire, we must leave at once. Time is of the essence," Link implored the ambassador.

"Very well," the ambassador said, rising from his chair and downing the mug of berry brew in the process, "Innkeeper, a voucher please."

"Yes, Sire," the innkeeper, replied, ducking down to retrieve a voucher from a shelf behind the bar.

The driver quickly dipped his bread in the honey bowl, took a large bite and then gulped down his hot tea before pushing his chair away from the table to follow Link to the door while the ambassador went to the bar to sign the voucher. The driver was not happy he did not have a chance to eat his meal and now he would have to wait until they returned to Granstone to quiet the rumbling in his stomach.

When the three exited the inn the sky was no longer bright with colors. It was growing dark quickly, and after helping the ambassador into the carriage the driver lit the lamps in anticipation of the night ahead of them. Link had entered the carriage from the side opposite the ambassador and had just settled in when the driver climbed up to his seat and reined the bush-tail to wheel the carriage south.

The sound of carriage wheels on stone soon gave way to the creaking of the carriage on the dirt road as they hurried south to Granstone with Link explaining the situation to the ambassador.

"And that is when Gribit asked me to intercept you," Link concluded.

"Thank you, Sire Fairy. You have given me a lot to think about," the ambassador said, stroking his chin as the carriage swayed side to side while the driver urged the bush-tail on.

"If you do not mind, Sire Ambassador, I would like to try and get a little rest on the way. I have not had much in the last couple of days," Link asked.

"Yes, of course you may."

Laying his head back on the padded headrest in the coach, with the rhythmic sound of the creaking and the swaying of the carriage, Link drifted into a light slumber.

◆ ◆ ◆ ◆ ◆

Croaker continued to sit with his back against the tree while the fairies began to collect their dead and help the wounded to an open area beyond the stand of trees. As he sat, he realized that his fatigue was not just from the physical exertions of the battle but that of the mental impact the fight had upon him. Though his training had prepared him well to defend himself, it had not prepared him for the remorse he felt for the taking of life.

"Sire Croaker, is everything all right?" the commander asked, sensing Croaker's distress.

Croaker looked up at the commander, a hollowness in his eyes, "Is it always like this?"

The commander suddenly realized that as a frog Croaker was a peacekeeper with the heritage of negotiation, and this must have been his first taste of combat. The idea that Croaker had not been in battle before had not entered his mind because of the way this young frog had fought.

"Sire, when in battle you must not let these thoughts enter your mind. It comes down to your life or theirs and what you had to do was no more than an act of harvesting grain or weaving mats," he said in a consoling voice.

Croaker knew the commander was right in what he said though the hollowness of his eyes went deep into the pit of his very being.

"I do not know if I will ever be able to accept those actions that way," he said, reliving the moment of plunging the dagger into the eye opening of his foe's helm over and over again.

"All warriors learn to deal with these events in their own way. They must, for it is what they have to do protect the citizens of their domain. Consider the alternative, the loss of those you care about if you do not act," the commander's words finally touching a place in Croaker's mind that gave him some solace.

"Thank you. Your words have salved the wounds of my mind," Croaker said, the light gradually returning to his eyes.

"Sire, your actions have saved many of my troops. Let that be a consolation to you," the commander pointed out.

The commander's words had brought him back from the depths of his despair and Croaker began to consider what must be done next.

"Sir, I have the casualty count you asked for," the ranking sergeant said as he approached the commander.

"What is the count?" the commander asked as the two departed for the area the dead and wounded had been taken, leaving Croaker still sitting with his back against the tree and Cloud Whisper at his side.

"We have eight dead and seventeen wounded. Of the wounded five are not serious but the rest will need to be carried on stretchers to the outpost," the sergeant reported.

"We will need to have enough troops to carry our wounded and dead back to the outpost with a security force to escort them. That will leave only a third of the column to gather up the enemy bodies. I would just leave them where they lay if I could but I am obligated to do something with them for the sake of the domain, even if it is the pixie domain," the commander calculated aloud.

"I will dispatch a detail at once, Sir," the sergeant said, anticipating the commander's orders. "I have already sent troops to gather the materials needed for the stretchers."

As Croaker watched the two fairies walk away his mind was on what he must do next; *I will have to take the body of this foe to Arklan. This enemy is unlike any of the inhabitance of the realm and they have dominion over the toads and slithers. It would seem that their intentions are to create conflict between the domains by making it appear that one domain has attacked another, though they will attack if they feel they should. In this they have shown us that we must prepare for either event.*

As Croaker went over his thoughts he found himself reaching for his canteen, as thirst and hunger overtook him, then mentally chastising himself for not considering Cloud Whisper first, "I am sorry friend. I should have given you a drink and offered nuts from my tack. You must be as thirsty and hungry as I am and you will soon have to carry an extra burden to Granstone when we leave. I will try to not think of myself first in the future." Croaker said, stroking the fur on Cloud Whisper's neck.

After a quick drink and some tack, Croaker stood and called to a passing fairy pointing at the body of General O'Dias, "You there. Secure that body to my mount while I talk with your commander."

"Yes, Sire," the fairy replied, taking the reins of Cloud Whisper and leading him to where the general lay.

"I will be taking that body to King Arklan. He will need to know who is behind these recent events," Croaker informed the commander and the sergeant as they looked out over the dead and wounded were they had been gathered.

"I will have a report for you to carry as well," the commander replied, "Sergeant. Have my orderly bring my supplies and place them by that tree.

"Yes Sir," the sergeant acknowledged his order and left toward a group of fairies he had given the task of weaving stretcher mats to earlier.

"Sire, it will take some time to prepare that report?" the commander said, turning his attention back to Croaker, "I know that you want to be on your way as soon as possible."

"I do not mind a short delay but I would like to get started soon."

Walking toward the tree, Croaker and the commander watched the orderly hurriedly set up a table and chairs. Light globes were being opened in the gray light of dusk as the Elgin Fire began flooding the area with it's blue-white brilliance, washing away the darkness where what meager amount of light left in the sky was being blotted out by the hills of the west and the tree stand at the gully's edge, while the fairies continued with their tasks.

The commander sat in one of the chairs, a soft sigh of exhaustion escaping his lips, his orderly placing the box that contained pen, paper and ink in front of him while another fairy placed one of the light globes on the opposite side of the table. In a motion of a task having been done many times before, he withdrew paper and pen from the box and then dipping his pen in the ink, he began to write.

Croaker thought about the long night that lay ahead of him and Cloud Whisper before they would reach Granstone and a chance to finally rest as he waited for the commander to finish his report.

"Sire Croaker, here is my report to King Arklan," the commander said, sealing the envelope with his ring stamp then looking up and handing it to Croaker.

Croaker nodded, taking the sealed report from the commander.

"I will have a couple of my troops accompany you," the commander said, thinking of Croaker's security.

"No, you will need all your troops to see to the dead and wounded. I am sure that Cloud Whisper and I will be alright."

"As you wish, Sire," the commander acquiesced, knowing that he really couldn't spare the troops he had offered.

Croaker quickly checked the body, making sure it was secure, then swung up onto Cloud Whisper and turned him to the east.

"A swift and safe journey, Sire Croaker," the commander called out.

All light from the sky was gone now as Croaker, in his white tunic atop his white mount, faded like a ghostly apparition into the darkness beyond the reach of the Elgin Fire before the commander turned away to return to his duties.

◆ ◆ ◆ ◆ ◆

The dim light of a single lantern hanging from a hook at the entrance of the stables acted as a beacon for the lone rider as he approached from the darkness of the border road. Reining his bush-tail up and swinging to the ground in a single motion, the pixie lashed off his mount at the hitching rail and entered through the open double doors. The pale red glow of the smith fires mixed with the yellow of the lantern and lighted his way inside.

Finding no one in sight he called out, "Sire smith, are you about?"

"I will be with you in a moment," a call came back to him from a stall in the rear of the stable, "I am tending to my animals."

The pixie returned to the doors and peered out into the darkness of the street, his eyes struggling to pierce the blackness beyond the reach of the lantern. He had been to Limonite many times before and had never seen the town without lights at night.

"How can I help you, Sire?" the smith asked, appearing from the stall area, an empty feed sack in one hand and swinging the gate shut behind him with the other.

"Why is the town without lights?" the pixie asked without responding to the smith's question.

"The lamplighter has been with the others at the Journey's Rest."

"The others?" the pixie asked, trying to comprehend why the lamplighter would ignore his duties.

"Yes, the whole town is there except for myself of course. I have to care for these animals you know."

"What is going on there?"

"Oh! There has been much coming and going the last couple of days. Our innkeeper, Sire Puck, arrived here earlier this evening with his companions, a young frog and the ambassador, from their trip to Lily Pond. It was his second trip since the missing children," the smith explained.

"Lily Pond! Missing children?"

"Yes, Sire. I have not gotten the whole story since I have to stay here and tend to the animals but you can inquire at the meeting if you like," the smith said as he walked over to a wall cabinet and pulled out a lantern, "You can use this to find your way, Sire."

"Thank you. Please see to my bush-tail, I have ridden him hard from Hillside."

"He will get the best of care, Sire," the smith assured the pixie while lighting the lantern then handing it to him.

When the pixie rounded the corner the babble of the crowd at the inn carried on the calm night air to his ears and lights from windows of the homes along the street speckled the darkness.

"I am the mayor of this town! I am an elected official! Why should an inn keeper be appointed to such a position?" he heard as he pushed his way through the pressing crowd.

"It is the wish of the Sage and that should be enough!" the ambassador countered.

"Puck has gained the confidence of Isalia," Webber chimed in, "Who else here can lay claim to that?"

"I believe that we should elect someone to represent us," a voice in the crowd shouted out, many heads nodding in agreement.

"The summit is to take place in three days. Do you think that all of the domain can elect someone before then?" the ambassador asked.

"I say we abide by the Sage's choice," another voice shouted out.

The room erupted into a loud buzz as differing points of view spewed forth as incoherent as the rushing white waters of the Winding Creek.

"Quiet!" the ambassador shouted, "Quiet I said. The Sage's choice will be accepted and that is that! Long ago the frogs became the arbitrators and our say is final!"

A hush fell over the crowd as if the air had been sucked from the room and moments that seemed an eternity passed before the ambassador spoke again, "I will need messengers to deliver this news to the rest of the domain."

"Sire Ambassador. I have just arrived from Hillside with a message for the mayor and militia and I am to take an answer back. I can carry yours as well," the pixie said, making his way through the crowd.

"What message have you for me?" the mayor asked.

Without saying a word the pixie extended his hand with a sealed message from the mayor of Hillside. Breaking the seal and reading the message a look of disbelief crossed the mayor's face.

"How did your mayor come by this news?" the mayor asked, handing the message to the ambassador, his gaze remaining on the pixie.

"A frog from the trade caravan to Feldspar delivered it before continuing on to inform the Sage."

"You will take no action!" the ambassador told the mayor then returning his attention to the pixie, "Your militia is not to take any action either. I want your mayor to understand that!"

A buzz of speculation rose in the crowd and someone demanded, "What has happened?"

"You can not expect us to not retaliate. Most of us had relatives in Feldspar!" the pixie protested.

Again, a call came from the crowd, "What has happened in Feldspar?"

"Quiet please," the ambassador raised his hands, "Quiet. It has been reported that an attack took place at Feldspar and it is believed that the fairies were the attackers. Now before anyone here reacts irrationally, I do not believe that the fairies were the attackers."

"How can you be so sure of that?" the pixie from Hillside asked.

"Because of information that has been received by the Sage and Queen Isalia. The very reason a summit has been called for."

"What the ambassador says is true. I was there at Lily Pond and learned of these things as well," Puck spoke up, "My youngest son was one of the children that went missing and I want to get those that are responsible and I believe that these incidences are related in some way."

The murmur of the crowd had grown louder when the mayor finally spoke again, "Sire Ambassador, it will be as you say for now. There will be no action taken by Limonite."

The lamplighter was the first to leave the inn and slowly individual points of light merged to wash away the darkness shrouding the streets as he made his way through the town, one lamp at a time.

CHAPTER THIRTEEN

The travel at night had been slow for Croaker and Cloud Whisper. The darkness and the added burden of carrying the body of General O'Dias added hours to their trek and now the dim gray of pre-dawn showed the two that they had arrived at the gates of Granstone.

"Who goes there?" a sentry called out.

"I am Croaker. Special liaison to the Sage and I am returning from the southwest outpost. I have urgent business with King Arklan!"

"See that he is who he says," the sentry called to the gatekeeper.

A small side door opened and the gatekeeper and two guards emerged through the opening with the blue white light of Elgin Fire from the guards light staffs flooding over Croaker and his mount, "It is the frog that was training with weapons!" he called back to the sentry.

"Allow him entry."

"Give me a moment, Sire Frog," the gatekeeper said as he and the two guards returned through the small door and the gray darkness engulfed Croaker once again.

A moment later the large southern gate slowly raised enough, allowing Croaker and his mount to enter, then descended to close behind them again.

"Please inform the King that it is imperative he come to the stables as quickly as possible and extend my apologies for disturbing him at this hour, but this can not wait until later. I will wait for him there," Croaker stated before proceeding to the stables.

The two guards looked at each other in disbelief that this frog was expecting the King to come to him. Long moments past before one decided that he should rouse the runner stationed at the gate and send him with the message to the King's quarters.

Croaker reined Cloud Whisper to a halt at the stable gate, dismounting to open the gate and lead him in to an empty stall.

"You can rest now, friend," he said stroking the fur on Cloud Whisper's neck, patting him gently, "I will find you some feed and brush you down."

Croaker had lain the imp general's wrapped body out near an empty wall in the main area of the stable and had taken the saddle and blanket off Cloud Whisper. He was in the final stages of brushing down his mount when the king and his guards entered the stall area of the stables.

"Sire Croaker!" The King called out.

"Your Majesty, forgive me, I will be right out," Croaker said, leaving the stall and Cloud Whisper to his feed, brush still in hand.

"Your Majesty," Croaker repeated, bowing slightly at the waist as he approached the King, "I have a report from the outpost commander for you and that package lying over there."

"Is that a body?" the King asked looking to where Croaker had pointed.

"Yes, Sire, it is an enemy the likes of which I have never seen before."

"Enemy? How did you come by this body?"

"Our column was ambushed on our return from the Rolling Hills and this was their leader. Cloud Whisper and I managed to slay him in the battle."

The King walked over to the body, knelt and unwrapped it, "What manner of creature is this?"

"I think it must be one of the imps that General Longhopper mentioned in his scrolls that Link told me about," Croaker surmised, "He had dominion over toads and slithers in the battle."

"Guard, bring me light," Arklan ordered.

The guard quickly brought his staff with the Elgin Fire globe atop it to the King's side allowing Arklan to inspect the body more carefully. Then Arklan, looking up at Croaker, noticed the cuts in the young frog's tunic from where he had been struck by arrow and blade.

"I see that you have fought hard. Guard, take Sire Croaker's tunic to the seamstress and have it repaired. He will need it for his journey to Lily Pond to report to the Sage after he has had a chance to rest and eat," Arklan said, speaking both to the second guard and Croaker, indicating that Croaker's travels were not over yet.

"Yes, Your Majesty," the guard accepted his orders while Croaker nodded his understanding of what he already knew he must do.

Still kneeling, Arklan opened the sealed report from the commander and read. As he stood again, he looked at Croaker with a greater respect for this young frog, "Sire, it would seem that we have much to thank you for from the commander's description of the events."

Croaker stood there not knowing what to say in response, uncomfortable with any praise and extremely tired, when finally uttering, "Your Majesty, I really could use some sleep and food now."

"Yes, of course. I will have someone finish taking care of your mount and I believe that your quarters are ready for you. I will have some berry brew sent to your quarters now and a meal will be ready for you when you arise. You must report all this to Gribit and show him this body as well. I will have the body loaded into a cart, and provide a driver and team, so your mount will not have to carry the extra burden any further."

"Thank you, Your Majesty. By your leave, Sire, I would like to find my way to my quarters now," with the King's dismissal Croaker bowed and departed the stables, handing the guard the curry brush as he passed him on the way out.

◆ ◆ ◆ ◆ ◆

Staring into the darkness of his chamber, Gribit's thoughts painted disturbing pictures in his mind. He was fatigued from lack of sleep. His thoughts had awakened him many times throughout the night, and the pressures of his position only added to his discomfort. Swinging his legs over the side of the bed he began pacing the floor, mumbling an unintelligible curse when bumping his leg into the nightstand and nearly knocking the water basin off. Over and over he thought about the latest information he received earlier in the evening about the attack on Feldspar from the trade caravan frog; *I do not believe that it was the fairies that attacked the town. The pixies already believe the fairies did it. They will want to retaliate and attack the Southern Field domain, which is exactly what they will do if they do not get the message about the summit before they take action. They may decide to ignore that message and attack the fairies anyway. We must prevent this from happening!*

Gribit's mind raced on. Events were happening faster than he could keep a rein on the domains to prevent an erroneous conflict from breaking out. Settling back down on his bed and squeezing his eyes shut, he tried to force sleep and push out the constant noise of his thoughts; *I really need to hear from Croaker and Arklan to know if they have discovered **anything** that can put light to the situation. I have only my suspicions and I am expected to have the solutions to events that have yet to unfold.*

Gribit lay there, taking slow deep breaths, when a thought came to him from somewhere hidden in the depths of his mind. Something he had heard or read when Link arrived with the message from Arklan; *Longhopper! I must collect the rings at the summit and go to Granstone!*

With his thoughts racing like tadpoles through the rushes of Lily Pond, with Old Big Fin hot on their tails, Gribit slipped back into his fitful sleep as the iridescent green radiance beyond the darkness of his chamber began to fade from the first light of the new day filtering its way down through the waters to the domed city.

◆◆◆◆◆

Fernon savored the faint smell of Nedalia's skin, a sweet fragrance tinted with vanilla, that mixed with the odor of the morning dew wafting on the light breeze through their chamber window. He reached out, cupping the loose strands of her hair that splayed across her pillow, and let the silky strands flow over his fingers as he drew his hand back.

Nedalia sighed lightly, opening her eyes and rolling toward him.

"Good morning," she said softly, reaching her free arm around his shoulder, pulling herself closer, and then gently pressing her lips to his.

"I did not mean to wake you," he apologized, yet happy with her response.

"It is time. We have a lot to get done today before you leave for the summit and I for Lone Oak," she reminded him.

"I know . . . I know. I just wanted to spend a few more moments here with you. I do not know how long I will be away," he confessed.

Nedalia's eyes sparkled with a smile as she kissed him once again while they lay in each other's embrace.

Their moment together was interrupted with the maid knocking at the chamber door, "Your Majesties, your morning meal is being set."

Fernon, feeling that time had passed too quickly, answered with a note of disappointment, "Thank you. The Queen and I will be there shortly."

"There is no need to be short with the maid. She is only doing her job," Nedalia gently scolded then smiled for the attention he wanted to pay her.

"You are right," he said, then thinking about the summit, "That report the ambassador gave of his visit to Lily Pond is troubling. If there are outside forces at work they nearly succeeded in starting a war."

"Five missing children in the Rolling Hills! Our missing children! Who could be that cruel?" Nedalia said, choking up at the thought, swinging her legs over the edge of the bed.

Fernon suddenly felt a pang of guilt for having brought up the subject. He had seen how hard Nedalia had taken the news as the ambassador relayed the conversations of the pixie from the Rolling Hills and the others in Isalia's meeting chamber.

"I am glad Isalia called for this summit. We will find out who is behind this," he reassured her, pulling on his trousers and sliding his tunic over his head.

"If the frogs were not involved I would not trust Isalia. Be wary anyway," she cautioned as she slipped into her dress while Fernon splashed cold water from the basin on his face.

"You know that I am cautious when meeting with *anyone*. Going into another domain you can be assured that I will be alert to *anything* suspicious," he said as Nedalia took her turn at her basin, gently sloshing the cold water to her cheeks then patting them dry with the soft cloth waiting on the stand.

"Yes, I know," she acknowledged, "We had better go now before the food cools."

As Fernon and Nedalia walked the short distance down the hallway to the dining chamber the smell of hotcakes and maple syrup filled the air. The damp chill of the morning had been lost to the warmth of the kitchen fires below and the bustle of the cortege as they brought the food to the dining chamber.

"I want to see General Oakon, the Commander of the Guard and Obrin when we have finished our meal," he said, to an attendant stationed near the doorway, when stopping to wait for Nedalia to enter first.

"As you wish, Sire," came the reply and with a nod and a curt bow the attendant hurried off to carry out Fernon's order.

Nedalia turned and smiled at Fernon, the informality of the attendant had struck her as humorous. The humor was not lost on Fernon, a broad smile crossed his face and he had all he could do to keep from blurting out a chuckle.

A kitchen maid brought in a pot of hot tea and poured Fernon and Nedalia each a cup asking "Will there be anything else, Your Majesties?"

"This is fine. We will ring should there be anything. See to the staff," Nedalia informed her.

When the maid left and they were alone, Fernon spoke, "I am going to have Oakon assign troops to scour the domain for slithers and toads. I want them to leave no leaf or stone unturned."

"I can not imagine toads and slithers working together. What kind of force could make them do that?" she asked, knowing that Fernon didn't have an answer either.

"The Sage believes he knows. In any event I want Oakon to keep the forces at the ready. Whether a ruse by one of the domains or not, I want to be prepared. If it is not, well then there is still a threat out there," Fernon said thoughtfully before taking a sip of his hot tea.

"I hope the children are alright. I will be glad to have them in my sight again," Nedalia said, pausing before taking a bite of her hotcakes.

Fernon reached down for the setting cloth to wipe away a drip of syrup from his chin whiskers, "I am going to have the

Commander of the Guard send messengers to all the cities to be on alert for slithers and toads."

"If they are lurking out there then no one is safe," she said with a sudden realization.

Swallowing down another bite of hotcakes and another sip of hot tea, Fernon gave thought to what she had said, "You are right. I will have to have the Commander assign escorts for all the trade caravans. I want you to have a larger escort back to Loan Oak as well."

"A larger escort? Is that really necessary?" she asked.

"For my peace of mind it is."

No more words were spoken while they continued their meal though Fernon thought about Obrin and the agents he had sent out; *I wish I had placed them sooner. I would like to have some intelligence reports. Obrin will have to make sure any information from our agents is sent directly to me via frog messenger.*

◆ ◆ ◆ ◆ ◆

General Broadstem glanced to the east from his vantage point high in the treetop palace, with the morning sun beginning to spill its rays through the breaks in the cloud cover that had blanketed the sky since yesterday. Returning his gaze to the ground below, he observed the queen and the ambassador approaching the waiting coach.

The ambassador made sure Airlein was seated after boarding before moving around back of the carriage. Passing the two rear guards flanking either side, he took his place beside her and the queen ordered the driver to proceed. The wheels crunched over the loose gravel road that led to the edge of Zarlan Grove and on to the summit at Lily Pond as they began their trip.

Broadstem watched the queen and her escort of four personal guards depart before returning to the war chamber to speak to his second in command awaiting his return.

"Colonel!" Broadstem barked as he marched through the doorway.

"Yes, Sir," the second in command responded, spinning away from the relief map to face the General and standing tall, understanding the tone of his commander.

"The Queen has left for Lily Pond and has taken only four personal guard. I told her it was a mistake to even go," Broadstem growled, "I do not trust that nymph queen, *Isalia*, and with the reports that we have received these past days … I doubt we can trust the frogs either!"

"Sir. The frogs have always been the peace…" the Colonel was cut short by the fire he saw in the General's eyes and the scowl that came across his face.

"I have considered these reports very carefully and I can see the obvious," the General growled in a low warning tone.

"Sir, *yes sir*! What do you wish of me?" the Colonel asked, having never seen him this agitated before.

"You will take command here while I go to Loamis. I will send word if I need anything. I will get to the bottom of things in spite of Her Majesty!" he said, both angry at the young queen's decision and concerned for her safety.

"I will muster an escort for you, Sir!" the Colonel said, raising his hand for a runner to carry his order.

"No! I will travel alone," the General motioned the runner to take his seat again, then turning to exit, "If any reports of strange activities come in, see that they are relayed to me at once."

"Yes sir," the Colonel called out as Broadstem vanished from view through the doorway.

CHAPTER FOURTEEN

"Sire Croaker believes this body is an imp from the description and glyphs in the forgotten chamber of the city. The messenger Link discovered the glyphs along with a couple of scrolls that belonged to a frog general, General Longhopper," Arklan said, pulling away the cover shrouding the body lying near the stable wall.

"A frog general! That would explain those curious statues by the city entrance," the Granstone Ambassador said, shifting his gaze from the body to Arklan, "I have often wondered why a frog in *that* particular attire was a part of those."

"Sire Croaker will bring the body to Lily Pond for all to view. The domains need to know of this foe," the king informed the ambassador as he replaced the cover and returned to a full standing position, waving the smell of decay away from his face, "Come, Sire. It is time we started our journey."

"Why wait to have young Croaker bring the body when we could have it transported along with us?" the ambassador asked, curious why the king would expect a young frog to be responsible for it.

"*He* defeated this foe in battle and it is *his* prize. Would you take the credit from him?" Arklan asked, glancing at the ambassador as they exited the stables.

"No! Your Majesty, I did not know it was Croaker that had fought him," he replied with a surprised look, his thoughts confused; *A warrior frog? A frog general? What would he learn of next?*

"Besides, I have other concerns on my mind," Arklan said, climbing up into the ambassador's coach which had been awaiting them.

The Ambassador walked back around to the stable side of the carriage, after Arklan had been seated, pausing a moment on the running board to look back at the stable entrance before entering to take his place beside the King. With a flick of the reins the driver urged his bush-tail on and the carriage pitched forward toward the main gate.

"Sire Ambassador, I have received reports that Airlein is amassing troops at Loamis. I do not know what her intentions might be so I have given orders for the Eastern Armies to be at the ready if they advance on our border," Arklan said as the carriage rolled through the main gate of Granstone onto the road north.

"Your Majesty, Airlein has many of her father's traits. She will use diplomacy before thinking of doing anything rash," the ambassador said thoughtfully, adding, "I am sure of that!"

"All the same, we will go to the eastern outpost before attending the summit at Lily Pond. I want to see the situation first hand," the king said, "She is young and her generals might influence her to make an ill-advised decision."

"I believe your concerns to be unwarranted," the ambassador disagreed, feeling a need to defend the young queen.

"With what has happened at Feldspar and to the returning column … I have no idea what could have possibly happened in *her* domain. There are forces trying to start a war between the domains!" Arklan reminded him.

Overhead the clouds were quickly being replaced by an endless blue while in the calm air the rhythmic sounds of the creaking coach and the soft padding of the bush-tail's footfalls on the hard packed ground played a languishing melody as the carriage and it's entourage of the king's security escort moved passed the silent grain stalks walling the sides of the road.

◆ ◆ ◆ ◆ ◆

Under the clearing skies of the new day the sounds of hurrying footsteps could be heard through the quiet morning streets of Limonite as a messenger ran to the stables and his awaiting bush-tail. All through the early morning messenger after messenger had repeated the scene from the first gray light to the now blue sky, lightly speckled with patches of white. As the messenger turned the corner onto the main street the sign above the inn door hung motionless in the calm air, the silence of the morning mirroring that of the interior of the inn itself.

The last of the pixie messengers was on his way to his destination, Whitewater, with the message the ambassador had written. As he had for each of the other messengers for all the other pixie towns, the ambassador had included in the message information of the coming summit, Puck's appointment to represent the Rolling Hills Domain and instructions not to take any actions without Puck's or his approval.

"Well, that is the last of them! I hope that the towns will do as I have asked," the ambassador said, worried about the call for militia at Hillside.

"If the other towns react to Puck's appointment with the same resentment that was expressed by the mayor of Limonite last night, then there is sure to be a problem," Webber mused, looking to Puck and then to the ambassador as they nodded in agreement.

"No one is leaving here without a decent meal," Puck's wife exclaimed, pushing open the kitchen door with her hip while carrying a tray of food, her son close behind with mugs and a pot of hot tea.

"Who knows what kind of food you will get at Lily Pond!" she continued as she neared the table.

"None as good as yours, Pamelia!" Puck smiled up at her.

Returning the smile, she hid the pain she felt over the fate of their youngest son. Pamelia served the food taking pride in her husband's selection by the Sage. It felt strange to her that she could experience both these emotions at the same time but she was determined that they would understand she supported her husband in the unexpected role he was about to play.

"Please, join us," Webber invited them as he stood and offered his chair next to Puck, "I will move over so your son can join us as well. We do not know how long Puck will have to be away!"

"Thank you, Sire frog," Pamelia accepted, directing her son to the kitchen, "Bring two more settings."

A pixie that was staying at the inn had heard the conversation and brought an extra chair from his nearby table as Webber found another at the empty table next to them.

"Thank you, Sire," Puck said, accepting the chair from the pixie.

"It is my honor, Sire Representative," the pixie responded, giving a quick nod of his head in respect then returning to the table where he had been seated, resuming his morning meal.

"It would appear that not all are against your selection," the ambassador noted.

"Puck has had the respect of many in this town long before these past events. I am sure they will understand why the Sage has selected him!" Pamelia said with pride.

"Ah, but that is this town. I wonder what the rest of the domain will think?" Puck questioned, reaching out to touch his wife's hand as she seated herself next to him.

"It does not matter. Gribit has chosen you for this. You have been accepted by the ambassadors and Isalia and by agreeing to their decision you are committed," Webber reminded him.

"Of course I will do what is expected of me, though it would be nice to know that the domain will accept the authority given to me," Puck sighed.

"Enough talk, let us eat," the ambassador said as Puck's son rejoined them at the table.

Aromas of fresh baked breads, hot grain cereal and honey tea filled the inn as Webber enjoyed the sounds of clinking eating utensils on baked clay dishes and bowls. Looking around the table he found that these were sights, sounds and smells that he was becoming accustomed to. This gave him a sense of ease and comfort he had thought he could find only at the waters edge in the warm sunshine with his friends Croaker, Lily Pad and Lotus.

It seemed to Webber that it had been long ago that he had last seen his friends at the shore's edge though it had only been a few days. Now with the thought of them he longed to be in their company once more without the worries and concerns that filled his mind.

"Sire Webber. Is there something wrong with the food?" Puck asked, breaking through Webber's thoughts.

"Oh, no, not at all. Why do you ask?" Webber responded, Puck's question pulling him back to the immediacy of his environment, his memories drifting in his mind like distant clouds floating lazily in the blue.

"You were staring into space and had not touched your food," Puck explained.

Embarrassed that he had let his mind wander, "I am sorry. Something came to mind that distracted me," he apologized, then quickly picking up his spoon he shoveled in some hot grain cereal so he would not have to explain further.

"I did not mean that you had to eat it all at once," Puck chuckled.

The others at the table tried to contain their grins while they continued with their meal as Webber swallowed down the cereal, smiling shyly as he pulled a chunk of bread from a loaf, not saying a word as he realized how silly he must have looked.

Webber's actions had brought a much-needed change of mood and relieved the tension that had built from all the travel and events, even though it lasted for only those few brief moments.

When the meal had ended Puck helped Pamelia and his son carry the dishes to the kitchen, it was a chance for him to have a few moments alone with his family. The ambassador scooted his chair back from the table, leaning back and placing his hands on his well-rounded midsection as if to ease the strain of the buttons of his waistcoat, showing that he was well fed and content. Webber continued to sip honey tea from the mug cupped in his hands, allowing his mind to wander back to Lily Pond and his friends once more, as he and the ambassador waited for Puck to return from the kitchen before they would start the return journey to Lily Pond.

◆ ◆ ◆ ◆ ◆

The sun hung low in the eastern sky, a disk of muted light in the constant haze of the wastelands. A hushed fuff-fuff-fuff broke the silence of the morning as a raven labored hard beating its wings to gain altitude with the added load of a rider.

Circling once over the cave palace below, Noma reined his mount north toward the caves west of Feldspar as he began his mission to the Endless Forest. In his pouch he carried a message from Lord DeMonas for General O'Dias.

Watching the marshes roll away under them, Noma's thoughts focused on his ambitions; *when we take the domains I will rule there. DeMonas can rule these marshlands. I will no longer let my brother intimidate me, though I do not have the strength to overcome him yet. I must make appropriate alliances and I think that I am making inroads with General O'Dias. If I can make him believe that it is to his benefit to align himself with me then I will have the power base I need.*

Spurring his raven on with his heels and leaning forward to allow his mount to gain speed, Noma's face twisted up in a sly grin as the prospect of the possible future he envisioned for himself unfolded before his mind's eye. Almost giddy with anticipation he looked forward to having more time with O'Dias to strengthen his influence on the general.

◆◆◆◆◆

Awaking with a groan, Croaker rolled onto one side trying to ease the pain and stiffness of his body before swinging his legs over the side of his bed. He ached in places that had never ached before, the havoc to his body these past few days had caught up with him in his sleep. As he sat, he rubbed his shoulders and back before trying to stand.

Still groggy, he wobbled his way to the basin to splash the sleep out of his eyes before returning to the bed to pull the bell cord summoning the page. As he sat on the edge of the bed it was like his mind was in a fog that had settled in around him and he couldn't find his way out and could only wait for it to lift away.

Croaker turned his gaze toward the door when he heard the quick knock and saw the door swing open and a young fairy slide though the opening.

"You rang, Sire?" the page humbly asked, giving a deep bow.

"Yes . . . have you seen my tunic?" Croaker asked, trying to clear his mind.

"Sire, it was sent to the seamstress when you arrived! I can send a runner to see if your new tunic is ready for you," the page informed him.

"Thank you. Have I slept very long?" Croaker asked, remembering he had to get to Lily Pond with the body of his foe.

"No, Sire. It has only been a few hours. It is still well before the mid-day," the page said, then asking, "Are you ready for a meal, Sire?"

Croaker sat a couple of moments dusting out the last of the cobwebs still cluttering his mind before responding, "Yes, I believe I am."

"Do you wish to take your meal here, Sire?"

"No, thank you. I can find my way to the dining area. It will give me a chance to walk out some of this stiffness," Croaker said, stretching his arms above his head before standing again.

"By your leave, Sire," the page bowed deeply before turning to depart through the doorway and scurry down the corridor.

Moving to the doorway, Croaker looked on, puzzled as to why the page would bow like that toward him; *if that is not the strangest. I guess I must be really tired. That cannot be anything at all. Has to be just my imagination.*

All along the way to the dining area fairies that he encountered would stop and bow as he passed them. The bustling noise of the dining area suddenly dimmed to hushed whispers as he entered. Croaker scanned the room as a fairy approached him.

"Sire. May I show you to a table?" the fairy asked eagerly.

"What *is* going on here?" Croaker asked, stunned by the reaction of the fairies to his presence, "Why is everyone *bowing* to me?"

"Sire. All have heard of your great deed!"

"What great deed?" Croaker asked with amazement.

"Sire. The guards that were present when you arrived have told of your deed. They heard what the King said as he read the commanders report," the fairy beamed with pride as she motioned Croaker to follow her, "Please Sire, I have a table just for you!"

Flustered by the attention, Croaker followed self-consciously to a table that was reserved for special dignitaries, a place of honor, and an exclusive staff to serve this particular table.

"Sire. What is your preference?" the fairy asked as Croaker sat.

"I have not thought about that. I would like some hot tea though. You may bring me what is on your morning menu. Thank you."

"Very good, Sire," she said, and the staff went about providing for his wishes.

As Croaker sat waiting, he surveyed the room and saw a familiar figure approaching his table.

"Sire Croaker. May I join you?" Link said, giving his comrade a bow.

"You *need not bow to me* Link and *yes* of course you may join me my friend," Croaker responded in embarrassment as he stood to offer a chair to his friend.

"It would seem that you have not only become a warrior but a great one as well," Link commented as he sat.

"If that is the case then it is because of you and the training you gave me," Croaker replied, "I want to thank you for that training, it, Cloud Whisper and General Longhopper's mail saved my life yesterday."

"I only showed you how to use your weapons. It was you that fought the way you did and that is why you are held in such high esteem my friend!" Link quickly pointed out.

Croaker did not reply. He sat staring at the all the food that was being brought to the table by the serving staff, "What is all this?" he asked.

"Sire. It is the morning menu you asked for," the fairy replied, stunned by his question.

"But I can not eat all of this!" then turning to Link, "I hope you are hungry, you can help with this."

"I will do my best, Sire," Link smiled back, "Be careful in what you ask for."

Laughter broke out and the fairy assured Croaker that he could eat just his fill of the choices provided.

Sipping hot honey tea, Link watched with amazement at how voraciously Croaker attacked the food in front of him. Croaker hadn't had a good meal since before leaving for Feldspar and his body demanded nourishment to replenish his physical and mental strength that were drained from the happenings of the previous day.

"You just might eat all of that at the rate you are going!" Link said with amusement.

"I did not know how hungry I was," Croaker confessed.

"Battle will do that," Link smiled his acknowledgement, "I went to the stables this morning and saw the foe you slew. He looks to have been quite a challenge."

"He must have been their leader. We fought hard and long and when he fell all his troops broke and ran. The commander and his troops were able to chase them all down and destroy them to the last," Croaker informed Link as he relived the battle in his mind.

Link sat quietly for a few moments seeing the distress in Croaker's eyes as he spoke about the struggle. Taking another sip of his hot tea, "King Arklan has asked me to accompany you to Lily Pond."

"I would like nothing better," Croaker's eyes lighting up at the prospect of having his friend's company once more.

After taking one last bite of the bread he used to sop up the yoke of his eggs, Croaker took a long drink of his tea to wash it down before leaning back in his chair with a sigh of fulfillment, "I feel much better now although my body still feels stiff."

Link waved the staff over to clear the table, "Sire Croaker has finished his meal, you may take the rest of this away now," then turning back to Croaker, "We can visit one of the heated pools for a short while. That should help loosen you up."

"Heated pools?" Croaker said, inquiring with surprise.

"Yes. We have four of them near the outer edges of the city two sublevels down. The level below that is where the fires are to heat them and the water comes from the main reservoir where all the rainwater drains. Passages only a little larger than the fairy that quarried them are channeled to empty into the large pool. The reservoir holds enough water to supply the entire city for half a year without being replenished. It is our greatest secrete asset should we ever be under siege. The builders of our city planned well," Link informed Croaker with pride.

"It will be good to get back into the water again, even if for only a short while," Croaker accepted then chuckling at an after thought, "I will not even have to worry about Old Big Fin!"

Thanking the staff for their service, Link led Croaker to the second sublevel and to a room at the outermost part of the city.

"We will have to be bathed here first," Link said as they entered the room.

Two attendants quickly came over to them to help them disrobe.

"This is Sire Croaker's first time here," Link informed them.

"Sire," one of the attendants said as she went to Croaker, "I will assist you. You not only must bathe before entering the pool but upon leaving as well."

"Thank you. Is there anything else I should know?" he asked.

"No, Sire. Please come with me, I will scrub you down."

Upon entering the room he noticed the air was warm and moist. The moss scrub with water felt good on his skin as the fairy scrubbed his back then his arms and legs.

"Why is it so warm in here?" Croaker asked, "Should it not be cooler down here?"

"Oh, that is because there is a space between the walls to allow the smoke to rise from the fires below," she explained, "There, you are ready to enter the pool now! I will see you when you are ready to leave, Sire."

Entering the room with the pool the air was even warmer and the dampness hung heavy in it. There were seven fairies chatting as they bathed until they saw Croaker. A frog at their pool was not an event that any could remember. Then one of the fairies recognized Croaker, "Sire, forgive us," he bowed his head, "Please join us."

The others, now realizing who he was, also bowed in respect.

"Please, do not bow to me," Croaker said feeling self-conscious once again, then looking at Link, "Is there no one that has not been told of me?"

"Sire, you will just have to get used to it." Link smiled.

Stepping into the pool, Croaker was shocked at how warm the water felt to his touch and was afraid it might scald him as he slowly sat. After a few moments he became accustomed to the water's warmth, felling it sink deep into his muscles as the stiffness slowly ebbed away.

Though the fairies asked him many questions about the battle, Croaker did not say much other than the fairies he had fought along side were as brave as any could be. He did not want the topic to be of him and he did not want to relive the battle again. For now he was content to sit there in the warmth and let his body relax and his mind wander freely.

"Sire. It has been an hour and we must finish our preparations for our trip," Link reminded him.

"Thank you, Link. This has helped a lot," Croaker, replied not really wanting to leave this wonderful pool, "Yes, of course we must get started."

Croaker and Link returned to the rooms with the attendants. The fairy greeted Croaker with a bow and began scrubbing him while his mind went through the progression of events that had happened since sitting at the shore of Lily Pond; *I am not the same now as I was only days ago. I wonder if I could ever be that frog again? No! I have experienced too much these past few days. Will Lily and the others recognize me now? I am not sure that I can recognize myself. I wish I could turn around and go back into that pool and let its warmth envelope me and escape back into those pleasant memories of Lily Pond and sitting in the sunshine. I am still tired and I hate the discomfort of everyone making such a fuss over me. What I did in battle does not make me feel good; I just did what I had to...*

"Sire. I have finished!" the fairy repeated again, breaking Croaker away from the quagmire of his rambling thoughts as he stood staring blankly at the wall in front of him, "Are you alright, Sire?"

Realizing that he hadn't heard her talking to him the entire time she was scrubbing him, Croaker turned and peered at her through the void of that place in his mind that her voice was drawing him back from before apologizing sheepishly, "Oh, yes. I am sorry. Thank you for your assistance," then, excused himself to rejoin Link for the return to his chamber.

The air around him now felt cool to the point of chill, accentuated by the soft blue-white light of Elgin Fire globes, as he and Link walked through the corridors and climbed the granite staircases. The thought of soon returning to Lily Pond had brought a new quickness to his pace and the coolness of the city faded from his mind. Along the way he politely returned bows with a nod of his head and a bashful smile whenever they encountered a fairy or group of fairies.

Entering his chamber with Link close behind, Croaker noticed two new tunics lying out on the bed. One was exactly the same as his first had been while the other was blotched with a pattern of the drab colors of grasses and earth.

"It appears that the seamstress remembered what you had told her, Link!" Croaker pointed out as he picked up the drab tunic, turning and holding it up for Link's inspection.

"Yes, now all you need is one for that mount of yours," Link smiled, "He stands out like Elgin Fire in the darkest of nights, for *all* to see."

"I know that you jest but if I could have a blanket mail made in the likeness of my own for Cloud Whisper . . . it would set my mind at ease. Do you know of a smith that could do that?" Croaker asked, realizing that his mount had not had the same protection as he in that battle.

"I do not know. I could inquire if such a smith exists," Link answered, "I have not seen that degree of skill until I laid eyes on your mail. I would think that you would also need a weaver that could work with those fine steel threads!"

"Maybe Gribit would know. We could ask him when we get to Lily Pond," Croaker said, satisfied that the Sage should have knowledge of such individuals.

"With all this new gear that you have now I believe we should stop at the saddler's to see if he has saddlebags that you can carry the excess in," Link said, scratching the back of his head as he looked over Croaker's gear then looking inquisitively at Croaker.

"I am glad you thought of that. It would make the traveling easier," Croaker agreed exchanging the drab tunic for the white one, then while sliding it over his head adding, "I do not believe that there is much chance that we will be going into battle between here and Lily Pond. I will pack the second tunic and mail in the bags when we get them."

Belting up his hip pack and then his sword, Croaker gathered up his helm, the drab tunic and mail, and looked the chamber over making sure he was forgetting nothing before he and Link started on their way.

◆◆◆◆◆

The sun was nearing its zenith as the mayor of Hillside ambled out of the city hall and through the throng filling the street as they parted a path for him. He steadily moved toward the town square to address the militia gathered there, still thinking deeply about the message he received only minutes ago from the messenger that had returned from Limonite. So far only Pellucere, the closest city to them being located in the Sand Valley to the west, had sent their militia to answer the mayor's call before a messenger from Limonite had reached that city.

A hush fell over the crowd as the mayor took his place on the speakers stand in the square but the quiet was broken by a nearly silent sound of breathing as the gathered masses seemed to breathe in unison waiting for the mayor to speak.

"I have received, only minutes ago, a message from the Sage himself," the Mayor started, but the women, children and elderly were so far back that they could not hear or understand all he said as the drone of insect wings was enough to drown out the words. They would have to learn what he said later.

"The message says that we are not to take any action unless instructed! It says that we are to take our instructions from the innkeeper from Limonite!" the Mayor continued, his face turning red and a growing scowl appearing as deep furrows formed over his brow.

After a long pause, "It says that *they* do not believe that it was the fairies that attacked Feldspar!" the Mayor's voice growing even louder, "I say that we were informed first hand at who did this deed by the caravan messenger and that it is our kin that were slaughtered! Why are we to take instructions from an innkeeper? When did the Sage become the ruler of this domain? I say we seek revenge and that we march *now* on the fairies! Are you with me?"

Like a giant clap of thunder a roar rose and echoed off the surrounding hills with a force that bent the nearby grasses of the fields as that of a sudden downdraft of a fierce storm passing over.

"We march. We march. To avenge our brethren we march," the militia members chanted, the sound of their footfalls in rhythm to the cadence, as they formed ranks and began marching east with weapons in hand.

CHAPTER FIFTEEN

Circling in a spiral decent, the raven carrying Noma landed on the rocky shelf at the cave entrance where they were greeted by the same large toad that had tended his bat when returning from the forest.

"See to his needs and have a bat ready for me when I leave this evening," Noma ordered.

"Yes, Lord," the toad responded as he led the raven away, averting his gaze from Noma, being sure not to make eye contact with the imp.

Entering the jagged mouth of the cave, Noma stopped for a moment to pick up one of the hand torches placed in a rack that had been anchored to the rock wall. With a flint and steel he carried in his pouch he sparked a light to the oil soaked wrappings. He watched the flame grow and flicker in the draft, before taking the first steps of the long walk deep into the caverns, allowing his eyes the time to adjust to the dim light.

Deep into the cavern Noma began passing stone pillars that had formed from ages of water dripping from ceiling to floor. Dancing shadows cast by his torch awaited his approach while maneuvering to try to stay hidden from his view, each retreating

233

behind the deformed pillar to which it belonged as he hurriedly passed by. Though he was tired and stiff from the long flight, there was quickness in his gait born from the anticipation of winning O'Dias' support when the time came to challenge his brother. In his haste his foot would occasionally strike loose gravel or stones causing the cavern to echo with skittering sounds like small creatures evading his approach causing him to grin at the idea that even the earth around him feared his wrath as he thought; *brother beware. My time is soon at hand.*

In the distance ahead, the glow of burning fires appeared in the darkness, like flashing eyes of unknown creatures that lay in wait, as he approached the main cavern of O'Dias' headquarters until the light merged with his own torch and the darkness faded away. *Now* he will begin his campaign for the general's alliance.

Noma noticed that there were fewer troops around the fires as he walked over to the table with the maps, looking for the general.

"Lord. I was not expecting you," a hard breathing voice spoke from behind Noma as the commander rushed over to greet him.

"I was expecting to see the General!" Noma responded when turning to see who had addressed him, "Where is he?"

"Lord, after you left a report came in that a column of fairies was approaching Feldspar. The General gave orders to ambush the caravan on its way back to Hillside while he led an attack on the column returning to the Southern Fields," the commander informed him.

"That does not answer my question, where is he?" Noma demanded.

"I have been going on the assumption that some of the fairies must have escaped the battle and that he is chasing them down. He should be back no later than tonight," the commander offered as an explanation.

Noma's mood had taken a distinct change as his face screwed up in anger. He had set his mind on convincing the general to ally with him against his brother and now he couldn't do that. Slowly his rage subsided with the thought that he would still be able to speak to O'Dias before he departed for the forest.

"When the general gets here I want to be informed immediately!" he snapped, "Have food and drink brought to me before I rest for the nights journey."

"Yes, Lord," the commander acknowledged the orders and called for one of the toads to get Noma's meal, "Will there be anything else, Lord?"

Noma simply shook his head no and flopped himself down in disgust into one of the chairs at the table.

◆ ◆ ◆ ◆ ◆

Gribit stood quietly gazing out at the patterns of light and shadow shifting across the surface of the dome, morphing from one form into another, as the rays of the sun filtered down to the city. He wondered if the call for a summit would bring all the rulers to Lily Pond; *Fernon has already arrived and I am sure that Arklan will be here since he has the best knowledge of the situation. Would Airlein arrive? She is young and her advisors might convince her not to attend. No, I believe that she will be here. She had sent word that she wanted to speak to me. As for Puck . . . I know he will be returning with Webber.*

Satisfied that they would all attend, he returned to his chair in the meeting chamber content in knowing that the three fairy rings he would need to open Longhopper's vault in Granstone would be available to him. As he sat awaiting Isalia's arrival to the chamber, other thoughts entered his mind; *I hope the talks go well. I do not know if or how mistrust from past conflicts would bias their approach to one another in conversation since this would be the first time the leaders would meet face to face. Will they part with the rings? We need to see those scrolls Longhopper stored in his vault.*

"And this is our meeting chamber!" Isalia said with pride and a wave of her hand as she entered the chamber, Fernon close behind, "From here you can look out over the city."

Gribit quickly stood, turning to face them, and gave a bow of his head as he greeted them, "Your Majesties."

They acknowledged his greeting and continued further into the room with Fernon following as Isalia led him to the opening, "To the left and right you can see the tunnel domes that lead to the lifts that moor the dock on the surface," she pointed out.

"Your city is truly a marvel to behold," he said, "And the way the light plays across the dome is a sight that I could never have imagined! I wish that Nedalia were here to see this."

Ever the diplomat, Isalia responded, "I am sure that I would be just as impressed at the sights of your Lone Oak."

Fernon smiled at her graciousness, a side to her he had not considered, and went to join Gribit while Isalia went to pull the bell cord near the door before joining them.

"Bring goblets and berry brew for our guests," the Queen ordered when the young nymph appeared at the door.

"Yes, your Majesty," the young girl bowed her acknowledgement then hurried off.

"Tell me of Nedalia," Isalia continued her conversation with Fernon as she crossed the room to take her seat near them.

A sparkle appeared in his eyes at the mention of his wife's name, a subject he could talk about for hours if allowed to, "What is it you wish to know about her?"

Gribit sat back with a sense of comfort as he silently listened to them learning more about each other, knowing that they were passing the time with social intercourse until the start of the summit when everyone present could speak of the events. For now they must wait for the arrival of Airlein, Arklan and Puck.

◆◆◆◆◆

Broadstem looked out over the fields to the west, a moving carpet of golden browns swaying in the breeze, allowing the greens and yellows of the stalks to randomly show through from beneath here then there. He stood, clenched hands on hips, before one of the oriels in the office he commandeered from his commander in Loamis. Here in the topmost floor of the tallest building in the town, this airy room was constructed with large oriels on each of the four sides allowing anyone to see clearly in all directions.

Below, he watched as a figure hurried toward his building from one of the little buildings near the edge of the town. He had been patiently waiting since the squad he had ordered out, when he first arrived, had returned and now hc hoped the commander would have the information he anticipated; information that would confirm his suspicions.

Returning to a table in the corner of the room with a large map laying open and spread out on it, he could hear hurried footsteps climbing the stairs.

"What have you got for me?" he asked as the commander stepped up into the room.

"Sir, the squad we sent into the Southern Fields Domain was able to surprise and capture one of Arklan's patrols along the border," the commander reported.

"What have they told you?" the general asked, "Have they said anything about how the frogs are involved with Arklan and Isalia?"

"No, Sir. When we asked, they appeared surprised by the question. They did not have any information other than what our intelligence has reported already."

"Keep a close watch on the frogs. I still believe they are up to something with Arklan and Isalia and that the pixies might be involved as well," Broadstem, instructed, "I believe that the Queen is walking into something in spite of my warnings. Is the battalion ready to move into the Southern Fields?"

"Yes, Sir, we can march on a moment's notice. We are awaiting your orders."

"I think that we should take this outpost on the trade road, that should give us enough prisoners to get some straight talk from Arklan," the General tapped a finger on the map, "We will move out from Loamis in fifteen minutes."

"Yes, Sir, I will ready the troops," the commander acknowledged before departing while Broadstem continued concentrating on the map, not bothering to look up.

The sun poured down from directly overhead washing away any shadows except those that filled the commander's mind when he stepped out into the street as he set out for the troop barracks to give the order to form up. He would follow the general's orders and so would his troops even though his thoughts were troubled; *there were things the general had said that lead me to wonder if this is the Queen's will or if Broadstem is following an agenda of his own. I have no way to tell which is the case and as long as I cannot see harm to Her Majesty then it will be as the general orders. . . .Watch the frogs? I cannot believe the frogs would be involved with anything that would cause upheaval since they belong to all the domains.*

"Sergeant, sound assembly," he ordered upon arriving at the barracks, giving no indication of his misgivings.

◆◆◆◆◆

Arklan grinned broadly when the ambassador opened his eyes with a start, his head twisting one way than the other, from the sudden jar of the carriage tossing after hitting a pothole in the road.

"What was that?" the ambassador asked excitedly, trying to get his bearings.

"The rains the other day must have washed out a hole in the road," Arklan said, still grinning.

"Oh, Your Majesty . . . where are we?" the ambassador asked, his mind still clouded from the unintentional nap and the sudden awakening.

"We will soon be at the eastern outpost on the trade road to Loamis."

"I am sorry, Your Majesty. The warmth of the day and the rhythm of the coach must have caused me to doze off," the ambassador apologized as the realization of where he was quickly set in.

"Do not concern yourself. It has given me the time I needed to consider the events and what I should suggest at the summit. Ah, there is the outpost coming into view now."

An excited flurry of activity suddenly erupted at the outpost with the recognition of the King's Guard in escort of the approaching coach. Guards brushed out rumpled uniforms with their hands as they stood to attention while a runner hurried to inform the outpost commander of Arklan's arrival.

The coach halted at the barrier arm just as the outpost commander came to a running stop near the side of the carriage to greet the King.

"Your Majesty," the commander said with a bow as one of the outpost sentry opened the carriage door allowing Arklan to step down.

"There will be no further need of formality," Arklan informed him as he returned the commander's bow, "I am here to assess just what the situation is from the reports I have received of Airlein's forces gathering at Loamis."

"Sire, a patrol from the area to our north has not reported in. I have raised the signal flags to alert all the other outposts and have sent runners to the next northern outpost and to the south in accordance to General Purslane's defense plan," the commander informed Arklan as he led him and the ambassador to his office.

"And what if the runners do not get to their destinations?" Arklan asked as they stepped into the commander's office.

Leading them to a map that hung on the back wall of his office, "They are an insurance in the event of a night attack or if there is thick fog. The signal flags are the main form of communications. They are set back in our territory and spaced at a distance from one another that allows each to be seen clearly by its neighbor. In this way it would only take minutes to inform the other forces throughout the domain where the need is and would allow for reinforcements and a pincer movement against the attacking forces, Sire," the commander pointed out on his map.

"It would appear that you were incorrect, *Sire* Ambassador. Airlein is being aggressive and it looks as if her actions are directed at us," Arklan said, giving the ambassador a cold stare.

"I am sure that I am correct about her," the ambassador stood firmly in his belief, "Commander, has there been any report of Airlein traveling to Lily Pond?"

"A report came in recently that a carriage with an escort was traveling in that direction. That does not mean that she was in the carriage though."

"I am sure that any action of her forces is not of her doing, Your Majesty," the ambassador looked at Arklan, his eyes and voice imploring the king to believe him.

"If that be the case then she is a poor ruler, not being able to control her military. In any event we have to prepare, anticipating where her forces are planning to attack our domain," Arklan said, stating the obvious in his opinion, irritation showing in his face that this was happening at this time, "Ambassador, if they are planning to move on us then I would need you to confer with them before any fighting can occur. We need to find out what their motivation is. This summit is too important to be upset by any actions that can not be brought under control!"

"I will do my best, Sire. I will leave for Loamis immediately," the ambassador agreed, already heading for the exit and his carriage.

Arklan stepped through the door watching the ambassador hurry toward the carriage, a smile coming to his face at the ambassador's shouting out orders with his waist-coated rotund belly belying the agility and speed he now displayed.

"King's Guard! Report to His Majesty. Driver, I will be going on to Loamis," the ambassador called out the orders as he moved toward the carriage. A quick bound and he was on the running board swinging the door open, "Hurry driver, there is no time to lose!"

An outpost guard swung the arm up allowing the carriage to advance. With a snap of the reins the bush-tail strained forward and the carriage was on its way, the portly frog pulling the door close behind him as he flopped back in the seat.

Returning inside, Arklan and the commander discussed the strategy they would need to use in the event the ambassador would not be successful in stopping Airlein's forces from attacking the domain when a runner entered with a message.

"Your majesty!" the runner said, surprised to see the king but still giving a quick bow before reporting to the commander, "Commander, we have received a signal from the western outpost on the Hillside trade road that a large force of pixie militia are approaching the border."

"The western forces will have to deal with that threat. We have our hands full right here," the commander informed the runner.

"Wait!" Arklan said, raising his hand, commanding their attention, "Signal them to not engage the pixies and allow them to march, but send updates on their progress. Have our western forces avoid close contact with the pixies while flanking them until they become a threat to our citizens. We must deal with Airlein's forces; they are the greatest threat at the moment. Maybe, just maybe, we can resolve this problem from the east before the pixies actually become a threat, allowing me a chance to talk with them," the irritation of these events all happening now, spread like constricting tendrils deep within his being, displaying itself in the tone of his voice.

"Yes, Your Majesty," the runner acknowledged Arklan's orders, "Will there be anything else, Sire?"

"No," Arklan said, after giving quick thought to what his response should be, and with that the runner bowed and hurried off to relay the king's commands.

Arklan stood for a moment with a vacant stare out the open door, a blank emptiness before him as his thoughts blocked out all images his eyes beheld, then began to speak, "The caravan messenger must not have delivered the second message to Hillside, or they refused to believe that it was an outside force that attacked Feldspar, and they still believe it was an attack by us."

"Attack on Feldspar?" the commander's question, showing his surprise to this information, penetrating the frustration of Arklan's thoughts, making him aware once more that he was standing in the commander's office.

"Yes, it is one of the reasons that a summit has been called for at Lily Pond, but this can be discussed when the time is right," he replied solemnly, suddenly aware he had spoken aloud what he had been thinking, "Now we need to concentrate on the threat from the east," Arklan continued, turning his head and looking back at the hanging map, prevailing upon the commander to refocus his attention on the immediate and most likely danger.

◆ ◆ ◆ ◆ ◆

"Alright, you know the procedure, take your positions and stand tall," the sergeant of the guard, barked out the orders as she watched the carriage and its escort on the southeast road nearing the stables, "Corporal, alert the stable commander that the Eastern Field Fairy Queen is arriving and have the canoes standing by."

Warrior nymphs, dressed in uniforms that glittered in the sunlight with iridescent colors, long flowing black hair draping like capes on their backs, short arm sword hanging from their belts and long white staffs in hand, took up positions along either side of the walking path from the stables to the waters edge. They stood at ease, staffs at their sides leaning toward the warrior at the right, as the commander; also in her regalia, took her position at the road's entrance to the stables, flanked by four warriors on either side of her.

The carriage driver reined the bush-tail to a halt as two nymph warriors, one from either side of the stable commander, stepped up to the coach door. The warrior closest to the front of the carriage opening the door while the other warrior took her position on the other side of it.

Airlein stepped out into the bright sunlight onto the running board and looked over the spectacle; viewing the reception, the stables and the glistening waters of Lily Pond itself at the end of the path leading to the water edge. As she placed her foot on the ground, the sergeant called out a single order, "Present!" In a single motion the entire reception came to attention as the staffs were raised and brought down with a stomp, completely vertical, producing a single thundering thud. Overhead, the drone of wings suddenly filled the air as dragonfly riders appeared and began hovering in place, the sunlight sparkling off the jeweled bodies of the dragonflies and the mimicking uniforms of their riders.

"Welcome, Your Majesty. Queen Isalia awaits you in the city. We have canoes to carry you and your escort to the dock and the tube lifts," the stable commander said with a bow and a sweeping gesture of her arm, pointing the way down the path to the waters edge and the awaiting boats.

"Thank you," Airlein, returned her bow, "You may lead the way."

As Airlein carefully stepped aboard the canoe, she heard the sergeant call out another single command, "Order!" Once again the warriors moved as a single entity to stand at ease with the drone of the dragonflies fading away, leaving only the sound of the water lapping against the side of canoes and the shore.

Airlein watched as a swirling eddy slid past when the nymphs, one fore and one aft, dug their paddles into the molten mirror that was Lily Pond, sending the canoe silently cutting through the water toward the floating dock. She felt as though she were soaring through the warm sunlit sky as she looked up into the blue, and let her thoughts flow freely; *this is so peaceful. It is hard to believe that armies of the domains are positioning themselves for conflict. I hope that Gribit and the others can give a clear picture of what is really happening. That is what this summit must be about.*

◆ ◆ ◆ ◆ ◆

The bush-tail strained at the harness as the driver spurred him on with flicks of the reins and commands of "Hup, hup." As they sped down the road, the ambassador's carriage suddenly tossed from side to side with jolts when the wheels of the coach hit a series of small depressions, causing the ambassador to reach out and grab a handhold on the open window to steady himself while muttering a slight curse at being buffeted about the coach's interior.

As they neared the town of Loamis, the driver suddenly reined the bush-tail to a halt. In the road ahead of them, General Broadstem and the battalion of fairies were approaching on their march to the border.

"Driver. Why have we stopped short of Loamis?" the ambassador, called out.

"Sire. There is an army approaching!" the driver responded excitedly.

Opening the coach door, the ambassador leaned out to see for himself, "By all the sages! I hope I can convince them to turn back," he uttered, nearly whispering the words, at the sight of Airlein's army moving toward them.

Stepping down from the carriage, the ambassador walked to the front of the coach and looking up at the driver, instructed, "Hold steady. I will speak to them," before he continued on to meet the approaching force.

The ambassador took a position in the road and stood with his hand raised, "Hold your army there!" he shouted.

Broadstem halted his troops, then he and the commander approached the portly frog that blocked their way.

"Ambassador, are you not in the wrong domain? Why do you stand before us?" Broadstem snarled the questions.

"General! That is *Sire* Ambassador to you! I will be treated with the dignity my position deserves!" the ambassador, snapped back, "You will answer my question first! Why are you moving against the Southern Fields?"

"Do not be so righteous with me. I *will* find out what you frogs are up to with these other domains" the general glared back.

Stunned at what he just heard, the ambassador could only stare back blankly for the next few moments before speaking again, "What we are up to? What kind of a question is that?"

"Explain the comings and goings at Lily Pond. Frogs escorting fairies and pixies in and out of Isalia's domain," Broadstem demanded.

"I need not explain to you any of these events, it is for Airlein to inform you. Is she not attending the summit at Lily Pond?" the ambassador said, wanting to put the general back on the defensive.

"Yes, she left early this morning, but she is young and inexperienced and I wonder about her safety," the general admitted his concerns.

"What has that to do with the Southern Fields?" the ambassador asked, puzzled by the general's actions.

"That is where all this began and I want answers!" Broadstem said, challenging the ambassador to give him the information he wanted.

"Sir. Is this action sanctioned by Her Majesty?" the commander interrupted, his suspicions of Broadstem's motives now at a peak.

Broadstem snapped his head around in the direction of the commander "Are you questioning my authority?"

"Sir, I will follow any order you give up to the point that it does not cross the line. That line, being any action that is not sanctioned by Queen Airlein. I *will not* jeopardize my troops because of your *personal agenda*," the commander said, resolutely.

"Of all the insubordination! You are going to challenge me?" Broadstem growled back, feeling his authority slipping away.

"No, Sir. I do not wish to challenge you. If we turn around now the troops need not know what has taken place here," the commander said, calmly.

"Listen to your second in command. All will be made clear when Airlein returns from the summit," the ambassador, urged the general.

"Why can you not answer my question now?" the general asked, still not trusting the frogs.

"Because, General, all the facts are yet still unknown. Much will be learned at the summit and all the leaders will act on that information, *not* on assumptions and rumors," the ambassador said, stressing the need for informed action.

"Very well, but what about this frog warrior I have heard of? Can you explain him?" Broadstem asked, as he reluctantly agreed knowing his commander would most likely mutiny if he did not.

"That would be Sire Croaker. I only have limited knowledge of him. I am told he is the personal liaison to the Sage and that he has fought an enemy, the likes of which I have never seen before, and slew their leader in the battle," the ambassador felt free to share this much information with the general.

It was not a lot of information but it allowed Broadstem to feel he had accomplished at least that much of what he had wanted to learn and could save face when giving the order, "Turn them around, Commander!"

The ambassador stood alone in the road as he watched the fairies march away from him, back to Loamis, before returning to his carriage. As he walked back down the road, he sighed a great sigh of relief that the commander had spoken up and between them they had been successful in averting a conflict. When he reached the carriage he quietly said, "Driver. We will be returning to the outpost and you may do it at a bit slower pace, I am too tired to be tossed around," then climbed aboard the coach and fell back into the seat, drained and exhausted now the confrontation had passed.

CHAPTER SIXTEEN

A cold chill ran through Croaker, though the sun's warmth on this clear day caused him to remove his helm.

"Would you mind taking this for a while?" he asked Link, reaching across the short space to his friend riding next to the cart driver, "It is getting too hot and uncomfortable to wear," he explained, as they tread northward on the shallow, cart packed, furrows of the road to Lily Pond.

Still unable to shake off the chill, he turned his gaze to the southwest skies and watched as a small cloud of black moved through the sky seemingly changing direction from one moment to another.

Link turned to see what had caught Croaker's attention, "Why are you watching that flock of birds?" he asked.

"I do not know why, but there is something about them that disturbs me," Croaker confided.

"It is just a flock of birds! Since you were in battle you are seeing trouble in normal events," Link chided him, smiling at Croaker's reaction to the birds.

Croaker turned his head back toward Link, "I had a similar feeling the night Feldspar had been attacked," he said somberly before returning his gaze to the ominous mass, watching until they disappeared from view as the tall stalks of grain lining the road blocked out the southwestern horizon, "It feels as though they are looking for something!"

"Probably which field to raid!" Link chuckled.

"Maybe it is as you say, nothing more than a flock of birds, but it is as if I felt a presence other than the birds," Croaker replied, wanting to rid himself of the tightness that was forming in his chest and the chill he felt in spite of the warm sun.

"I saw only birds, Sire. Relax and enjoy the ride. Cloud Whisper does not appear to share your apprehension," Link said, trying to allay his friend's anxiety.

"Yes, you are right. He did sense the ambush at the gully before we were attacked," Croaker agreed, but still took a quick look over his shoulder again anyway.

"Ho!" the cart driver commanded his bush-tail, with a sudden pull of the reins, as a fairy messenger appeared a short distance in front of them. The messenger had flown over the fields from the northwest and landed in the road when he caught sight of Croaker riding Cloud Whisper alongside of the cart.

"Greetings. Where are you bound?" Link called out.

"Sires. I …I carry a message to Granstone," he responded, not taking his eyes off of Croaker and his mount, "Pixie militia have crossed into our domain on the Hillside trade road. We have had orders to report on them but not engage unless they become an immediate threat to our citizens."

"I had a messenger sent to Hillside to prevent this from happening," Croaker said abruptly, adding, "He must have been ambushed as well. I wonder if the caravan made it back to Hillside? If they had they would have informed them that it was an outside force that attacked Feldspar and made it look as though the fairies had."

"Deliver your message. Sire Croaker and I will see what we can do," Link told the messenger, "Safe journey."

"And a safe journey to you, Sires," the messenger said with a bow of his head toward Croaker, then continued on his way to Granstone.

"We are nearly to the junction of the trade roads. Do you think that we can intervene without doing battle?" Link asked, "We *are* carrying the body of the foe you defeated."

"It is worth a try. I think that I should take the time to put on my mail though. In the event we do not get the opportunity to show them who the real enemy is," Croaker agreed.

"If they are as stunned by your appearance as the messenger was then that could give us a good chance to talk without them attacking," Link said.

"Cloud Whisper and I will ride out ahead of you and call you forward if I can get them to listen," Croaker instructed while retrieving his mail from his saddlebags.

As Croaker unbelted his sword and hip pack, laying them across his saddle in front of him, Link asked, "Do you think that wise?"

Taking off his tunic before sliding into his mail, Croaker said, "If there is to be trouble from them, then you will be able to retreat. It would be best that I am between you and them since I have this protection and you have none. Cloud Whisper and I will follow when you are far enough away."

Link nodded his agreement; *we are not to engage the pixies and I should not be the cause of that engagement.*

After replacing his tunic, Croaker re-belted his hip pack and sword as the driver flicked his reins and the cart moved forward with the bush-tail straining lightly against the harness.

"Link, hand me my helm," Croaker said, reaching over toward the cart to retrieve it.

Prepared for the pixies, Croaker's concern continued to center on the flock of birds causing him to look at the sky over his left shoulder once more. Though no longer there, the apprehension of them continued to shadow his thoughts as he lowered his helm over his head. Forcing his mind back to the immediate problem of the pixies, he urged Cloud Whisper to move several lengths in front of the cart. He felt this would allow a safe distance for Link and the cart driver, should they encounter the pixie militia unexpectedly.

By the time they reached the junction to Hillside, Croaker felt confident he would be able to deal with the militia as he thought back to his encounter with the pixies and frogs of the trade caravan at Feldspar. He had placed himself in the position of authority, though it was not a conscious thought at that time, and would do so again since now he knew from that experience that he would be accepted in that role.

Croaker waited at the junction until the cart came up alongside him, "The pixies have not made it this far yet. It is my hope that we do not have to go far before we encounter them. I would like to make Lily Pond by this evening if possible," he said, staring down the Hillside road.

"We will have to travel much faster than we have been, Sire," Link answered.

"Driver, can your bush-tail take a faster pace?" Croaker asked, turning his gaze toward the cart and riders, wanting to see the driver's response as well as hear it.

"Yes, Sire. He is strong and has good stamina. We have made many trips together," the driver said with pride.

Satisfied with the driver's evaluation of his bush-tail, Croaker said, "I will take a lead again. Remember, when we meet the pixies, you hold back until I summon you."

"Yes, Sire," the driver acknowledged the plan, as Croaker and Cloud Whisper turned west.

◆◆◆◆◆

The sun poured down on the militia like warm honey, clinging to the troops, as they marched eastward, the sound of their footsteps dampened to nearly a muffle by the standing grains lining either side of the trade road. The border crossing had found the fairy outpost deserted when they crossed into the Southern Field domain. With no opposition they continued on, with the mayor wondering what the fairies might be up to.

"Sire, should we not have scouts? Why would the fairies abandon the outpost?" the commander of the Pellucere militia inquired, as they marched side by side at the front of the troops.

"I do not know why they would leave the border open, Commander. As for scouts . . . where would you have them scout? I do not intend to lose any militia unnecessarily flailing around in the tall grasses of the fields and I can see far enough down the road in front of us," the mayor responded.

"Where do we march, Sire?" the commander asked, looking around at the tall stands of grain to either side and the empty road, both in front and behind the militia.

"We will follow this road until we encounter fairies, be they on the road or we come upon a town," the mayor said sharply, irritated that the commander would even ask such a question.

"What is that Sire?" the commander asked pointing at a bright white glow approaching them on the road ahead, "That is no fairy, Sire!"

As the militia and the white object drew nearer each other the mayor held up his hand to stop the troops. Soon they could see that it was a bush-tail, a white bush-tail carrying a rider that was also in white and wearing a helm, polished silver bright, that glistened in the sun. Several lengths behind the rider, a cart came to a stop as the rider held up his hand.

"What and who be you?" the mayor shouted his question, as they were still a good distance apart.

"I am Croaker . . . Liaison to the Sage and first warrior frog since General Longhopper, who became the first of the Sages," Croaker shouted back, "I have much to discuss with you, may I approach?"

The mayor stood dumbfounded at what he had just heard, then looking around to see if he had entered some kind of trap and seeing none, said, "Approach, Sire Croaker. Be forewarned that any treachery will bring a swift response."

Croaker nudged Cloud Whisper to move closer until they were only a couple of arm's length away from the mayor and the commander, "Tell me Sire, who are you?"

"I am the mayor of Hillside and in command of the militia," the mayor informed Croaker, "and what of that cart that lays back?"

"*That*, you will be made aware of if you are willing to listen to what I have to say," Croaker spoke, with an authority that compelled the mayor to feel subordinate.

"Sire Croaker, since when have the frogs changed their ways? First a dictate from the Sage and now before me is a frog warrior."

"I know not of Gribit's dictate, but I have a need to know if the second messenger from Feldspar arrived with his message. Also what became of the returning caravan?" he asked, his steady gaze fixed upon the mayor.

"Second messenger? Returning caravan? None but a frog messenger arrived at Hillside, telling of the fairy attack, until I received that message from the Sage," the mayor said, confused by this revelation, "How is it that you have knowledge of these things?"

"In the early morning two days ago, a young pixie was found near death along the Southern Field Fairy border. Scouts tended him and brought him to their healers. In his delirium he spoke of monsters attacking his town and killing all. I was requested to investigate. When I arrived at Feldspar I encountered the caravan master and offered to help in burying the dead. He told me a messenger had been sent to Hillside to tell of a fairy attack. It was then that I had him send a pixie messenger to inform you that it had not been the fairies that attack," Croaker explained.

"So say you! If not the fairies, then who?" the mayor asked, not believing Croaker's story.

"A force from outside the realm of Lily Pond. Of this I have proof, carried in the cart," Croaker said, looking back over his shoulder.

"How do you come by this proof?"

"We were attacked, when returning to the Southern Fields, by slithers and toads who were led by a creature the likes of which I have never seen or heard of before. In the battle I was able to defeat this foe and now have his body in that cart. I was on my way to Lily Pond with it when I learned that you had marched into this domain. That is why I am here now," Croaker explained.

"*We* were attacked? Who was with you?" The mayor asked, suspicious of Croaker.

"I led a column of fairies since we did not know what to expect. They *also* helped in the burying of your kinsmen. You would know all this if the caravan had made it back to Hillside. They must have been ambushed as we had been. I suggest that you send a party to find them when you return to Hillside," Croaker said, now giving the mayor his direction to go.

"I will see this body you carry before I go anywhere!" the mayor said, still not believing Croaker.

Croaker turned in his saddle and with a wave of his arm, in a motion toward his position, the cart started slowly forward. When they were near Croaker and the pixies, Croaker motioned them to turn the cart so it faced the way they had come.

"Sire Mayor, have your look," Croaker said, and the two pixies moved to the back of the cart as Link left his seat to uncover the body.

The Mayor looked at the body and then at the Pellucere commander, a questioning look on both their faces, then back to Croaker, "What is he?"

"From information we have obtained through the scrolls of General Longhopper, we believe that he is an imp. My companion, Link, discovered ancient artifacts and glyphs that tell a story of a great conflict with these beings long ago," Croaker informed them, "It is from this discovery that I have obtained my war garb, my weapons and helm. It was my companion that taught me the use of these weapons that I was able to defeat this foe in battle. There were many others of his kind that rode rats in the force that ambushed the column I led to Feldspar."

"Sire Croaker, we will return to Hillside and I will have a party sent to search for the trade caravan that is missing," the mayor said, the commander nodding his agreement as well.

"Tell your search party to be alert at all times. These are fierce fighters as well as cunning. I believe it was their intent to cause the domains to fight one another by making it look as though one had attacked another," Croaker cautioned, "Now I must hurry to Lily Pond and the summit that has been called. The leaders will need to view this foe as you have done."

"Sire Croaker . . . that was the message from the sage, though he did not put a name to the foe. His dictate was that we take instructions from Sire Puck, an inn-keeper from Limonite," the mayor said, before turning to order his militia to turn back to Hillside.

"I met Puck at Lily Pond, he travels with your friend Webber," Link said, covering the body once more, then stepping over the back rest of the cart to take his place beside the driver again.

The cart pulled away, back to the east and the trade roads junction, with Croaker and Cloud Whisper watching on as the mayor and the commander explained to the militia what had just occurred, waiting until the order had been given for the militia to march before they turned and hurried after the cart.

◆◆◆◆◆

"Over here Sir! I saw him go under the brush!" a fairy warrior called out as he chased after a slither.

"You there, circle around to the right!" the commander shouted out to the five fairies on the right of the warrior that had sighted the slither, then facing the troops on the left shouted out, "The rest of you circle from that side. Do not let him escape!"

The forest crackled with the sound of troops beating the brush as they closed a circle around their prey, making sure that the slither could not slip past them. Soon one of the warriors called out while pointing out the location, "There he is!"

A swish of arrows filled the air, several finding their mark, impaling the slither and pinning him to the ground as he wriggled violently in twisting coils until finally giving one last twitch as the life left its body.

"Sir, that is one more that will not be bringing harm to our children," the fairy that had first sighted the slither smiled back at his commander.

"I wonder how the others have done in finding these vile creatures. That makes two that we have uncovered and destroyed," the commander spoke his thoughts, then ordered, "Send a messenger back to Broadleaf to report our success to General Oakon while we continue on to the north."

"Yes Sir," the sergeant at his side acknowledged.

As the echelon of troops moved north, searching the forest floor as they went, their senses were acutely active. With the momentary excitement of the chase now over, the sounds of the forest were both relaxing and intense at the same time. The rapid ta-ta-ta of a woodpecker hammering at a hollow tree reverberated throughout the forest and the scratching sound of beetles skittering through the leaf clutter would draw the attention of the closest fairy. The still air was filled with the odor of damp moss mixed with the smells of ground flowers and decaying litter that had fallen to the ground, and a cool dampness clung to their flesh as they pressed forward in their search while constantly scanning the sun dappled shade of the forest floor that lie in front of them.

A desperate slither raced along the ground searching for cover as the fairies approached the brush he had fled from only seconds ago. Frantically he slid from rock to brush, avoiding any open ground, until he found an abandoned burrow at the base of a tree. It was perfect. The opening was concealed by plant growth and fallen debris and with any luck the fairies would not find it or him and so he wriggled his way deep inside and waited for them to pass.

Long after the sound of the fairies had faded deeper into the forest, the slither went to the burrow's entrance and tested the air. *How many of us had managed to escape the fairies*, he wondered. They had passed him by and the forest was growing darker now, the daylight fading, and so he began his trek to the rendezvous location where on the ensuing night he would meet with Lord Noma to give his report.

◆◆◆◆◆

Only the whisper of a breeze sighed through the streets of Feldspar as the sun dipped below the hills to the west. If there had been anyone there they would have seen the flock of ravens circling in the rich glow, descending until they disappeared behind the hills.

As the flock landed in the trees to roost for the night a lone raven broke away from the others and landed on the ledge by the cave entrance and an imp dismounted. After releasing the raven to go roost with the rest of the flock the imp entered the cave entrance, lighting a torch to see his way, and began his walk into the depths to report to his commander.

Reaching the fires of the large cavern the imp doused his flame, his eyes searching for his commander. Seeing the commander pacing back and forth near the command table, his head down and eyes fixed on the cavern floor at his feet, the imp was in no hurry to bring him the news of his search for General O'Dias. Slowly he approached the commander then spoke, "Sir," he said quietly, then repeated a little louder, "Sir."

The commander looked in the direction the voice had come from, "Yes. What news have you for me?" he asked, recognizing the imp he had sent searching.

"Sir, I searched the fields to the east and even went south to the swamps of our land . . . I . . . I could not find any sign of General O'Dias or his troops," he said, a cowering tone in his voice.

"No sign at all?" the commander asked, disbelief exuding from the commander's question.

"Sir, I searched each area more than once and nothing was to be found," the imp assured him.

"There must be some clue to the General's whereabouts!" the commander said, the trepidation in his voice was evident at the idea he would have to tell Lord Noma of this information, "You are dismissed! Get out of my sight, before you disappear!"

The idea that the general and his troops could have been defeated was unthinkable to the commander so this possibility never occurred to him as he went to arouse Noma from his rest to make the trip to the abandoned mines north of Millville.

"Lord, it is time for your trip. I have instructed that a bat be made ready for you," the commander said, waking Noma.

"I will speak to General O'Dias first!" Noma said, throwing off his cover as he stood.

"The General and his troops are still in the field Lord," the commander lied.

"It is not like him to have to take this much time to chase down an enemy," Noma snapped, irritated that he still could not have his talk with O'Dias.

"Lord, would you like to have fruit and berries before you leave?" the commander asked, wanting to change the subject from the general.

"Yes, but I will have my talk with him when I return from the meeting with the slithers. I do not want him to find another reason to be gone. Is that understood?" Noma glared at the commander.

"Yes Lord," the commander responded quietly.

CHAPTER SEVENTEEN

The dusky blue of the western sky donned a robe of velvet black and wisps of high clouds lightly veiled the sliver of the crescent moon as the first of the stars began to shine when Croaker and his companions caught sight of the lights flickering on at the Lily Pond stables.

Foremost in Croaker's mind was the need to reach Lily Pond with the body of his foe and so they had pushed on through Weavertown not stopping for food or rest.

"I will be well rid of this foul cargo, Sire Croaker," Link said, glancing back over his shoulder to the back of the cart.

"It will not be long now and the nymphs can have care of that body," Croaker agreed.

There was no pomp upon their arrival at the stables, just the stunned look of the nymph guard at the sight of Croaker.

Recovering from Croaker's appearance in battle garb, the guard finally spoke, "Sire. We have been expecting you," she said, lowering her hand, "King Arklan of the Southern Fields told us to expect you when he arrived shortly before last light," then turned away from them calling out, "Send for the rulers as directed. Sire Croaker has arrived with his cargo!"

267

Croaker dismounted Cloud Whisper as a runner sped along the path to the shore while Link and the driver stepped down from the cart, "Please see to the needs of our bush-tails," he said, handing his reins to one of the stable hands that approached.

"Sire, you are to wait here for the rulers. The others may leave for the city if they wish," the nymph guard informed him.

"Sire, I will stay with you. The driver my go on since he has finished his task," Link said, nodding his head at the driver to go on his way to the city.

"You will want to leave the cart outside the stables," Croaker told the stable hand that took up the reins of the cart's bush-tail, "We will stay with it," he added as they followed behind.

◆◆◆◆◆

The simple grandeur of the meeting chamber impressed Arklan as he and the ambassador entered with the nymph escort announcing their arrival. Arklan noticed the green hue of the city, which he had seen as he made his way from the tunnel dome, was growing deeper when his gaze went to the opening that looked out on the city. The green transformed the limestone to a glowing emerald and tinted all that the light fell upon. Across the room Isalia stood to greet them, breaking away from her conversation with Fernon and Airlein. As she approached Arklan, his eyes momentarily went to the full wall tapestry behind them that depicted the daily life of the nymphs very much like the glyphs in his hall at Granstone.

"Welcome to Lily Pond Sire. We had been expecting you much sooner," Isalia said, offering her hand to him, palm down.

"My apologies Your Highness. The ambassador and I were delayed by an incident on my eastern border that diverted us there," he replied, taking her hand in his and tilting his head forward in a bow, "Allow me to complement your troops on their welcome to us at your stables."

"Thank you, I hope you will enjoy your stay in our domain. May I introduce you to the others?" she asked.

All in the chamber had stood and the Granstone ambassador went to join Gribit, Puck, Webber and the other ambassadors that had congregated in an area directly across from the chamber opening.

Leading Arklan back to where Fernon and Airlein were standing, Isalia asked, "We have already had our meal but would you like me to order a meal for you and the ambassador after the introductions?"

"That would be fine. We have not had the opportunity to stop and dine since we traveled straight here after the incident had been resolved," Arklan replied, though he had not given it any consideration because of all the thoughts of the events that have taken place.

"King Arklan, this is King Fernon."

"Cousin, at last we meet," Fernon bowed his head, "It has been too many generations since our family split."

"Let us hope that will not be the case from this point on," Arklan said graciously.

"And this is Queen Airlein," Isalia said, looking toward the young queen.

"Yes, we need to talk, after I meet the rest of the participants," he said, giving her a stern look.

"Sire?" she replied, puzzled by his attitude and his apparent lack of respect, "Of what do you wish to discuss?"

"We will talk in a few moments!" he said, before turning away to meet the Sage and the group around him.

"Sire, this is the Sage, Gribit, and the pixie representative Puck," Isalia said, indicating each in turn, "The rest of this group are the ambassadors and Gribit's young friend, Webber."

After the introductions, Isalia ordered a meal for Arklan and the Granstone ambassador then asked if Arklan would join her, Fernon and Airlein in conversation.

"I would like that very much, though I must speak to Airlein first if Her Highness would join me?" Arklan replied loud enough for the young queen to hear him.

Airlein nodded and started across the room as Isalia went to rejoin Fernon while the others were seated once more, "Sire, just what is it you wish to discuss with me and maybe you can explain your hostility towards me!"

"If not for the ambassador . . . our domains would be at war this very moment!" Arklan huffed, looking over to indicate the rotund frog sitting next to Gribit, "*Who* is in control of your army?" returning his gaze to Airlein, "Had he not been able to turn your general around . . . I do not even wish to think of what would have happened."

"*I* am in control of my army. What do you mean? Turn my general around, around from what?" Airlein said, shocked by this revelation.

"Your general was marching against my domain with his troops! I had received word that your forces were gathering at Loamis before I left Granstone and that is why I diverted from my trip here, to assess what was happening. The ambassador has assured me that you had no knowledge of this and that is why I ask the question, *who* is in control?" Arklan answered, as if to scold a child.

"This is the first time General Broadstem has taken any kind of action without my authority and it *will* be the last," Airlein said, a calm control in her voice, "Furthermore, grumbling at me will not make a difference in how I deal with him and *be assured* I will deal with him."

"Forgive my irritation," Arklan said, "It is just that at that same time I had pixie militia marching into my domain from the west," swinging his attention to Puck and the ambassador of that domain, "I was grateful when a messenger from the troops I had observing them delivered a message to me, when we had reached the crossroads, that Sire Croaker had altered his course to intercept them and had been successful in turning them back to the Rolling Hills."

271

"I assure you Sire, we had no knowledge of their actions. In fact we had sent a message to the other cities to take no action without hearing from us," Puck said, standing and gesturing with his hand toward the ambassador, "I fear that the mayors of those cities do not accept me as the representative of the domain. In all things outside our lands we have depended on the frogs to represent us . . . this is new for us and I am sure that for some it will take time to accept it."

"Time! I fear that we have precious little of that. When Sire Croaker arrives you will understand my concerns. Sire Croaker carries with him the body of our true enemy, the body of the foe he defeated in combat near our southwestern border." Arklan said, moving his gaze around the chamber, looking from one to the next until he had engaged all the representatives.

"A frog in combat! Unheard of," Fernon, voiced what many of the participants had thought at that moment.

Holding up his hand as he stood, even though he too could not imagine his young friend doing battle, Gribit said, "*Not* unheard of. It was a very long time ago that we frogs fought alongside the fairies and pixies to overcome a foe that we drove from these lands. With the events that have been happening of late, I believe that this foe has returned."

At that moment a runner from the stables entered the chamber, "Your Majesty," she said, stopping to bow, "Sire Croaker has arrived with his cargo and waits at the stables as requested by King Arklan."

"Thank you. Inform him that we are on our way," Isalia said, dismissing the runner to return to the stables.

Fernon stood quickly from his chair to walk over to Isalia, Arklan and Airlein at the runner's announcement; anxious to see this enemy that has control over the slithers.

"Let us see this foe," Gribit said, motioning to Puck, Webber and the ambassadors to join him as he followed Isalia, Airlein and Arklan with Fernon close behind them, to the chamber entrance.

"Sire, you and the ambassador will have to wait a while longer for your meal," Isalia, apologized to Arklan as they entered the corridor.

Arklan dismissed her concern with a wave of his hand, "A meal at this time is not important. I am sure the ambassador will agree with me," he said, looking back at the ambassador who nodded in agreement.

As they walked the streets of the domed city, on their way to the tube lifts, the green luminescence flooded over and clung to all it touched. To those that had never been to Lily Pond before the atmosphere conveyed a feeling that the assembly was moving through a strange dream world where one wanted to both linger in it and wake from it at the same moment.

Arklan stood looking out over the waters of Lily Pond as he waited for the rest of the group to take their turn in the lift, the whisper of a cool damp breeze brushing across his face. On the distant shore he saw the stable lights competing with the fireflies flittering here and there through the tall shore grasses. Above, thin veils of wispy clouds moving across the black sky were increasing, softly glowing like distant ribbons of Elgin fire from the sliver of moon, blotting out stars here and there as they passed in their flight. Conversations of frogs floating on the air and, from the forest side of the pond, an occasional hoot of an owl provided a sense of well being in the realm.

Odd this contrast of the serenity of the night and the reason we are going to the stables, Arklan thought to himself as Isalia stepped up close to his side.

"I do not often get to enjoy the peacefulness of nights like this. I spend far too much time in the city below," Isalia said, almost in a whisper.

"I could enjoy it more if it did not belie the turmoil that is brewing just beneath the surface of our perceptions. This outside enemy is cunning . . . he tries to make us fight each other and more than once he has nearly succeeded," Arklan said as he continued to gaze at the shore.

"That is why I called for this summit. I believe that we need to form alliances with one another because of this threat," Isalia agreed.

"I have a similar idea about that but I think it should wait until we are all sitting down for the discussions," Arklan said, turning to face her.

The last of the delegation stepped out of the lifts as six canoes were brought alongside the dock. Isalia and her guard embarked on the first. As her canoe silently slid away toward the stable shore, Arklan followed with his guard in the next followed by Fernon then Airlein, each with their guard. Puck, Webber and Gribit shared the next canoe with the ambassadors boarding the last.

♦ ♦ ♦ ♦ ♦

Croaker and Link watched as the procession approached from the water's edge, nymph warriors along the path snapping to attention, bringing their staffs fully upright. The stable commander had met the group at the landing and was leading them to Croaker and Link as they stood next to the cart outside the stable doors.

"Your Majesties, I hope you will forgive the late hour of our arrival. A detour became necessary along the way," Croaker said as he and Link bowed when the procession had reached their position as the royal guards formed around them.

Acknowledging Link with a nod, Isalia turned her attention to Croaker, "And you must be Sire Croaker," Isalia said with admiration, as Croaker stood in his battle garb, his helm tucked in the crook of his left arm, "I have been told of your deeds in battle as well as your diplomacy with the pixies by King Arklan when he informed us of the nature of your detour."

"I am humbled by your praise," he said with a slight bow.

"May we view the foe you slew?" she asked.

Link went to the rear of the cart and lifted away the covering that concealed the body of General O'Dias, the foul smell of death escaping into the night air in a rush. The assembled group quickly turned their heads away, covering the faces with whatever each had at hand, for a brief moment until the night breeze cleaned the air of most of the odor.

O'Dias' malevolence appeared even greater in death than it had in life. His avocado face was distorted in a frozen scowl with needle sharp canines projecting from under his lips and the remains of his gashed eye, where Croaker's dagger had pierced deep into his skull, along with the black mail he wore brought a cringe to those that viewed him.

"Arlen's fate!" Airlein gasped, and then quickly turning her gaze to Croaker, "You defeated that? How?"

"Your Majesty, with good fortune and excellent training from my friend here, Sire Link," Croaker said, indicating Link with a gesture of his hand as he explained, "This . . . this enemy . . . nearly caught me unaware when he attacked with his battle axe as he swooped down from above on his bat. Cloud Whisper avoided his attacks until we were able to get the advantage and take the offensive."

"Cloud Whisper? Who is that?" she asked.

"He is my mount, my bush-tail . . . my friend. He is being cared for in the stables," Croaker said proudly, nodding in that direction.

"I will give you all the details of the attack I received in the report from my outpost commander when we sit for our discussions," Arklan broke in, "It is late and we still have to dispose of this body."

"My stable commander will tend to that," Isalia said, the commander nodding her acknowledgment of the order, "I think we should return to the city for rest. We can start our talks in the morning."

"Your Majesties. Before you return, I must ask you for your domain rings," Gribit announced, "I am now *absolutely* certain that I must see the scrolls in Longhopper's vault. I can leave now for Granstone if I can be provided with a carriage and driver."

"What scrolls and why would you require our rings?" Airlein asked, puzzled by Gribit's request, "And who is Longhopper?"

"Longhopper was general of the frog forces I spoke of earlier. He became the first of the Sage. He had the three fairy domain rings made as keys to his vault in Granstone and left instructions, that if needed, the rings were to be given to the Sage at his request," Gribit informed her.

"How is it you have knowledge of this and we do not?" Airlein asked.

"I received this information in the copy of the scrolls that King Arklan had sent to me after their discovery in Granstone," Gribit explained.

"I will not be giving up my ring. However I will accompany you and see this vault and scrolls for myself!" Fernon said defiantly.

"I agree with King Fernon," Airlein said, "I would see these scrolls as well!"

"Sire Gribit. We would all accompany you to Granstone in the morning and have our summit there, if that meets with Queen Isalia's approval?" Arklan suggested.

"If there is information about this enemy that would help us in understanding and defeating him then I have no problem with your suggestion," Isalia agreed.

"Sire Puck, as representative of the pixies, do you agree as well?" Gribit asked, not wanting this pixie he had chosen to represent that domain to be discounted.

"Yes, of course. It would be the most efficient use of our time rather than having to wait for your return to relay what you have learned," Puck replied, understanding that Gribit would not allow him to be excluded from any of the decisions.

"Then we shall leave for Granstone in the morning. Commander, have all our transportation ready for us at that time," Isalia ordered, "Now let us return to the city and rest for our journey."

"Croaker, you will make the trip with us as well," Gribit informed the young frog as they walked to the shore and the awaiting canoes, "We will need your input at the summit since you have met this foe in battle."

"King Arklan has all the information I could tell you in the report from his commander," Croaker said, and then lifting his tunic slightly for Gribit to see, he asked, "Do you know of a smith that can do this kind of work? I wish to have a blanket of mail made for Cloud Whisper. Not just any mail, it must be of the quality of my own."

"I have heard of one such smith, a fairy smith, in a village just north of the head of Slither Clearing. He has retained the crafts of old," Gribit said after giving thought to Croaker's question for a few moments before they reached the canoes, "I will ask Fernon to send word to him of your need."

"It would be better if I were to go there myself. The smith would need to measure Cloud Whisper and I have a definite idea of how it should be made after seeing the mail that protected the bat my foe rode upon," Croaker said as he carefully stepped into the canoe to take his seat.

"Very well then, although I will expect you in Granstone five days from now," Gribit agreed as he sat next to his young friend, "We will speak to Fernon when we are back in the city."

"Do you wish me to accompany you Sire?" Link asked.

"I can see no reason that you should not," Croaker said, happy to have his friend travel with him, then asking Gribit, "Is there any reason that you can think of?"

Gribit could not help but smile at the close friendship that had formed between these two that only a few short days ago had met at his pad; *if friendships like this can be formed so quickly then there is hope this gathering of the rulers will allow the domains to set aside their differences to confront the problem facing all of us.*

Answering thoughtfully as the canoe silently slid away from the shore, "I can see none."

◆◆◆◆◆

Noma shrugged up his shoulders as the cool wind pressed his back. Behind him to the east the lights of Pellucere were fading away as the first of the lights of Millville appeared before him. The high wispy clouds were being covered from view as the lower, thicker, clouds of the rains chased him through the night.

I should make the abandoned mines before the rain catches me. I will be glad to light a fire before I sleep. What is O'Dias up to? He should have returned before I left. Has my brother anticipated my intentions and summoned him back to the palace cave to make sure that he is aligned with him? Is the commander keeping this from me? So many questions . . . Am I letting my mind find things that are not? No, he will be there when I return! Noma thought, then leaning farther forward on his bat he urged him on, "Faster, faster!"

CHAPTER EIGHTEEN

Croaker woke to the voice of a nymph calling his name from the entrance to his chambers, "Sire Croaker. The others are waiting for you! Will you be much longer?"

The long day and the short night had caught up with him and sleep was clinging hard to his eyelids like weights preventing him from opening them more than small slits. The muted light that filtered through the thin slats of the woven cattail leaf shutters within his chamber was enough to burn into his fogged mind as he tried to rub the sleep away, "Yes, yes, thank you. I will be there shortly," he muttered, swinging his legs slowly over the side of the bed as he sat up.

After a few moments the lingering urge to close his eyes and drift back into the cocoon of darkness finally gave way and he began to see clearly. Standing, he shambled over to the stand that held the water basin and splashed some cool water on his face, shaking off the last of the lingering sleep, before crossing the chamber to open the shutters of the window that looks out over the city.

As he looked out over the city it was nearly as dark beyond the dome as when he arrived and the once bright green was now a

281

pallid pall that clung to the city, much like the sleep that had clung to him.

Yet another long trip to places I have never been before that I must undertake . . . at least Link will be with me, Croaker thought to himself as he turned away from the window to retrieve his gear that he had laid out on the chest at the foot of his bed.

He had considered not wearing his battle garb but thought better of this since Link was his companion and not of Fernon's domain. Donning his mail to be prepared for any eventuality and deciding that he would wear the formal tunic, he had learned from his previous travels to expect the unexpected, as he thought about those who had already seen him in it and how they reacted; *wearing this and riding Cloud Whisper could provide enough of a pause in any potential situation giving us a chance to avert needless conflicts.*

After belting his hip pack and sword he reached down and scooped up his helm, tucking it in the crook of his left arm, before opening the chamber door.

"Sire," the waiting nymph said, "I am to escort you to the dining area."

"Thank you. Is the city always this dark in the daytime?" Croaker asked as they walked the corridor, "I would have thought it brighter!"

"*Oh no,* Sire, it is only like this when there is a rain above. Very little sunlight to filter down," she informed him.

The chorus of voices slowly faded when Croaker and his escort entered the dining area, heads turning his way to see this unusual sight. From the prominent tables, where the rulers were seated, Isalia motioned him to join the delegation.

"Your Majesty," Croaker said, bowing his head as a kitchen nymph pulled out an empty chair at the table for him to be seated.

"Sire Croaker," Isalia said, acknowledging his bow with a nod of her head, "please be seated."

"Would you find a place for this?" Croaker asked, handing the kitchen nymph his helm before taking his seat, then turning his attention back to the delegation, "I am sorry to have kept you waiting."

"It is quite alright, Sire Croaker," Isalia said, smiling at him, her eyes indicating her understanding of all he had been through in the past two days.

Across the table Airlein was handing a sealed message to a frog messenger, "See that General Broadstem receives this. Look for him in Loamis first but if he is not there go to Zarlan Grove. Send any reply to Granstone."

"Gribit, Link thought it nothing yesterday when we saw a large flock of birds in the distance to the southwest but I felt a presence amongst them. I had the same feeling the night Feldspar had been attacked. When I was attacked, it was from above as my foe rode a bat. Sire, take heed and watch the skies!" Croaker cautioned the Sage.

"Your warning is well taken," Gribit said solemnly, and then adding, "I have a letter for you to carry to the smith from King Fernon. It will introduce you and Link and instructs him to expedite your request. He will be found in the village of Juniper, north of the head of Slither Clearing. You will follow the trade road to Broadleaf then pass Bale's Hollow to Raven's Roost. From there you will stay on the north road until you reach Juniper. You will have to travel fast, it will be two days there and three to return to Granstone!"

"I would need to have at least one more day should we encounter any delay. We would need that much extra to arrive in Granstone," Croaker said, protesting the tight schedule Gribit had to set for them.

"Very well then, six days. No more though. Events are happening to fast and I believe it is necessary for you to be in Granstone as soon as possible. If you can make it there and back to Granstone in five, then all the better," Gribit nodded in agreement, still urging Croaker to hasten his travels.

"We will do our best to make it that soon," Croaker said, wanting to reassure the Sage.

Croaker began to eat the hot grain cereal and bread, dipping the latter into the bowl of honey provided, which had been brought to him while listening to some of the conversations of the others at the tables. Fernon and Puck were sending frog messengers to their domains to let their wives and others know that they would be going to Granstone as he took a long sip of his hot tea.

284

"I wonder if Lily or Lotus would recognize you if they saw you! You have changed so much in these last few days," Webber said, marveling at the change in his friend.

"I wonder sometimes if I could recognize myself," Croaker agreed, "though the same could be said about you, since you have changed also."

"I still miss sitting at the edge of the water, enjoying the sun and the girls!" Webber confided.

"So do I, Webber, so do I," Croaker said, his voice trailing off as he lamented before taking another long sip of hot tea.

"We will have those days again," Webber said, trying to reassure his friend.

"Are you to Granstone?" Croaker asked.

"Yes. I am traveling with Puck. He and I have traveled together since the day after you left," Webber informed Croaker, "I see that you also have a new friend, Link. We have talked when he was last here."

"Yes, I would not have survived the battle if not for his training and my bush-tail, Cloud Whisper. Both are friend to me!" Croaker said, taking one last bite of bread and the last of his tea.

◆ ◆ ◆ ◆ ◆

Thick clouds blanketed the sky above so heavily that it was almost as dark as the night had been. A steady rain poured straight down, hitting the waters of Lily Pond with such frequency and force that the sound of each drop fused together with the others in a single continuous roar like that of the rapids.

Near the southern shore a slither slides unseen through the tall grasses and into the water. Weaving his way through the rushes, he begins his trip to the rendezvous location in the forest where he is to meet Lord Noma. Crossing the water would be the shortest route and so he swims with a purpose, believing he will ingratiate himself with the goblin prince with the information he has gained from watching the Lily Pond stables.

The previous night he had seen the frog warrior arrive and overheard what had been said. When the detail, the stable commander had formed, left to bury the body he followed silently. There were a few minutes when the nymphs were distracted, as they dug the grave, that he was able to get close enough without being seen and recognized the body to be that of General O'Dias. He was certain this was information for which Lord Noma would be grateful.

◆ ◆ ◆ ◆ ◆

After finishing their morning meal, Croaker and Link were the first to leave for the tube lifts. The nymph operating the lifts suggested that they would want to put on their slickers because of the hard rain above.

"There will be a covered canoe to take you to the stables, Sire. Your mount is being readied for you and one for the fairy as well," she informed Croaker, "He will not want to fly in this weather and it appears as though it will not change for most of the day."

"Thank you," Croaker said as he slid his slicker over his tunic before entering the lift, "Sire Link will have to decide for himself how he wishes to travel."

"If the weather is as she has said then I am most grateful for the mount. Without it I would not be able to keep up with you," Link said, giving a nod to the nymph before entering the lift.

Stepping out onto the floating dock it was as if they had stepped under a waterfall and the visibility was poor from the darkness of the day and the heavy rain pouring down.

When the canoe came alongside the dock, Croaker saw that it had arched ribs, fore and aft, that a spider silk canopy was stretched over with the sides just high enough for them to duck under to be seated. Once in the canoe, he could see that it had been equipped with an outrigger on the far side to compensate for the loss of stability from the canopy.

The rain pounding against the taut covering was like being inside a drum with someone beating a relentless rhythm while the nymphs dug their paddles into the water and pulled for the stable shore.

"I have never been in rain like this before," Croaker said, almost yelling at Link to be heard over the sound, "I hope it will ease up some before too long!"

"Yes Sire, this amount of rain will make it very difficult for our mounts," Link agreed.

As they landed on the shore a low rumble of distant thunder rolled through the air and the wind began to blow, driving the stinging cold rain against what little exposed flesh they presented to the elements. Croaker was thankful for his slicker and the graveled path as they trudged their way to the stables against the driven rain.

Once inside the stables they shook off the cold rainwater that still clung to them as a stable nymph brought them drying cloths.

"Your mounts are ready, Sire," she said, holding the reins of Cloud Whisper and a gray that trailed behind her, "He is a magnificent animal, Sire!"

"He is truly that," Croaker answered, wiping dry his face, "and he is much more. He is my friend."

"The roads will not be fit for carriage or cart. At least we will have the wind and rain at our backs, Sire," Link said, as he stood looking out the stable doors.

"Well, with the way the wind is blowing now it might move this weather out though it would be near the direction we are headed," Croaker answered Link, looking up at the sky through the doors, before swinging up unto Cloud Whisper and gently patting him on the shoulder, "I am sorry friend, but we have no time to wait this out."

Link swung up onto his gray and followed Croaker out the stable doors and as the veil of rain engulfed them the stable nymph called out, "A swift and safe journey, Sires!"

The bush-tails took long arching strides as they sped through the rain, their paws throwing up fountains of spray behind them. The furrows were filled with water and if not for the wall of grasses to either side it would have been easy to stray from the road.

Croaker and Link leaned forward, low and close to their mounts, to limit the resistance so their bush-tails would not tire too quickly. If Cloud Whisper and the gray could keep up the pace, they ought to reach Fernon's domain in about half the time it would usually take, then the forest should offer them some shelter from the unrelenting rain.

♦ ♦ ♦ ♦ ♦

The buzz of conversation filled the dining area as the delegation sat finishing their morning meal while workers from the late night shift were arriving to have theirs.

Finishing his morning tea, Gribit watched as a nymph messenger approached Isalia. He had been in conversation with the ambassadors as the messenger arrived and others in the congregation were preparing to return to their quarters before starting their journey to Granstone.

"Your Majesty," the nymph said, bowing before offering Isalia a message.

Isalia nodded as she reached out for the envelope. Opening it, she studied the message for a moment before dismissing the messenger.

"Your Majesties, Gribit, Sire Puck, I have just received word that the rain has made the roads impassable for carriages and carts. I believe that we will have to wait until tomorrow to travel to Granstone," she informed them.

"We can begin our talks here," Fernon said, "There are some things that I would like to discuss!"

"And what would that be?" Isalia asked, not caring for Fernon's tone of voice.

"You have had citizens of my domain held captive from past skirmishes for a long time now. I would like to have them released so they may return home," he said, a sternness in his demand.

Nodding in agreement with Fernon, Airlein said, but with a more diplomatic tone, "Yes, I too would like the return of *my* citizens as well, it would go a long way in developing an atmosphere for mutual talks."

Isalia hadn't expected this subject to come up at this time though she knew it would eventually, "And you Sire Puck, do you wish the same?" she asked, a hint of irritation in her voice.

"I believe that is a subject for future talks. Right now we need to address the immediate problem we face," he said, thinking about what had happened to the children of his town and the citizens of Feldspar.

"Sire Puck is right. I also have citizens that Isalia has in her custody but we can negotiate their release at a time that is more appropriate," Arklan spoke up.

"Yes, we need to discuss this foe that is at our door but we can still discuss getting our citizens back," Fernon said, standing strong on this issue.

"This is a most sensitive subject. My domain is not ready to give up these fairies and pixies and I believe that many of them would not want to return to their previous domains. *This* has become their home," Isalia said, the look in her eyes showing that she would not yield on this.

"Enough! We are doing exactly what this foe wants us to do. True, the armies of the domains are not fighting but *you*, the leaders, are arguing. That is nearly the same thing," Gribit said, "Until we can read General Longhopper's scrolls to learn more about this enemy then the talk should be about getting to know and understand each other. It is imperative that we work together!"

The delegation became quiet as Gribit's words struck home with each of them understanding that he was right about what needed to be done. No progress could be made if they could not get beyond these issues that separated them though these would be hard to set aside for any one of them.

Slowly quiet conversations began amongst them as the tension eased and for now they were back to concerning themselves with this common threat.

◆◆◆◆◆

It was late afternoon when Croaker and Link reached the outpost of the forest fairies. The winds had calmed down to a slight breeze and the rain had diminished to a soft steady drizzle.

291

Cloud Whisper and the gray were at a slow walk, their wet fur matted close to their skin, as a guard watched them approach through the open door of the roadside shelter. Wisps of gray smoke from the warming fire, burning in the fireplace within the shelter, left a pungent odor in the air as it escaped through the chimney and wafted its way into the tree cover of the forest.

Glancing up at the sky and giving a little sneer, the guard stepped out into the drizzle as Croaker and Link pulled their mounts up to a halt at the barrier arm.

"What is your business, Sire frog?" he asked, seeming not to notice Croaker's warrior garb, "and state the reason for bringing this foreign fairy with you!"

"I am Croaker and this is my companion, Link. I have a letter from King Fernon for our passage through your domain," Croaker said as he retrieved it from his pack.

After scanning the letter, and seeing Fernon's signature and seal, he handed it back to Croaker, "Welcome to our domain, Sire Croaker, and your companion as well."

"Is there a place to rub down our mounts? They could use some rest before we continue on and we would like to dry them down as well," Croaker asked, looking away as he returned the letter to his pack.

"There is a small stable in back of the shelter," the guard said as he raised the barrier arm, "You can put them with the frog messenger's mount. He is inside taking some hot tea. He arrived only a few minutes before you, long enough for him to tend to his mount. He has just sat down."

"Thank you," Croaker said as he and Link dismounted, leading their mounts to the stable.

"I will have hot tea ready when you have tended to your mounts, Sire," the guard said as he returned to the shelter.

After drying the bush-tails off and combing them down, Link found the mixture of nuts and grains while Croaker grabbed up two oak buckets to retrieve water from a trough just outside the stable.

"That will take care of them. Now let us have some hot tea!" Link said, using a dry cloth to wipe himself damp dry, "and a sit near that fire will feel good as well."

Croaker nodded his agreement as he hung his cloth on a wall hook near the doorway to dry, "We will stay just long enough for Cloud Whisper and your gray to rest. I want to make Broadleaf before it is too dark to travel. We can find an inn there."

The Shelter was much larger than it appeared. It was a structure of stacked logs with milled board flooring and the windows were made of the translucent spider silk as those he had seen at Weavertown. Stepping up into the entrance Croaker could see that there was a large room with a fireplace on the back wall and at the end of the room was a doorway to another room. On either side of the fireplace were metal doors that covered the ovens and there was a metal arm that swung a caldron over the fire.

A second fairy sat near the messenger frog in chairs that were arranged in a semi-circle in front of the fireplace as the guard poured two mugs of hot tea from a pot he had retrieved from a metal plate that was over the front edge of the fire.

"Here you are, Sires," he said as he handed Croaker and Link each a mug, "If you like we have some fresh bread left over from our lunch that our cook baked this morning. It is on the table."

Croaker looked to the other end of the room and saw that is was set up as a dining area for more places than he thought would be there.

"How many of you are there?" Croaker asked, surprised.

"We are a full complement, Sire. Four shifts of guards and two cooks. Why do you ask?" the guard replied, uneasy about the question.

"I was surprised by the size of your shelter. Where are the others?"

"They are in the barracks room. Some sleeping and others just relaxing," he replied, indicating the door at the end of the room.

"You did not seem surprised by my attire when we arrived," Croaker said, curious about the guard's lack of reaction to him and that he had not made any mention of it since.

"There has been talk of a frog warrior. I thought it to be nonsense until I saw you sire," the guard said in a matter of fact tone.

Croaker and Link moved over near the messenger and sat looking at the flickering flames dancing on the logs, grateful for the heat that radiated from the fire and the hot tea they drank.

The frog messenger looked over to Croaker and Link, asking, "Are you two going to Lone Oak?"

"No. We will be going north from Ravens Roost," Croaker answered.

"Will you be leaving soon? If you are, then may I accompany you to Ravens Roost?" he asked, "The journey goes better with company!"

"We rode our mounts hard through the rain until it finally let up. They need some rest but we cannot take much time for it. If you are able to wait, then yes, you may accompany us," Croaker said and turning to Link, saw his nod in agreement, then added, "We will be finding an inn at Broadleaf for the night, will you be stopping as well?"

"Yes. That is what I had planned to do. We can stay at the Golden Leaf Inn. It is comfortable, has fine food and has a stable for the bush-tails," the messenger said, letting Croaker and Link know that they would not have to search out a place to rest.

There was a sudden snap as the fire found a bit of sap in the wood, sending sparks shooting up and out, breaking the silence that had followed the conversation. Croaker looked over his shoulder to find the guard that had greeted them and saw that he had returned to the open door and was watching the road, as he had been when they arrived.

CHAPTER NINETEEN

Though the journey had been much easier for the trio after leaving the outpost, as they traveled the forest road, it felt considerably longer with the forest growing dark much sooner than usual as the thick clouds that still blanketed overhead blocked out most of what light that would have penetrated the forest canopy. The light rain had finally stopped before they had resumed their journey and only a few drops fell from the leaves overhead now, when disturbed by the occasional breeze.

"Sire Croaker, if you would follow me, the Golden Leaf Inn is near," the messenger said as they entered the town of Broadleaf.

"Night is setting in fast, here in the forest. I can see lighted windows already," Link said, his eyes taking in the town as the buildings revealed themselves from between the trees before blending into the forest again as they passed them by.

Groups of fairies were stopping to watch in quiet curiosity, as Croaker and his companions passed them by, their whispered conversations soon being heard behind the trio as the fairies speculated about the frog warrior and his white bush-tail in the company of a fairy, unusually riding a bush-tail, and another frog.

"It would seem that you have not been heard of in Broadleaf, Sire Croaker. They do not know what to make of you and your bush-tail!" the frog messenger said as he turned his mount down a side street.

"I am getting quite used to that and I was expecting it," Croaker replied, his tone matter of fact.

"Here we are, Sire!" the messenger said, pulling his mount to a halt in front of a large two story building, a sign shaped like an oak leaf hanging out over the walk at the front entrance that read 'Golden Leaf Inn', "Though there usually are, we should make sure that rooms are available before we take our bush-tails around back to the stable."

"Link, would you stay with our mounts? I will go in with the messenger," Croaker said swinging down from Cloud Whisper and handing the reins to the fairy.

Link took the reins, nodding acceptance of the task, "Yes, Sire."

The main room was alive with music and singing as they entered the inn. In the far left corner a group of fairies played ocarinas, harps and mandolins while others sang along. In the center of the room several fairies danced while others sat a tables, some eating and others deep in conversation. A young fairy carried a tray of drinks, as she maneuvered through small groups and around tables, to be delivered to patrons that sat across the room.

Walking over to the bar, Croaker followed the messenger as he approached the innkeeper. The level of sound decreased as more of the fairies noticed Croaker in his helm with his sword dangling below the bottom of his slicker.

Catching sight of the frogs approaching, the innkeeper, surprised by Croaker's attire stared for a moment before speaking, "Sires, what can I do for you this evening?"

"We will need three rooms for the night and a meal prior to that," the messenger replied stepping up to the bar.

"Three rooms?" the innkeeper questioned, seeing only the two frogs.

"Yes. We have a fairy companion traveling with us. He is waiting with our mounts which we need to stable as well," Croaker spoke up, "and we would like those rooms as far away from this commotion as possible."

"Yes, Sire frog, I have three rooms upstairs, at the end of the hall," the innkeeper informed him, while looking Croaker over very carefully, "What would you have for your meal?"

"If you have one, your house special will be sufficient along with some hot tea and berry brew," Croaker said thoughtfully.

"You will find water and feed for your mounts in the stable, Sire frog. Will there be anything else?" the innkeeper asked as he drew a berry brew for the fairy that had been waiting patiently since the frogs arrived.

"No. Thank you, Sire. We will see to our mounts now," Croaker said, as he and the messenger turned toward the entrance.

The brief lull of the crowded inn ended as the noise level increased with the fairies resuming their activities when Croaker and the messenger began retracing their steps to rejoin Link and care for their bush-tails.

"Link, we have found rooms," Croaker said, taking Cloud Whisper's reins from his friend, "The patrons are a noisy lot but the rooms, I have been assured, are well enough away that we should be able to get some rest."

After grooming and feeding their mounts they returned to the inn. Once inside they removed their slickers and once again the room quieted upon seeing Croaker's tunic and Link's attire.

"That fairy is not of the forest!" the innkeeper glared, "What is he doing here and why is he in the company of frogs, and for that matter what sort of frog are you Sire!"

"Silence, innkeeper. It is sufficient that he *is* in our company and as for myself . . . I believe that all can see what sort of a frog I am," Croaker said with an authority that surprised the innkeeper and all the patrons, "Now we will have our meal."

"Yes, Sire frog. My apologies, Sire. I have a table for you over there," the innkeeper said softly, pointing out the table, stunned by Croaker's rebuke, then calling out to the young fairy waiting on the tables, "Catkin, show our guests to their table."

"Alright father. I will be with them in a moment," she replied, gathering up the empty goblets onto her tray from the table she was waiting on, "I just have to return these to the kitchen first."

Catkin maneuvered her way through the crowd with her tray so quickly and easily that it was like watching a dancer glide across a stage. Her sandy blonde hair and cerulean eyes held a sparkle of mischief that was echoed by the sly smile that crinkled up the corners of her eyes making it difficult to look away from her.

"Sires, please follow me," she said, her voice like a cooing dove, upon returning from the kitchen, all the while watching Link from the corner of her eye. After seating Croaker and the messenger, "and you Sire . . . Sire, what shall I call you? How do you find the forest?"

"My name is Link. I find it very different from the fields and Granstone."

"Your meals are ready Sires, I will be back with them shortly," she said starting for the kitchen then turning for a moment, "and Sire Link, you can tell me of the fields if you like when I return."

Link flushed warm from Catkin's attention then suddenly felt the necessity of searching out the innkeeper. Feeling relief when he saw that the innkeeper was busy attending to the patrons at the bar, his redness deepened when he noticed Croaker and the messenger smiling at his discomfort.

"It would appear that you have an admirer, Link," Croaker said, somewhat jovially.

Catkin returned to the table with a large platter containing three bowls of hot mushroom sage soup, six boiled finch eggs, a loaf of fresh baked bread and a bowl of honey.

"I will be right back with your drinks," she said, giving Link a wink before returning to the kitchen.

Croaker and the messenger struggled to hold back a chuckle as Link's face turned red again. Link glared at the two frogs, saying, "The food is here. *Eat*," then grabbing one of the finch eggs he took a bite. Croaker and the messenger burst into laughter as they each reached for their bowl of soup.

Catkin brought the tray of drinks and as she placed them on the table, was summoned by another patron across the room, "Sire Link, I have to take care of that table but will be back as soon as I can," she smiled.

Link did not have a chance to say a word. He sat there wondering how he should handle her advances; *it is not that she is unattractive, but I have met the one that I would choose if I could. I do not wish to hurt her feelings but I do not wish to encourage her either. If she continues, her father has shown already that he has distain for me, what problems would that bring about for us.*

Catkin returned as they were drinking the last of their berry brew, "Sires, can I get you anything more?"

"No, thank you. We will take our leave and go rest now. May I request that we be aroused prior to the sunrise?" Croaker said, pushing his chair away from the table to rise.

"It will be done, Sire frog. Sire Link, if you could take the time, would you be interested in a game of quills?" she said, showing that she would like his companionship for the evening.

"Quills? What is that?" Link asked, having never heard of the game.

"See those two at the end of the bar?" she asked, pointing at two fairies standing, facing the wall at the far end of the bar where there was a space between the end of the bar and the wall to their side.

"Yes."

"Well, they are playing quills. They toss the quills, which have been feathered and weighted and must be a finger and a quarter long, at the target on the wall. The target is made of several layers of braided grasses. There are five rings with the center ring large enough to accommodate six quills. Each ring from that point is quadrant off and subdivided with alternating colors of green and brown. One player is brown and the other is green. The center ring is black and has a point value of five for each quill that lands in it. The further out the ring, the point value decreases by one and any quill outside those rings looses a point. Each player takes a turn tossing his quill and tries to hit his color or the center ring. The other player may neutralize the point by landing his quill in the same place his opponent landed. The first player to reach fifteen points wins the match." She explained, as they watched the two players toss and retrieve their quills and repeat the process.

"That is very interesting and I always enjoy a good competition, but I must retire with my friends," Link politely declined, leaving Catkin stunned at his rejection.

"Will you be returning?" she asked.

"We are on a mission and I do not know where that will take us. A good night to you," Link said, turning to follow after Croaker and the messenger.

As they walked the hallway to their rooms, Croaker suddenly stopped and turned to Link, "There is something wrong. I have that feeling again that I had the night of the Feldspar attack and when watching that flock of birds."

"Sire? We are nowhere near the southern fields or the rolling hills!" Link reminded his friend.

"That does not matter, I have that feeling and I am sure that there is something wrong. Just what it may be I do not know," Croaker said, his apprehension growing stronger with each passing moment.

◆◆◆◆◆

Earlier in the evening the dark figure of Lord Noma astride his bat silently ascended unseen into the murky sky from the abandoned mines north of Millville. Turning east toward the forest he had felt a sense of pleasure at being able to leave the mines earlier than planned, due to the heavily overcast sky, which allowed him to not drive his bat too hard to reach the rendezvous with the slithers. Now, as he approached the edge of the forest, he was glad to have this part of his trip nearly completed as he could think only of his anticipated meeting with General O'Dias.

Descending under the high canopy of the forest, Noma and his bat darted through the trees making sure that there were no fairies near the clearing were the rendezvous with the slithers was to take place. After carefully checking a wide perimeter, Noma reined his bat to land in the small clearing where moments later three slithers appeared from the underbrush.

"Where are the others?" Noma demanded, surprised to see so few of them.

"Lord . . . Lord, we are what is left I fear. The . . . the forest fairies have been hunting us down!" one of the slithers hissed out the words, "I barely escaped them myself."

"How did they know to hunt you?" Noma snarled, his yellow cat eyes glaring in the dark.

The slither did not want to answer. He had no wish to tell him that they had not mentioned the warning that was sounded when one of them had been sighted near Lily Pond.

"I want to know how they knew to hunt you!" Noma demanded, his anger rising quickly as the corner of his lips curled up exposing his needle sharp canines, "Tell me now or you will pay for not speaking up."

Before the slither could answer, another slither appeared from the undergrowth from the south, "Lord, I came as quick as I could. I was watching the stables of Lily Pond and what I have learned you will want to know."

"Does it explain why the fairies have been hunting you?" Noma asked, turning his gaze toward the new slither.

"It may, Lord. I saw a frog warrior arrive there last night with a fairy companion and a cart," the slither started to explain.

"A frog warrior!" Noma snapped, "What do you take me for. Some kind of fool!"

"It is true, Lord," the slither protested, recoiling from Noma's wrath, "There was a body in the cart Lord. I saw it. It was General O'Dias."

It was as if a bolt of lightning had hit Noma. He stood there, silent and in disbelief at what he had just heard; *the general . . . dead. What am I to do for an ally against my brother? What am I to tell DeMonas? How could this happen? What about O'Dias's troops?*

"Tell me all of what you have learned," Noma demanded and began pacing back and forth as he listened to the slither's report.

"The frog warrior rode a white bush-tail. I heard him tell of the battle near Feldspar and how he killed the general. He spoke of how the general's troops broke and ran when O'Dias fell and how the fairies that accompanied this frog had chased them down and destroyed them all," the slither recalled, "I was able to get close enough to see that the body was the general before the nymphs buried him. I knew that you would want to be informed about this, Lord."

Noma stopped in his tracks, his anger now directed at a new foe, a foe that had taken away his chance to move against his brother, "I want this frog warrior dead. There will be a reward for the one that kills him and brings me proof. Lord DeMonas wants you to continue with his original orders. Send your reports to the Feldspar caves. I will have toad messengers available at the rendezvous locations in each of the domains. Do not fail me, I want that frog dead!"

Without another word Noma mounted his bat, reining him into the night sky heading directly to the caves west of Feldspar. It would be a long flight for him as he thought about what had been learned. Upon reaching Hillside a tight-lipped smile crossed his face as the thought occurred to him that he could talk to the commander at the caves and make him an offer of promotion to general if he would ally himself to Noma. This idea now gave him new hope of acquiring control of these lands that they were about to go to war for and displacing his brother.

◆ ◆ ◆ ◆ ◆

Croaker lay awake in his bed, the strong feeling of uneasiness not allowing him to rest. What was it that brought about this feeling of apprehension he wondered. If it was a presence, then how could it be here in the forest, far from where the attack on the pixie town and his battle had taken place? Finally, as the night wore on, the feeling began to subside and eventually fade completely away. He was now able to close his eyes and sleep.

CHAPTER TWENTY

The morning air was cool and a veil of fog, reaching from the ground to the canopy above, shrouded all it touched. Trees and shrubs a short distance away appeared as ghostly figures as Croaker, Link and the frog messenger carefully followed the path to the inn's stable to ready their bush-tails for the trip to Ravens Roost.

"You have traveled this domain many times. Will this fog burn off soon?" Croaker asked the messenger, turning his head side to side and up toward the canopy, "If it stays like this we will be long to Ravens Roost."

"It will thin more as the day warms, Sire," the messenger replied, breathing in deeply as if to sample the air, then pointing up and to the east, "I would say before the sun reaches there."

Cloud Whisper seemed restless and eager to go as Croaker saddled him.

"Did you feel the presence last night too?" Croaker asked his mount, giving him a pat on the shoulder, "I fear we need to heed these feelings my friend, though others may think them foolish."

As the trio led their bush-tails to the front of the inn, Link and the messenger both had a look of amazement as they watched Croaker leading Cloud Whisper ahead of them.

"Sire Croaker, you two nearly disappear from view!" Link said, a hint of excitement in his voice, "And you are only a few steps ahead of us."

A smile crossed Croaker's face. He now knew of an advantage he might have under these conditions, "That could be useful, Link, very useful indeed."

Catkin stood by the door of the inn as they brought their bush-tails around the corner of the inn to the street. Swinging up onto their mounts they heard her call out, "A fair journey sires. And Sire Link, I still wish to have you tell me about the fields and Granstone if someday you return."

There were only a couple fairies out in the heavy morning mist as they turned off the side street onto the main road north. The fog was already lifting some, just as the messenger had said it would, and the fairies stopped to watch them pass by and then slowly fade away into the rolling white haze.

The travel would be slow until the fog burned off. Croaker and Link allowed the messenger take the lead, since he and his bush-tail had traveled this road many times before, believing that his bush-tail knew the road well enough to not stray from it.

As they approached Bale's Hollow the fog had dissipated enough that they were now moving at a much quicker pace. Croaker looked up through the open areas of the canopy and could see patches of blue through the thinning mist and felt it would be only a short while until their mounts could run to make up time, "If we can pick up the pace, we should be able to have our mid-day at Raven's Roost," he called out to the others.

"I think there is a good chance of that, Sire Croaker," the messenger replied, "This fog *has* lifted considerably already."

"It will be a nice change to not be wet," Link said, "Even with our slickers, more than a day's worth of rain and this dampness has become very disagreeable!"

"I thought it was rather nice . . . I felt right at home!" Croaker chuckled.

♦ ♦ ♦ ♦ ♦

"Lord, it is time," the words found their way into Noma's consciousness as the commander repeated them again, "Lord, it is time. I have sent a toad to ready your raven."

"Did the toad messengers get off as I instructed?" the imp prince asked as he swung himself up into a sitting position on his cot, his eyes watching the lashing tongues of flames from the cavern fires leaping into the air and drawing back again, "I want to talk to you before I leave."

"Yes Lord. I sent three toads to each of the locations you instructed," the commander reported then, both puzzled and worried, asked, "What do you wish to speak to me about, Lord?"

"Kallose! That is your name, is it not commander?" Noma asked, his stare like piercing needles in the commander's brain, then not waiting for an answer, "Can I trust you to be loyal to me?"

"Lord?" the question surprising the commander, "Yes, Lord. Why would you need to ask?"

"When I arrived, I told you of O'Dias's death and the fate of his troops. A general will be needed to replace him. Would you want to be that general?"

"Yes, Lord. I believe that I am ready to assume that rank!" Kallose eagerly agreed.

"If I speak to my brother about you then I must know that you would be loyal only to me! Not to my brother, only to me! Is that understood?"

Kallose now knew exactly what Noma wanted from him, "It will be as you ask, Lord. *Your* word will be my command," he said slowly and calmly.

Noma's eyes narrowed as the corners of his mouth curled up into a slight smile, "Good! Now have some berries and grubs brought to the table. We will eat before I leave!"

◆◆◆◆◆

The sun was beginning to dapple the forest floor as it neared its zenith when a slither found a suitable hiding space overlooking the southern road out of Raven's Roost. It had been a long trip from the rendezvous clearing and twice he had to evade the fairy patrols as they searched the forest.

Carefully he coiled himself in the small space he had found, where the sun would pour out its warmth on him for most of the day, and settled in for his watch of the comings and goings of the fairies. For now he planned to watch, but when it was dark enough he would move in closer to the fairy village to overhear conversations to see if any important information could be gained.

He had been there only a short while when the nearly muffled sound of padded feet in a hurry from the south caught his attention. Three bush-tails and riders were approaching Raven's Roost and to his surprise, one of the bush-tails was as white as the drifting puffs of clouds on a warm, languid summer's day. When they were close enough to him, he saw that the rider of the white bush-tail was a frog wearing a helm and white tunic; *that must be the frog warrior Lord Noma wants us to kill. He is with two other riders so I cannot strike now. Should I follow them or should I return to the rendezvous clearing to report his whereabouts? I would have to wait there until the toads arrived. What should I do?*

After the riders past by he gave out a long, low, hiss at his frustration, then left his secure place of concealment to follow; *if they continue north from Raven's Roost then I will return to the rendezvous clearing. If they continue on to the forest fairy king's palace or return south then I will follow and if the chance presents itself . . . I will do Lord Noma's bidding.*

His mind made up, he felt better as he quickly and silently glided through and over the undergrowth and ground clutter of the forest.

◆ ◆ ◆ ◆ ◆

The frog messenger brought his mount to a halt at the stables and smithy below the treetop village, "Sire, Croaker, we can tend our bush-tails here before we climb the spiral stairs to the village," he said, pointing out the stairs that wound around and up a large tree.

The sounds of cottage industries filled the air, drifting down from above mingling with the sounds of the smith at work. The high walkways that circled the buildings that wrapped around the trunks of the trees also connected one tree to another at several levels forming a network that caught Croaker's eye as he peered up into the canopy. He could see movement of fairies as they went about their daily chores, traveling from tree to tree.

"This is a busy place. What is it they do here?" he asked, shifting his gaze back down to the messenger.

"They do many things, Sire. There are the gatherers; they collect spider silk, honey, wood for buckets and a number of other things. Then there are those that are spinners, weavers, coopers and many other crafts not to mention the inn keepers and of course the smith," the messenger said, reaching for the corral gate.

"It sounds a lot like what takes place in Granstone," Link commented.

"Sire Frog, you are back again . . . and you have brought friends," the smith greeted the messenger, as he stepped out of the smithy into the corral area, scrutinizing Croaker and Link as he approached them.

"Yes, this is Sire Croaker and his friend, Sire Link. We will be stopping for our mid-day before continuing on. Will you see to the needs of our mounts?" he said, handing the smith the reins of his mount as Link closed the corral gate behind him after entering.

"They will be fed and brushed," he assured the trio, "and may I comment on your magnificent mount Sire Croaker, he is a rare one."

"He is that indeed, Sire smith! But more than that he is my friend. His name is Cloud Whisper," Croaker said with pride, reaching out and patting his mount on the shoulder before the smith led the three bush-tails to the stable.

"There is an inn, 'The Perch' it is called, at the top of those stairs and they serve fine food, sires," the messenger informed them as he led the way.

"Do they have any young maids to distract Link?" Croaker chuckled, watching the fairy's face redden.

The inn was built differently than any other building Croaker had seen in his travels. It circled the tree with a roof of shakes sloping away from the trunk, though at its peak there was a short slope toward the trunk allowing for a space between the building and the tree. Toward the far side of the tree and left of the entrance they faced, a chimney protruded up. Hanging well over the exterior wall, the eaves were still high enough to let an adequate amount of light enter the windows.

Once inside, Croaker saw that the dining area was deep enough to have an arc of tables following the curve of the room and booths along the outside windows. To his left, patrons at the 'L' shaped bar kept the innkeeper busy as a young fairy carried a tray of food through the kitchen door. To his right was a door next to the back wall leading to a hallway and a dozen guest rooms.

The innkeeper stood motionless, a freshly poured goblet of berry brew in his hand, when he looked up and saw the trio taking a seat at an open booth near the entrance. The fairy, that was waiting for his beverage was one of a group of five troopers that were taking their mid-day break from searching the forest for slithers, turned to see what had stopped the innkeeper cold.

The room quieted as others turned to see what they were staring at when the trooper walked over to Croaker and his companions.

"What manner of dress is that for a frog?" he asked Croaker, "and would you explain this foreign fairy, Sire frog?"

Having been challenged about Link's companionship before, Croaker did not take offence at the trooper's remarks.

"Sire fairy, I am Croaker, Liaison to the Sage, Gribit," he informed the trooper.

"I am accompanying Sire Croaker on a mission to Juniper, and I would have you know that he is the first frog warrior since General Longhopper, first of the sages," Link quickly interrupted.

"This should explain our presence here," Croaker said as he retrieved the letter from his pouch, "This letter from King Fernon should set your mind to rest."

"My apologies, Sire Croaker. With the events of late, being on constant alert and chasing down slithers, we are all on edge and we have never known of a frog warrior before . . ." Croaker cut him short, holding out his hand for the return of the letter.

"No need to apologize Sire. It is well that you are alert and you should stay that way, for events are unfolding that will require it."

"What events?" the fairy asked, surprised by Croaker's cryptic revelation that only further fueled his curiosity of what must be happening and how it was connected to so many slithers being in the area.

"I am not at liberty to discuss any more than I already have, Sire. Now we would like to order our mid-day so we can continue on our way without further delay," Croaker said, motioning the waitress over to their booth.

"Of course, Sire. By your leave," the fairy bowed his head and returned to the bar.

As they sat in conversation while awaiting their meal, they could hear whispered conversations of the patrons of the inn and were aware of the many quick glances in their direction.

From a group of fairies close to them Croaker could hear,

"Can you imagine that, a frog warrior!" one said.

"And his tunic . . . did you notice his crest?" another said.

"Look at the sword he carries, it is like no other. Even the king does not have one finer!" yet another observed.

"What field domain do you think the fairy is from?" the first asked.

Croaker stopped listening to the fairies whispering amongst themselves and gazed around the inn's dining area. It was a warm atmosphere that was tempered by the light of Elgin Fire from small globes lighting the darker corners where sunlight was not strong enough to light the area. He noticed a chandelier, consisting of many of these small globes strung together in a circle, hanging in the center of the room. He guessed that it was for night and dark days.

After finishing their mid-day meal, Croaker asked the innkeeper for a voucher to sign.

"Did you find your meals alright?" the innkeeper asked, "If you come back to Raven's Roost I hope you will stop here again, sires."

"This has been my favorite stop," the messenger said.

"Thank you Sire, your hospitality and food will not be forgotten," Link said graciously.

"We will return in a day or so," Croaker informed him, "I can understand why the messenger chooses your inn to stop at, Sire."

They left the inn with the patrons still buzzing about them.

After descending the spiral stairs to the stables, they found that the smith had their bush-tails ready and waiting for them.

"Sires, I hope you enjoyed your mid-day. Sire Croaker, your bush-tail has been acting nervous for the past few minutes. He keeps looking to the back of the stables," the smith said as he handed the riders their reins.

"Did you check to see if there was anything there?" Croaker asked.

"Yes, Sire, but I found nothing," the smith replied, glancing back in that direction, "Is he usually like that?"

"Only when he senses danger. If you can catch them before they leave, I think you should tell the troopers at the inn to check out the area," Croaker advised the smith.

"Yes. Sire," the smith agreed, turning to call his young apprentice to fetch the troopers as Croaker and his companions mounted their bush-tails and rode north.

"Have a swift and safe journey," the smith called out as he raised his hand in a wave.

Reaching the north side of the village, the messenger bid Croaker and Link farewell as he turned his bush-tail onto the road that led north-east toward Lone Oak Croaker and Link continued on, north to Juniper, unaware of the slither watching from the undergrowth of the forest.

◆ ◆ ◆ ◆ ◆

Noma did not press his raven to hurry; he had no desire to be the one to tell DeMonas that O'Dias had been killed. As they soared over the wastelands, he thought; *how could our information be so wrong? The frogs were not known to be warriors, yet it was a frog that slew our best general, a general that has never had an equal in battle. Will DeMonas still want to follow his plan after he learns of this? What else is there that we do not know?*

CHAPTER TWENTY-ONE

The late afternoon air hung still with the sounds of young fairies at play echoing throughout the trees. The merriment of their laughter, touched all those that heard it, like the sound of rippling waters of a babbling brook as it washed over and around the smooth worn stones of its shallow bed. Soon other sounds from the village mixed with the carefree joy as Croaker and Link neared Juniper.

Slowly the laughter faded as the young fairies caught sight of Croaker and Cloud Whisper. While peering through the forest growth at the brilliant white cloud that seemed to be floating between the patches of light and shadows along the road leading to their village, whispers of astonishment at this strange sight began to replace the once heard laughter.

"Sire, Croaker. It would appear that we are being observed," Link smiled, nodding his head toward the trees along the road where the whispers came from.

"Link, how many times must I tell you that you need not call me sire?" Croaker reminded his friend, "and yes, I believe we will be expected in the village now."

"I am only showing my respect for your station, Si . . . my friend."

"Now, that was not that hard to say. Was it?" Croaker smiled.

"Even so, I will continue to address you as Sire when we are among others," Link said, a tone of resolve in his voice.

Croaker still felt uncomfortable with the formality between them but now fully understood there would be no changing his friend's mind on the subject, "Very well then, since you are so set in your ways, so be it!" he sighed.

Curious fairies were beginning to line up along the road that passed through their village as Croaker and Link approached. A youth hurried ahead of them, excitedly alerting the inhabitance that a white bush-tail carrying a frog dressed in a white tunic were entering their village. It was only when they came to see this strange sight, they noticed the frog was accompanied by a foreign fairy also riding a bush-tail.

Seeing the sword that hung from Croakers side, a stately fairy presented his self as Croaker and Link reined their bush-tails to a halt, "I am the Regent for this village, Sires. What can we do for you?"

"I am Croaker, liaison to the Sage, Gribit. This is my friend and companion, Link, from the court of Arklan, King of the Southern Fields. We are here on a mission to see your smith," Croaker explained as he retrieved the letter from his hip pack, "King Fernon sends this letter of passage with us."

"You will have our full cooperation Sires!" the regent said when seeing the king's seal, then turning to the fairy next to him, "Get the smith. Tell him not to tarry."

"You have traveled far. Would you take your evening meal with my family, Sires?" the regent continued, handing back the letter unread.

"It would be an honor, Sire," Croaker accepted, with Link nodding in agreement.

"The honor is mine, Sires," the regent said, then waving at the crowd of fairies that had gathered, "Go back to your activities. There is nothing more for you here."

Croaker and Link watched as the fairies dispersed, some looking back for a last look at them when the regent spoke again, "When the smith arrives we can go to my home to talk. I would like to know why it is that the King should have dealings with a Southern Field fairy and a frog that wears battle garb."

"Sire, have your patrols not been this far north?" Link asked.

"Patrols? No, we have not seen any patrols. What would they be searching for?" the regent asked, surprised by this information.

"There is a force that threatens the entire realm of Lily Pond. At this moment all the rulers have gathered and are on their way to Granstone for a summit," Croaker informed him, "We can give you more details later but for now you must keep a close eye on your children."

"Our children? Why?" the regent asked, puzzled by Croaker's instruction.

"Children from Broadleaf and the town of Limonite in the Rolling Hills domain have disappeared and are believed dead by slithers," Croaker told him, "and in the town of Feldspar, a pixie town in the Rolling Hills, all but one had been killed. A boy that managed to escape was found near the border of the southern fields and his delirious ranting led to my leading a column into that town to investigate. The force that had attacked that town ambushed us on our return to the southern fields."

"Why have we not heard of this before now?" the regent asked in disbelief.

Croaker was about to answer when the fairy the regent had sent after the smith and the smith flew up to the group in the road.

"Sire, you sent for me?" the smith asked.

"Yes. This is Sire Croaker and Sire Link. They are here to see you," the regent informed him.

"Sire's, what do you wish to see me about?" the smith asked, studying Croaker and Cloud Whisper very closely.

"I am told you retain the old knowledge of drawing out fine steel thread for mail. I would require enough to create mail for my mount," Croaker informed the smith while reaching out the letter to him, "I have a letter from King Fernon, requesting you to assist me in this. I would like it to be as well made as my own."

"As your own?" the smith asked with surprise.

Croaker dismounted and unbelted his sword and hip pack then lifted his tunic. The smith and the regent could only stare at the shimmering mail for long moments before the smith asked, "How did you come by this, Sire?"

"That is too long a story for now. Can you create mail like this?" Croaker asked, wanting to know that this trip had not been in vain.

"No, Sire. I can only draw out the threads. To have a mail that fine you will have to go to Ravens Roost and see the weaver, Heddle. She is the only weaver I know of that will be able to help you. It will take some time to gather the minerals I will need to add to the iron. They are very rare and will have to be imported from the rolling hills mines, Sire," he informed Croaker.

"Time is of the essence. Since your King is at Granstone, then your regent will have to prepare a letter for whomever you send to obtain these materials. I will sign it as well for safe passage into that domain. It must be fairies, not frogs, for like I have said; time is of the essence and fairies can travel faster with their flight," Croaker instructed, "When the threads are ready then send them to the weaver you have told me about. I will leave instructions with her on how the mail is to be constructed."

"Sire, I will need to know that as well! If I am to make enough thread," the smith pointed out.

"Very well, I will go with you to your smithy. Link, you can go with the regent. When the smith and I have finished, I will join you at his home," Croaker said as he re-belted his sword and hip pack before leading Cloud Whisper to follow the smith.

◆◆◆◆◆

The cool dampness of the large cavern mirrored Noma's feelings, at the prospect of telling Lord DeMonas of O'Dias's fate, as he approached the heavy wooden door to the entrance of his brother's chambers.

"What news do you have to report from your meeting with the slithers?" DeMonas demanded from his knurly root chair, when he saw it was his brother entering his chamber.

"The news is not good brother," Noma said, his voice hesitant, "General O'Dias and a column he led against a force of fairies, that entered the pixie domain at Feldspar, have been defeated."

"The General defeated!" DeMonas shouted in disbelief.

"Yes brother, and the worst is that O'Dias was slain along with all the troops he led," Noma said, his eyes focusing on the floor of the chamber to avoid making contact with his brother's.

"O'Dias dead! How can this be? Who could have defeated him?" the goblin king's questions' sending a chill down Noma's spine.

"A slither reported to me that a frog warrior transported the general's body to the Lily Pond stables and related how he had killed O'Dias in battle," Noma informed DeMonas, "I gave orders that this frog should be killed on sight."

"A frog! You tell me a *frog* defeated O'Dias? Frogs are not warriors! This can not be true!" DeMonas raged, his footsteps loudly drumming through the chamber as he paced to and fro past the fireplace, while each snap and pop from the burning logs sent flames leaping wildly, as if to emphasize the king's ire.

"My Lord, brother, I have more bad news. The domains know of our presence now and the forest fairies are hunting down the slithers," Noma continued his report, dreading to say each word, "and we must think of replacing O'Dias."

DeMonas glared at his brother and then spoke as if he were slowly pouring bile from his soul, "Are you telling me that our plan has not worked? If that is the case then we will have to take a more direct approach. As for replacing O'Dias, I suppose that *you* have someone in mind?"

"I thought that O'Dias's second in command, Commander Kallose, could be made general. He is filling that position already, Lord," Noma offered, trying not to indicate that he was pressing for that result.

"Another had come to my mind, although what you say does make sense. Alright, I will send promotion papers with you on your return to the Feldspar caves," DeMonas reasoned, then motioning Noma to follow to the military quarters, "Come, we must meet with the generals and make new plans how we will assault the domains now that they are aware of us. That they are separate domains still works to our advantage."

Noma followed closely, relieved that DeMonas was thinking about strategy rather than unleashing his wrath on him.

◆◆◆◆◆

The procession from Lily Pond had started out at the first gray light of day and now the sun was fading behind the rolling hills of the west as they approached the main gate to Granstone.

The hard rain of the previous day had taken its toll on the road to the great city making the travel slow for most of the day as bush-tails strained against their traces whenever wheels would get mired in the muddy road. Once they had traveled beyond Weavertown the sun began to dry out the roads and travel became somewhat smoother.

A message from the northern outpost had been sent to Granstone and the guardsmen were dressed in their finest uniforms to greet the king and his guests as the coaches entered the city. Granstone citizens maneuvered themselves to get the best view of the royals, and their entourage, as they disembarked their coaches, for this was a sight that had not been seen in any of their lifetimes.

Gribit was the last to step down, following the ambassadors, when Arklan spoke, "Welcome to Granstone. You will be escorted to your quarters where you can freshen up before the evening meal. If you have need of anything, just ask your escort and he will get it for you. My sergeant of the guard will show your personal guards to the military quarters."

Arklan led the way across the bailey and through the second palisade, past the fairy sculptures emerging from the wall that the new comers gazed at with wonder, and into the market place. Airlein, Fernon and Isalia paused at the statues of the fairy, pixie and frog holding up a single torch.

"If I had not met Croaker, then this would have indeed astonished me," Airlein said as she reached out her hand and passed it lightly over the statue closest to her.

"The meaning of the trio holding the torch is evident. It takes all in the realm to secure and maintain the light of life," Fernon mused.

"But what is the meaning of two identical statues?" Airlein asked.

"I can only speculate, but I think it means that any effort has to be doubled to secure the outcome," Isalia said, venturing her best guess.

"Maybe it simply means that history will repeat itself," Gribit said, leaving the group of ambassadors to join the royals in their conversation.

"It has been a question of debate by our best scholars ever since I can remember," Arklan said, "We will have time for this discussion later. We have more urgent matters to consider first; though I believe that these statues have a bearing on what we must do."

"Yes, indeed. I trust you have laid your finger upon it, Sire," Gribit said, nodding his head in agreement and with that the procession continued on to their quarters.

"Will there be anything you require, Sire?" the escort asked, holding the chamber door open as Gribit entered.

"When dinner is ready, please show me the way to the dining area," he requested, then abruptly sat on the edge of the bed, "I think I will rest until then. The trip was rather tiring."

The escort nodded his understanding as he closed the chamber door, "Yes, Sire."

As he sat there in his chambers, Gribit thought; *I hope that Croaker and Link will not be delayed in getting here. If it was this wearing on us, then it must have been much harder on them to travel in that rain. At least we encountered no problems on the way here from this foe. I watched the sky from my carriage and saw nothing that could have been a threat. Now that we are here I cannot see an enemy entering this city, indeed, a slither would be hard pressed to even attempt it. Tomorrow, tomorrow we will find Longhopper's vault and read the scrolls that are stored there!*

◆ ◆ ◆ ◆ ◆

As the last light of day fades away, a toad hurries through the tall grasses of the southern fields toward the southwest. He is returning to the caves west of Feldspar to report on a sighting he had made. He and two other toads had been on their way to the rendezvous location they had been ordered to when by chance they saw the procession of carriages with royal guards, from the three Fairy domains and the nymph domain, heading south to Granstone.

"We should return to the caves to report this," he had said to the second toad.

"We were ordered to the rendezvous site and that is where I intend to go!" the second had said, "If you want to return then do so. I will not suffer the imp's wrath for not doing as ordered."

"Neither will I," the third toad said.

"You two do what you will, I am going back! If this is not reported it will be *Lord DeMonas* that we will have to suffer, should he discover we did not report this."

CHAPTER TWENTY-TWO

The glow of Elgin Fire from the guardsmen's staffs filled the corridor, pushing back the persistent darkness, as they took up their stations along the way to the chamber at the corridor's end.

"It is this way, Your Majesty!" the smith said as he led the way, directing the royal party to the forgotten chamber deep within the city, "It is just where my father and his and our fathers before had said it would be, Sire."

Opening the chamber door and reaching up to twist the wall globe open, the smith announced with excitement, "In here, Your Majesty. This is where the messenger and I found the artifacts."

"Thank you. You have done well, Sire Smith," Arklan said, entering the chamber with Gribit and the others close behind, "You may return to your smithy now."

"Guards, locate any other wall globes and open them," Arklan ordered, his voice echoing off the walls, "Let us see just how large this chamber is."

"We must go to the back wall. That is where Link said we would find the glyphs," Gribit said, taking the lead.

The guards found globes at either end of each isle both left and right of the entrance and when each of the globes were opened, releasing its light, the darkness waned revealing a much larger chamber than it was thought to be. Soon the light became as intense as daylight while maintaining the coolness of moonlight.

"A chamber this large! How could it have been forgotten for so long? How could I have not had knowledge of this?" Arklan wondered aloud.

"There must be enough armament here for thousands!" Isalia said with awe, looking across rows of granite shelving and all the bins contained by each, "The frogs must have been a formidable force!"

"Who would have even guessed that was the case? The arbitrators for peace . . . a warrior force!" Airlein said, a tone of disbelief in the realization, even after seeing the statues, that Croaker had not been the only frog to become a warrior.

"I will need your rings now," Gribit said, after locating the triangle of openings for them that Link had described.

One by one they surrendered their rings to Gribit who in turn inserted each into its proper opening; but when he placed the last one, nothing happened.

"Nothing, nothing has happened! Did you place them correctly?" Fernon asked, a flush of frustration rushing out of him.

"Were there no other instructions?" Isalia asked.

"Do you mean to say that we wasted our time?" Airlein questioned, her sudden display of impatience surprising them all.

"I am sure the answer is here for us to find if we just look," Gribit reassured them.

As they studied the glyphs, Gribit noticed that there were three banner carriers amidst the conflict, a frog, a pixie and a fairy. On each banner were two written lines and all three banners together giving a cryptic message; which he read aloud as he moved his gaze from one to the next:

Let each that resonates find its home

Amidst the turmoil of this epic fight

All is to be learned within the tome

As each will turn from dark to light

Unveiling that which may be unknown

So brings to light a clearer sight

"What can that mean?" Arklan wondered.

"Let each that resonates . . . What resonates?" Airlein asked.

"A bell resonates. It rings . . . ah . . . that must be the three rings," Gribit reasoned.

"And the turmoil of this epic fight must mean the glyphs before us!" Fernon surmised.

"Yes, that much we already know. We had to find where the rings would find their home," Gribit responded, "The next line is self explanatory, but what of the fourth?"

"As each will turn from dark to light . . . but it is already light in here, how can they turn from the dark?" Airlein puzzled at the line.

"Could that mean to rotate the rings a half turn?" Isalia asked.

"I think that could be the answer," Gribit said as he began turning the first of the rings until it was upside down, when the sound of a click could be heard.

"That must be the answer," Arklan said, reflecting the excited anticipation of the others as Gribit rotated the next ring.

When the third ring had been turned, there was the sudden sound of whirring from somewhere deep within the wall, then a large section of the wall receded a short distance then slid to the left, presenting an entrance to the vault that lay beyond. A rush of stale air gushed out momentarily causing the group to gasp as it sucked the oxygen from where they stood.

"Guard, loan me your staff," Gribit said, reaching out his hand to the guardsman closest to him, while peering into the dark opening.

Surprised by the request, the guard looked to Arklan for instruction and seeing the king nod his approval, handed the staff to the Sage. Entering the opening, Gribit saw a short staircase leading down into the vault, which he slowly descended with Arklan close behind.

"Wait there!" Arklan told the others as he looked back over his shoulder, "We will see if there is room enough for all to enter."

Inside the vault they found a small granite table at the far end. It had been carved out of the wall with a granite bench rising out of the floor. On the wall behind the table was a set of light globes, which Gribit quickly opened. After the dust settled from Gribit's action, the light from all the globes filled the vault. On the walls to either side were a honeycomb of bins carved into them, most filled with ancient scrolls. The thick layer of dust covering everything in the vault would have to be carefully removed before they could investigate the scrolls.

"Guard, send for someone to clear away this dust," Arklan ordered.

"Yes, Your Majesty. Right away," the guard acknowledged the order and passed it on until it had reached the last guard at the base of the stairway at the corridor's end.

"The vault is small with room for only three comfortably," Arklan informed the others as he re-emerged from the vault, "We will have to wait until the dust of the ages has been removed. I believe that we should transport the scrolls to the great hall where we can all examine them."

The others agreed though they felt they should stay and supervise the gathering and transport of the scrolls.

◆ ◆ ◆ ◆ ◆

The morning light slowly washed away the darkness at the rendezvous clearing as the slither patiently waited for the toad messengers to arrive. He had traveled all the afternoon and most of the night from Raven's Roost and had not hunted for food in his single-minded thought of how to deal with the frog warrior. Though tired and hungry, he had to be sure that the message for the assistance he required would go to the Feldspar caves as soon as possible.

Testing the air from his place of hiding, he soon caught the scent of toad on his flicking tongue; the messengers had finally arrived.

"I have been waiting for you!" he hissed as they entered the clearing, "I have a message for you to carry back to the caves!"

Startled by the slither's sudden appearance from the undergrowth the toads spun to face him, drawing their swords as they did.

"In our own good time!" the toad in charge said angrily, re-sheathing his sword, "We have just arrived from a long journey and will have our rest, *squirmer*."

"Do not speak to me of your arduous journey, I have had one of my own. You will deliver this message at once!" the slither spoke, his voice a constant threatening hiss, while circling the three toads then coiling before them and slowly rising into a striking position while looking them directly in the eye, "or suffer the consequence."

"And what consequence would that be, *squirmer*?" the toad asked, distain for the slither dripping from his words, his hand ready to draw his sword again.

"I have traveled day and night without food and toad can easily be on my menu. You will deliver what I have to say and without further delay."

Armed as they were, the three toads did not want to try their luck against this slither.

"We could take the message to the Rolling Hills rendezvous and let them relay it to the caves," one of the other toads suggested to their leader, "We will not have to travel very far that way."

"That is a good idea. That is what we will do," the leader said, turning his gaze back to the slither, "What is this message that can not wait?"

"I have sighted the frog warrior that Lord Noma wants killed. He was traveling north, from Raven's Roost, accompanied by a fairy. I believe that they will have to return to Lily Pond and I will require a scout raven and rider to alert me. I will also need rat riders to attack the frog and whoever is with him when they come out of the forest. I will be waiting near the road from Lily Pond to Granstone; they should look for me there. We will do the bidding of Lord Noma and he *will* have his prize," the slither explained, "Do you understand this message?"

"Yes, the message will be delivered," the toad leader answered, then designated one of the others to be on his way to the Rolling Hills.

"Do not fail," the slither said, his eyes fixed on the toads, "and now I must eat so I go to find something *tastier* than toad."

◆ ◆ ◆ ◆ ◆

The pleasant aroma of hot battercakes, fresh brewed rose tea, and honey wafted through the house from the kitchen. The sound of eating utensils clattered on wooden plates in the dining area, competing with the giggles of the regent's young children peering in from the adjoining room.

"Sire's, there is plenty more. Would you like more hot tea?" the regent inquired, immediately turning to face the kitchen door without waiting for an answer, "Viola, would you bring our guests more hot rose tea and some of those fresh strawberries we gathered yesterday. The berries should go well with their cakes and honey."

"Sire, you and your wife will spoil us with this fine fare," Link smiled, wanting to show his appreciation for their hospitality.

"My friend is right, Sire," Croaker, agreed then exaggerated, "We may not need to eat for several days after this fine feast."

"My wife is a very good cook and it is a pleasure that she is able to share this with such honored guests," the regent said, looking up at his wife and smiling with pride, as she joined them at the table.

"You do carry on so!" she said to her husband, blushing at his pride in her.

"I hope your sleep was restful, Sires. You have not had much time to rest and it is a long journey to Raven's Roost," The regent commented.

"I found the bed you provided was very comfortable, Sire," Croaker said, "I hope that our mounts are rested enough as well. They have the burden to carry us."

"Our village smith takes excellent care of the stables, and any mounts he boarders there, besides retaining the old knowledge of the forge," the regent reassured Croaker.

"Now that you brought him up, see that the fairies needed to obtain his minerals get an early start," Croaker reminded the regent.

"I will see to it immediately after your departure, Sire," the regent assured Croaker while reaching into his tunic, producing a packet with his seal from an inner pocket, "I have the letter of passage we drafted and signed last night right here."

Hearing a knock at the door as they talked, the regent's eldest son rose to answer it, "Come in, Sire Smith. They are at the table having their morning meal. You may join them."

"Thank you," the smith replied as he went to the entrance of the dining area, "A good morning, sires. A good morning to you, Viola."

"Have a seat. I will get you a cup of hot tea," Viola said, scooting her chair back to stand, "Would you like some battercakes?"

"Thank you, tea will be fine," the smith said, pulling out a chair from the table and sitting, "I have already had my morning meal. Sire Croaker, I have your mounts ready for you. They are waiting by the staircase at the foot of the tree."

"Have you chosen those you will send to the Rolling Hills mines?" the regent asked, reaching out the packet he still had in his hand, "I have their letter of safe passage here."

337

"Yes, they are preparing themselves at this moment, Sire," he said, a smile crossing his face, "They are almost like children at the idea of this adventure."

"It is time we must be going, Sire. Thank you again for your hospitality," Croaker said, he and Link excusing their selves as they stood to leave, as Viola entered from the kitchen with the hot tea for the smith.

"Remember, Heddle is a village elder but she is still the best weaver in the forest, Sire!" the smith said, turning in his chair as Croaker and Link exited the room.

"She will be afforded our utmost respect, sire smith," Link said, pulling the outer door closed behind him.

◆ ◆ ◆ ◆ ◆

"Look there, the toad enters an opening to that cave," the fairy scout quietly said, pointing in that direction.

"That must be where the forces that attacked our column came from. There, over there, I see a toad sentry near the entrance," the second scout said, both excitement and apprehension in his voice, "I am glad we decided to follow him into the rolling hills."

"I knew it was the right thing to do. He was traveling so fast that it had to be urgent business he was on. He made no effort to be stealthy," the first said.

"The commander will want this information as soon as possible, we should leave now," the second said, turning and silently slinking back toward the southern fields, his companion close behind.

◆ ◆ ◆ ◆ ◆

Deep within the caverns of the cave, the messenger toad approached Commander Kallose with his report about the sighting he and his companions had made.

"What has happened? Why have you returned? Where are the others that you left with?" the imp commander asked, not giving the toad a chance to answer, his unusually thin and angular avocado face glaring down on the toad, "I gave you orders!"

"Sir," the toad answered, fear coursing through his entire body at the tone in the commander's voice, "The others continued on to the rendezvous site. I returned, when they would not, to report something we saw."

"Well, what is it you saw that caused you to disobey orders?" Kallose growled when the toad seemed to pause to long for his liking.

"We chanced to see several carriages on the road to Granstone, Sir!" the toad started to relay.

"And why would that be of any importance to me?" the commander broke in, his face contorting as his left eyebrow rose, showing that his patients for the toad had grown thin.

"Sir, as I was about to say, they were all royal carriages with full complements of guards for each. One was guarded by the nymph queen's personal guard, three were fairy carriages from each of those domains with a couple extras mixed in with them," the toad completed his report, desperately trying to hide his fear of the commander.

"Nymphs in the fairy domain! How can this be?" Kallose asked, suddenly shaken by this news, "And you say the other fairy domains as well?"

"Yes, Sir," the toad said, relaxing some with the commanders change of tone, then looking for favorable recognition, "I hope that Lord DeMonas will be pleased with this information."

A fierce scowl came across Kallose's face, realizing that he would have to be the one to inform DeMonas about this, "This news will not please the King at all. This does not bode well with his plans, but I will tell him of your vigilance."

CHAPTER TWENTY-THREE

General Broadstem stood at the large oriel, facing to the west of Loamis, as he watched the messenger below hurrying toward the building he was using as his headquarters. His mind was on the message Airlein had sent him two days ago. She had been much more forceful in her reproach of his actions than he thought she could be; *she has truly grown more than I gave credit. I wonder why she did not say why they moved the summit to Granstone? What of this enemy that the Granstone ambassador and Airlein have both mentioned? I have not had any other information that indicates a force is out there somewhere . . .*

The General's thoughts were interrupted when the messenger topped the staircase entering the room, "General, I have an urgent message from one of our patrols, Sir!"

"Yes, what is it?" Broadstem asked, turning away from the window.

As if to answer the general's last thought, "One of our patrols, one to the southwest of Loamis, encountered two toads, Sir," the messenger paused for a quick breath, "the toads had crossed into our domain from the southern fields and were headed in a direction that would take them south of Zarlan Grove. When the patrol approached them, the toads drew weapons and one of our scouts was killed before they themselves had been dispatched."

"Toads? They must be part of this force that is threatening the domains, why else would they draw weapons?" Broadstem spoke his thoughts.

"Sir?" the messenger looked puzzled at the general's comments.

"Nothing. Thank you. You are dismissed!" he said, flicking the back of his hand at him while returning to the oriel. Standing with clenched fists braced against his hips, he began staring in the direction the skirmish had taken place; *where could the toads have come from? We have not seen any in this domain for . . . let's see now . . . longer than I can remember. I better send a report of this to Granstone and see if Airlein is all right in the process. Who knows what has been happening there. I do not like having her where I am not able to protect her.*

✦✦✦✦✦

The sun had climbed to just beyond mid-day as Croaker and Link entered the northern side of Raven's Roost where they could hear an industrious group of fairies in the canopy above singing a soft melody in harmony with the rustling leaves as they were busy gathering spider silk that would later be spun into threads.

The fairies paused from their work to watch the unusual sight of a frog warrior attired in white, matching his mount, with sunlight glinting off his helm whenever he happened under a ray that found its way through the leafy roof above. When Croaker and Link had traveled beyond their location, they could hear the fairies take up their enchanting song again and knew that they had returned to their work.

As the riders encountered homes along the road, their presence attracted young fairy children that excitedly flew down and circled around the pair, as if to be a chaotic escort for Croaker and Link, while the two continued on to the stable where they had stopped on their journey to Juniper.

"Sire Frog, what manner of dress is that for a frog?" one of the youths called out, "I have never seen a frog dressed such as you!"

Croaker simply smiled and said, "I am the first warrior frog since General Longhopper of a time long past!"

His statement astounded them, leaving them with looks of amazement and occasional whispered comments amongst themselves; no one had ever told them that frogs had been warriors.

"Do any of you know a weaver by the name of Heddle?" Link asked, "And where we could find her?"

"Sire Fairy, why do you ride a bush-tail?" another of the youths asked Link, ignoring his request, "Is your ability for flight handicapped?"

"I ride to be a companion. Now, can any of you direct us to the weaver, Heddle?" Link asked again.

Glancing at one another, the children began to gleefully giggle with an unspoken understanding of a new game to play, then suddenly flew off in all directions without another word.

Croaker let out a chuckle, his face broadening into a huge grin, "We can ask the smith when we arrive at the stable," he chortled, making light of Links exasperation at the children's antics.

"The children of Granstone would have been helpful if a stranger had asked for directions," Link grumbled then he too had to grin.

"Ho there, Sires!" the smith's apprentice called out from across the corral, over the rhythmic sound of the smith's hammer ringing against steel, as Croaker and Link reined up their mounts at the enclosure's gate, "My master will be out to greet you in a moment. I must to fill the feed troughs and see to the care of the animals," before entering the door to the stables with the feed sack slung over his shoulder.

Croaker swung down from Cloud Whisper and opened the gate, leading the white bush-tail into the empty corral with Link following close behind with his gray.

The sound of the hammering steel ended abruptly and moments later the smith appeared through the doorway of the smithy, wiping away the sweat and soot from his forehead with a coarse linen rag he had pulled from under his belt. After pausing a moment for his eyes to adjust to the brighter light of outside, "Welcome back, Sires. I trust your trip went well?" he inquired, jamming the rag back under his belt, while striding over to Croaker and Link.

"It did indeed, Sire Smith!" Croaker smiled back at him, then asked, "And what did the troopers find after we left?" Croaker had been wondering what Cloud Whisper had sensed before they had left for Juniper. The question had stayed in the back of his mind until now, as much as the feeling of uneasiness he had when they spent the night at Broadleaf.

"The troopers had found nothing, Sire. They said there were no signs of anything or anybody to be detected," the smith informed them, "Are you going to stay a while, here in Raven's Roost, Sires?"

"That will depend on a weaver named Heddle. Since I have made mentioned of her now, could you direct us to her?" Croaker asked, glancing up and raising his hand with palm up while turning in an arc, gesturing at the spider-web of walkways throughout the canopy above them.

"Yes, she is one of our elders, Sire," the smith said with a smile, "If it is her you go to see, then you will be here a while. She can talk a flittering insect into a stupor!"

Link broke out into a sudden laugh as he pictured the old weaver, as he imagined her, stopping a fly in mid-flight simply by speaking to it. His laugh was so infectious that Croaker and the smith found themselves laughing along with him, although not sure what they were laughing about.

After hearing the smith's warning about Heddel's tendency to ramble and given the length of time since they had last eaten, Croaker decided with the aid of the aromas drifting down from the inn, to take the time to eat first. "We will put up our mounts for now, Sire Smith," Croaker said, bringing his laughter back to a mild chuckle, "I believe that we will enjoy that inn's fine fare again before we seek her out."

The smith was more than just a little curious why this frog warrior and foreign fairy would be looking for a weaver; not just any weaver, but *Heddle*, so he offered, "I will be glad to escort you myself, Sire. That will give me enough time to finish the new drawknife I have been working on for the cooper. His place is on the way to Heddel's and I can use a break from the forge," he said, while taking the reins of Croaker and Link's mounts and began leading them to the stable, adding over his shoulder, "If that is alright with you?"

"It will be our pleasure to have your company, Sire," Croaker said as he and Link both nodded their agreement before turning to the spiral stairs that led to the inn.

Croaker and Link had found a table near the back of the dining area of the inn and were nearly finished with their meal when the smith entered.

"There you are!" the smith said, squinting his eyes to adjust to the dimmer light inside, as he located them after a few brief moments, "I will be right with you, Sires. *Barman*, bring me a mug of that stuff you so kindly call ale," he called out jovially.

"Have your seat you slow witted fool. I will bring it over to you!" the innkeeper shouted back, feigning indignation, "Who is minding your smithy and stables?"

"You know full good and well it is that boy of yours that wanted a true profession," the smith chortled, as he sat at Croaker and Link's table, laying the new drawknife he made on it with a thump, "not follow your mistakes."

The smith winked at Croaker and Link and smiled slyly as he lean toward them and said in a low voice, "Pay us no mind. He is my brother and has more sons and daughters than can work the inn. Two of them are as you, warriors in the king's army."

"Spreading talk about my young ones, are you? Take a wife and then you can talk about your own for a change," the innkeeper mocked irritation as he pounded down the mug, splashing ale over the sides, then smiling at Croaker and Link, said, "You should choose your company with a little more discretion, Sires."

The good-natured banter between the brothers continued even as they exited the inn. "Our first stop is the cooper's, Sires. It is this way," the smith directed them, taking the lead on the walkway leading into the forest away from the main road below.

A light breeze rustled the leaves of the canopy, as they moved from walkway to walkway, and the hush sound it made mixed with the sounds of cottage industries and children at play along the way. It carried a freshness in its scent of forest flowers and pine that was so light and refreshing that Croaker hadn't notice the distance they had traveled when the smith said, "The cooper's workshop is there . . . down there, on the ground level."

Croaker saw light wafts of steam escaping through vents near the top of the workshop as the smith led them down a spiral staircase, much like the one they had used to get to the inn, that wound its way around a large tree not far from the cooper's workshop. From inside they could hear whirring and scraping sounds along with the dull thumping of wooden mallets striking against wood and the sharp sound of metal on metal of hoops being driven. Entering through a service door at the end of the building, Croaker saw a fairy sitting on a stool to his left, his leg pumping a treadle that drove a lathe. As the fairy worked a cutting tool along a rest, shaping the wood that spun in the lathe, chips flew to the sound of thack . . . thack . . . thack, until it smoothed to a buzz. Beyond this fairy another was working in a similar manner at another lathe. The smell of hot, damp oak filled the air as staves were being heated over burning cressets, to later be bent when pliable enough, near the side of the workshop below the vents. In front of Croaker and across the large workshop three fairies sat astraddle the ends of shaving horses as they pulled drawknives, like the one the smith had made, shaping staves for kegs and buckets. Not far from them, three more fairies were at various stages of preparing headers, either dowelling planks together, at a treadle driven band saw cutting them in circles or cutting the basle. Still others cut chimes or hammered the metal hoops that another fairy had riveted on the bick iron.

Croaker had never given thought to how much went into the making of a keg or bucket and so he watched in amazement to the constant movement and talking of the craftsmen, even the apprentices that worked brooms sweeping up chips and shavings to feed the fires of the cressets.

"Welcome, Sire Smith! I see you have brought along companions," the master cooper said as he approached them from his office space in the far corner of the workshop, "You two must be the ones that passed through Raven's Roost yesterday. The description I have had of you, Sire Frog, was not exaggerated."

"This is Sire Croaker and his companion from Granstone, Sire Link," the smith introduced them.

"Are you here to see me?" the cooper asked, wondering what they would want with him if they were.

"No, Sire Cooper. Sire Smith is good enough to escort us to see the weaver, Heddle," Croaker replied, "and since your shop was on the way he wanted to stop here first."

"I have the drawknife you ordered for your new apprentice," the smith said as he handed the master cooper his handy work, then reaching down and opening the draw strings of a small pouch that hung from his belt, "Here are the pin rivets you will need for the pull handles."

"Thank you. He is in the process of making the pull handles as we speak," the cooper said, indicating the fairy that Croaker had first seen when they entered, then looking at Croaker and Link,

"The other journeyman is turning an oak canteen on the other lathe. What is it you wish to see Heddle about, if may I ask?"

"I need some special weaving done and was informed that she had the skill necessary," Croaker said, and was not going to tell him or the smith more than that.

The master cooper could infer from Croaker's manner that he was not going to learn more about their visit to Heddle, so he asked Link, "And how do you find our forest compared to your fields, Sire Link?"

"Different, but very pleasant, Sire," Link said as diplomatically as he could.

"Ah, well said, Sire Link!" the master cooper smiled, "I am sure I would find your fields equally pleasant!"

"We must be going, Sire. Our time is limited," Croaker apologized to the master cooper and looked to the smith.

"Yes, of course," the smith answered, then informing the cooper, "I will have the dish steel strips you ordered in two days."

"We can make due till then, but no longer than that. You need to get a couple more apprentices of your own!" the master cooper suggested, somewhat indignant that he might have to wait for his needs because the smith didn't have enough workers to keep up with the demands on him.

"Do not fear, I will have them for you!" the smith replied, upset with the tone of the master cooper, "You have grown your operation far too large. There is no other industry here in Raven's Roost that compares, Sire."

"It is the most efficient of the industries here, Sire Smith. Others would do well to take my example by combining," the master cooper stood resolute in his conviction.

"This is discussion for another time. I must see Sire Croaker and his companion to Heddle's. Good day," he said, turning and leading the way out and back to the walkways in the forest canopy.

As the trio entered Heddle's workshop, an easy feeling came over Croaker as the sounds covered him like the waters of Lily Pond while taking a swim. Young female apprentices standing at either side of a large loom, positioned in the middle of the workshop, were shooting a shuttle like a well choreographed dance with Heddle's actions; which created a sound much like a melody from a musical instrument as it slid across the warp threads, combining with the deep base thump of the loom itself, as the batten packed the weft when the Master Weaver pressed the pedal at the base of the loom setting the warp for the next pass.

The once youthful beauty of the aged weaver at the loom had only been enhanced by her years. Hair glistening as brightly as polished silver in moonlight, tucked behind pointed ears as delicate as flower petals, and flowed over her shoulders to cascade down her back where it parted at her wing base like the water of a high mountain falls spilling onto a rocky outcrop. Her skin, though not as taut as it was in her youth, still glowed warm despite her age and her full face carried none of the harsh lines expected of one of her years. Thin dark eyebrows and long dark lashes set off her almond shaped eyes that glistened like clear emeralds from a light deep within.

Without looking away from her work to see who had entered, "Be a dear and pour me a draught of wine from the skin on the hook. I have worked up a thirst."

Quickly looking around, Link found the hook with the wineskin above a narrow table against the outer wall. The table held several mugs and a bucket of water with a ladle handle protruding over its rim. Picking up one of the mugs and uncorking the skin, Link poured a good swallow before handing it to the elder weaver who signaled her apprentices that she was suspending the operation before accepting the mug Link offered.

After tipping the mug to her lips and feeling the flush of warmth it provided she turned, looking first at the kind individual that had fulfilled her request, "You are a dear! What might your name be?"

"I am Link. I come from the court of Arklan, of the Southern Fields, in the company of Sire Croaker, liaison to Sage Gribit," he introduced himself and his friend.

"Master Smith, how nice of you to accompany my guests," she smiled at his presence in the doorway. Then moving her gaze to Croaker, "Ah, what is this? A frog in warrior clothing! How unusual!"

"Master Weaver Heddle, if you will excuse me, I must return to my smithy. If I do not fill Master Cooper's order I will never hear the last of it!" the smith apologized and with a courteous bow of his head turned to exit the workshop.

"Sire Smith! Thank you for your assistance. We will return to your stables when we have finished our business here," Croaker said quickly before the smith was out the door.

"Be a dear again and fill my mug with some of that water. The wine fortified me but I still need to quench my thirst," Heddle asked Link, nodding in the direction of the bucket, then asked Croaker, "And what is it that I can do for you, Sire Croaker?"

"If you will permit me," Croaker lifted his tunic, revealing his mail, "I have been informed that you have the knowledge to weave mail such as this."

Heddle's eyes fixed on the shimmering garment, "I have been taught how to weave in that manner but I do not have the kind of thread that is required. I do not know of any that exists, Sire," she apologized, reaching out to run her fingers across the fabric.

"I have seen the smith in Juniper that knows how to make the threads. He is the one that has sent me to you," Croaker explained, "When the thread is ready, he will deliver it to you. The mail I require is for my mount. I want him to be as protected as myself when we enter into battle."

"Your mount!" Heddle's eyes widened in surprise, "With whom are you to do battle?"

"Are you aware of the search for slithers?" Link asked, as he handed Heddle the mug of water, then explained, "They are part of a force that threatens all the domains of Lily Pond. Sire Croaker has already fought in a battle in the south of the Rolling Hills, near the southern fields, and defeated the leader of that attack."

"Then the rumors I have heard *are* founded in truth, though not completely accurate, but based on truth none the less," Heddle let the words slip quietly from her lips.

"Yes, the entire pixie town of Feldspar had been wiped out and when I led a column to investigate, we were attacked," Croaker informed her.

"I trust that what you have been told will remain in this room? At least until after the summit that is being held at Granstone," Croaker scanned the apprentices for their assurance as well as Heddle's.

"Most certainly, Sire, I can see no need to feed the fires," she assured him as he watched both the apprentices nod the affirmative to his question.

"Sire Croaker, I will have to see this mount of yours. I must take his measurements for a proper fit," she informed him.

Heddle began shaking her head in disbelief that she would be weaving with materials that had so long been unavailable that it was kin to myth, "At long last I will be able to employ the knowledge and loom that has been passed down from my forebears for its true purpose, not just for training."

"You will not be using this loom?" Croaker looked puzzled, wondering what the difference could be.

"No, Sire, this loom is one of three in the domain that was built at the time the material for the domed city of the nymphs was

354

built. We needed to be able to produce extremely large panels of material in a short period of time. The crafters could not accomplish that with their small looms in their homes," she said, "The loom I speak of was made before that . . . a time long forgotten."

"Master Weaver, Heddle . . ." Croaker started to say when she interrupted him.

"Please, Sires! I would much prefer you call me by my given . . . *Heddle*," she smiled, her hand raised motioning Croaker to stop speaking.

Croaker smiled knowingly, "Heddle," he began again, "We have to be on our way south as soon as possible. We are limited in the time we have available to us."

"You will need to stay in Raven's Roost for the night, Sire. It is already late in the day and by the time I make the necessary measurements of your mount you would have to make most of your trip to Broadleaf in the dark of night, or sleep out in the forest when you tire."

Giving thought to her suggestion, Croaker conceded, "You are right, we can take a room at the inn above the smith," then smiling at Link and giving his friend a wink, he teased, "You can see Catkin tomorrow when we have our mid-day in Broadleaf."

CHAPTER TWENTY-FOUR

Gribit paced the granite aisle below the half round table in the great hall, his left hand closed in a fist and pressed into the small of his back while his right hand cradled his chin as he pronouncedly leaned forward in his stride. His thoughts ran deep as he awaited the arrival of the domain leaders. They had brought the scrolls up from the vault and had read all that day and late into last night learning about the imps and a history long forgotten to all. Still, after all this, Fernon and Airlein continued to concentrate their energies on their grievances with the other domains.

Isalia has had the least direct problems from the imps, other than Airlein, and she is able to see the necessity to concentrate on solving this problem. Fernon . . . Airlein . . . they see the threat that is out there, yet still they bicker about issues that can be resolved at a later date. I must get them to focus on the real problem of the imps, that is our greatest threat at the moment. Why won't they see it?; these thoughts nagged at him as he tramped back and forth as if he were making a deliberate effort to wear a rut into the granite beneath his feet.

"Sire Gribit!" the greeting coming from the side entrance to the hall, behind him, causing him to turn abruptly as it startled him out of his focused thoughts, "We did not see you at the morning meal."

Gribit watched as Webber and Puck approached him, "I ate early, in my chamber," he said absently, "I kept waking throughout the night and finally decided to call for something to eat before coming here. My thoughts have been many."

"We have learned a lot from the scrolls about this enemy that threatens us," Puck agreed, "Now we have to decide how to use this information to our benefit."

"I wish Airlein and Fernon would be of the same frame of mind," Gribit flicked the back of his hand into the air, showing his frustration that they did not set this as their priority, turning and taking a couple of paces before turning back, "They keep harping about their citizens that Isalia has interned and land that should rightfully be theirs. All problems that can be addressed at a time when the greater threat has been dealt with."

"We pixies have the same grievances, but I want justice for my son and the other children, both pixie and fairy, and all those of Feldspar that had been pointedly destroyed to provoke conflict between the domains. For this reason I will maintain my attention on this vile force that threatens us," the anger and determination flowing from Puck like a fountain with no valve to control it.

Gribit reached out his hand and placed it on Puck's shoulder, for in that moment Puck had allowed himself to loose constraint and grieve for his son.

"It is a wonder that you have maintained yourself for this long. Release it now, we understand," Gribit's voice was low and soothing, as Webber also placed his hand on Puck's other shoulder.

The voices of Isalia, Fernon and Airlein rang throughout the great hall as they entered, while Puck was gathering his composure once again.

"How many times do I have to tell you . . . I have no knowledge of who brought about your parents deaths . . . just because that incident took place near our border . . ." Isalia growled at Airlein, furious that she continued her implied accusation that it had to be either her, Arklan or Fernon that ordered the deed or had knowledge of it.

"I, like Isalia, gave no such order or have any knowledge of who had perpetrated that deed but I most certainly would have acknowledge it, had I ordered it," Fernon said in a strong and deliberate tone, his eyes narrowed in intensity as if to punctuate the truth of what he was saying.

"I just want to know who!" Airlein's frustration and hurt rose to the surface, her royal bearing displaced for the moment by the young girl that had lost her parents, "How can I trust any of you if . . ."

Gribit interrupted her with a raised hand as he turned toward the group. "Airlein," he said sympathetically, "Enough of this discord. Think of what is happening now. I have to believe it must have been the imps. Since none of the domains take credit for the deed, and with the tactics the imps are using now, then they most likely were trying to do then what they are trying to do now . . . get us to fight amongst ourselves . . . and you are doing exactly what they want. We must join together against them as was done in the time before, as written in the scrolls."

"If they are trying to insight us to fight each other then they must not be of any great strength. I believe that we can concentrate on resolving issues such as return of our citizens and land that is rightfully ours," Fernon said, glancing at each of the others for confirmation of the direction they should be pursuing.

"Fernon makes a valid point," Isalia nodded in agreement, "If the imps were stronger, then they would attack us in force."

"Have you learned nothing from the scrolls?" Gribit's frustration at their reasoning bubbling up within him, "They are devious creatures. They will not expend themselves if they can get us to deplete our strength against ourselves. They are truly the real problem we must consider!"

All heads turned toward the back wall with the glyphs as Arklan entered the great hall through his private entrance, "Please take you places at the table," he motioned with an arc of his upturned palm as he proceeded to his chair, "I have just received a message that there is a force of unknown size of toads, and possibly others, that are bivouacked in a cave west of Feldspar."

◆ ◆ ◆ ◆ ◆

The mid-day streets of Broadleaf were quiet, except for an occasional fairy running an errand or on their way for their mid-day meal, as Croaker and Link approached the Golden Leaf Inn.

The journey from Raven's Roost had been pleasant but Croaker's now familiar feeling of apprehension returned.

"Why do you keep glancing to the south?" Link asked, seeing Croaker's uneasiness as they walked their mounts around to the stable.

"That feeling is with me again. It is not strong though . . . it is like a hint of a cold breeze that has found its way deep in my bones," Croaker said, almost in a whisper, "It is faint but it is there!"

"A warm meal and hot tea is what you need," Link said assuredly, trying to alleviate Croaker's unease, "It has been a long and busy journey with no time to relax."

"I am sure you are right," Croaker said, opening the gate to the corral as a young fairy came out to greet them, "We will be staying only long enough to have a meal. See that our mounts are fed and brushed."

"Yes, Sire Frog," the young fairy acknowledged, taking the reins of Cloud Whisper and the gray then leading them into the stable.

"Well now, I believe that there is a certain fairy that would like to see you again," Croaker teased Link, deliberately trying to change his mood and smiling at the displeased look on his friend's face at his remark.

"Croaker, I know you jest but you do not know my reasons for the way I feel. She is full of life and easy on the eyes and would be a very good prospect if I had not already met the one that

I would have as mine, though *that* does not appear to be a possible future for me," Link replied wistfully, a distant look in his eyes as the two walked toward the inn.

"I am sorry my friend. As you have said, I do not know," Croaker apologized.

Croaker pondered the possible reasons why Link believed that he could not have the one he wanted and who she might be; *could it be someone I have not met? Or . . . is it someone that . . . maybe it is her.* All this allowed Croaker's thoughts to wander back to Lily Pond and the tall grasses swaying in the breeze while sitting near the sunny shore in the company of Lily, and he knew *Lily* would be the one in his own life.

The warmness of Croaker's thoughts was fleeting as they were quickly clouded with the tinge of apprehension, which he still could not define, creeping back into his mind; a hint of a distant presence, a malevolent presence that once again drew his gaze to the south.

The inn was much more subdued than the night they had stopped to rest as the patrons carried on quiet conversations during their mid-day meal. Catkin was busy waiting tables near the entrance and her father was out from behind the bar waiting tables in the back of the room when Croaker and Link entered.

"Sire Frog and Sire Link. Welcome back." Catkin said when turning to see who had entered, her smile broadening at the sight of Link. Then with a gesturing nod of her head, "There is a table over there . . . by the fireplace. I will be with you as soon as I have taken care of this table."

"Perhaps you should let her know that you are not interested in her," Croaker said, pulling out a chair from the table.

"I tried to let her know that I was not interested the last time we were here. I do not believe she will accept that," grinning, Link shook his head in frustration as he sat, "I think that she has made up her mind about me and nothing can change it. It will most likely be easier dealing with this enemy that is threatening the domains than dealing with her."

"You will just have to try my friend," Croaker chuckled, "or just accept her attentions, wanted or not."

"Well, at least I will not be coming back this way again, I can tell her that I will not be seeing her after this since I am returning to my domain," Link said, relieved that he had found an answer to his dilemma.

"You do not know that for sure. Did you ever think that you would be here now, in the forest domain, at any time in the past?" Croaker's question pointing out the way events can lead to unexpected outcomes.

"No."

Catkin had taken her empty tray back to the bar and stood for a moment looking at the table where Croaker and Link were seated. She had a sly glint in her eyes as she pressed out the wrinkles of her apron with her hands and then brushed a stray lock of hair behind her ear before heading for her objective. Her gaze was mainly fixed on Link, this handsome fairy from another domain who was traveling with a *warrior frog* and must be a warrior as well from the way he carried himself.

"May I take your order, Sires?" she asked, her voice as sweet as a melody as she bent down close to Link, then almost in a purr as she moved her head near to his ear, "It is nice to have you as our quests again."

Link flushed and quickly looked to Croaker, a pleading look in his eyes for help from his friend, who had all he could do to keep from laughing at his friend's discomfort.

"Ha hum," Croaker cleared his throat, "We will have two of the house specials, some hot tea, bread and honey."

"Right away, Sires," she smiled, acknowledging the order while looking across the table at Croaker, then added, "It is nearly time for my break . . . would you mind if I joined you? I have many questions to ask your friend, Sire Frog."

"We would be delighted to have your company," Croaker responded, dismissing the contrary look on Link's face.

Link watched Catkin as she returned to the bar with their order, "Did you have to? I know you could see how she was acting toward me."

"You can answer the questions she wants to ask you. It is not just her, the others might be offended," Croaker looked around the room to indicate the fairies having their mid-day, "We can not afford to alienate any of the forest fairies by appearing to be anything but congenial if they are to be allies. The fact that you are here with me now is a great stride toward that end and we do not want to undue the good of that simply by rejecting her company."

Link looked at Croaker with a realization of the growth in this young frog that was even greater than he had previously thought, "Yes, Sire. You are right and I will do my best to deal with her attentions in as tactful way as possible."

"Two specials, bread and honey and tea for three!" Catkin called out to the kitchen, pulling her apron bow loose before removing it and laying the garment unceremoniously across the end of the bar. Looking at her father, she explained, "I will bring them their tea now, including one for myself, and I am taking my break at their table."

"I have seen how you look at this fairy of the fields from the first time he entered our inn. I do not want you to get hurt," the innkeeper said with concern for his daughter, "You know nothing more than he is a warrior that is traveling through our domain. True, he must be held in high regard by the king to be permitted to travel in our domain for reasons we do not know, but that is all we know. He may already have a mate from where he comes or will not take any for that matter because of the way he lives."

"I know my own mind father and . . . *he is* very handsome," she said, glancing in Link's direction, "Besides, I want to find out things about the southern fields that the frogs cannot tell us, and if I can attract his interest . . . then this break will be just what I hoped for," she confided.

"Yes, you do know your own mind daughter, but do not hope for what might not be possible. Now, here is the tea, go talk to your field fairy and ask your questions about his domain, I have had my say," the innkeeper nodded in the direction of the table where Croaker and Link were seated while handing Catkin a tray with the pot of tea and three mugs that had been brought from the kitchen, "I will bring them their meals."

"Now, Sire Link, tell me of yourself and your domain. Things that Sire Frog cannot," Catkin said as she placed the tray and its contents on the table.

"Sire Croaker can tell you nearly everything I could. He has learned many things that other frogs have not had the opportunity to about my domain and myself as well," Link informed her as he poured a mug of tea and offered it to her as she sat.

"Sire Croaker, you are more unusual than I had thought but that should be expected since you are the only warrior frog I have encountered," she said to Croaker with a look that was a mixture of surprise and admiration.

"I will not be the only one! I am simply the first since a long time past," Croaker informed her.

"Sire Link, what of yourself? How did you come to travel with a warrior frog?" she asked before blowing softly across the lip of the mug to cool the tea before taking a sip.

"I am a messenger for King Arklan and was sent with a message to the Sage at Lily Pond. Sire Croaker was there at my arrival and the Sage sent him to be his liaison. Since then Sire Croaker asked me to train him in the use of weapons and now we travel together as friends," Link looked across the table at Croaker, "He has become a hero to those of my domain thanks to his deeds in a conflict with an enemy that has invaded the Rolling Hills and the other domains."

"My friend trained me well!" Croaker interrupted.

"I would still like to know about you," Catkin said, trying to put the focus of the conversation back on Link, "Forgive my asking, but are you with a mate?"

Link flushed at the question then answered as politely as possible, "I do not have a mate though I have met the one that I would have as mine. You are very attractive and a delight to be around and if your interest is of that nature then I must apologize if I have misled you in any way."

"No, Sire Link, you have not and I am sorry if I have made you uncomfortable," she said, reprimanding herself for her boldness, "Please, tell me of your southern fields."

CHAPTER TWENTY-FIVE

The afternoon sun labored to burn through the thick haze that hung over the marshes of the wastelands as the armies of the goblin king were gathering. Toad foot soldiers, and those that pulled and operated the siege machines, which numbered in the thousands were bivouacked near the wet fringe of the marshes while the imp rat riders and archers were situated on higher, dryer ground. Stationed high on the plateau above, near the cave palace, were the military quarters of the goblins where Lord DeMonas was holding a strategy session with his brother and the generals.

Lord Noma and the five imp generals sat quietly waiting for Lord DeMonas to speak while he paced back and forth as he considered their suggestions and how those might benefit the way he wanted to conduct the assault on the domains.

"How long before we have a full complement of troops for each of the army groups?" DeMonas stopped, his yellow eyes glaring at the generals, demanding, "And are they ready to march?"

General Mordant, the senior general, hesitantly spoke up after looking at the others and seeing that they did not want to speak in fear of incurring the king's wrath, "The rest of the troops

367

will arrive in the next five days, Lord. We had to conscript toads from the factories in the far south to meet our needs and it will take them that long to reach here. We will march when you say, Lord, and they can be used to pull the siege machines since they have not been trained for anything else," he added.

"Then we will march in six days from now. Mordant, you will lead the center army group to the border south of Granstone. You can assign the others, and I want only one to lead the west group. He will meet with our new general, Kallose, at the caves west of Feldspar," DeMonas instructed before motioning his brother to come to him, "Here are General Kallose's orders. A raven has been readied for you so I want you to leave immediately. See that he receives them before you meet with the slithers again!"

"Yes, brother, it will be done," Noma said, taking the message pouch while suppressing his urge to grin, having succeeded in his cunning manipulation of his brother, as he turned to leave.

◆ ◆ ◆ ◆ ◆

The muted light of the forest road gave way to the bright sun that washed over the land beyond the end of the canopy where the forest trees yielded to the fields. Though the dappled shade of the forest road was cool, it could not account for the cold dread that clung to Croaker as if it were a shroud being drawn tighter around him with no way to struggle free. Cloud Whisper too, was moving with hesitation in his step the closer they came to the forest's end.

"Your muscles are tense, you can feel it out there too," Croaker said softly as he leaned close to Cloud Whisper's ear, then sitting upright again and turning to speak to Link as his right hand unconsciously went to his sword, "We must be alert Link! That feeling has engulfed my being so intensely now that I truly believe there is imminent danger. Cloud Whisper senses it as well."

Link nodded his understanding. He had been noticing that the closer they got to the border of the Forest domain and Lily Pond, the quieter Croaker became as his focus on something unseen to the south increasingly distracted him from their conversation.

They could see activity at the outpost shelter as they approached. A guard was standing near the barrier arm as another appeared from the stables behind the main building. The second guard stopped and watched as Croaker and Link drew nearer the outpost, "The frog warrior and his companion are returning!" he called out, causing the guard at the barrier arm to look up from his near stupor, of standing in the warm afternoon sun, and turn his head toward the forest and the approaching riders as yet another guard poked his head out the opening of the shelter doorway.

"All has been well here?" Croaker asked looking around at the relaxed atmosphere of the outpost as he reined up Cloud Whisper and swung down to the ground, "Have you seen anything out of the normal?"

Surprised by Croaker's actions and questions, the guard at the barrier arm swiveled his head about slowly then focused back on Croaker, "No, Sire Frog, although," he paused to look up as he recalled the shadow that had passed over several times, "I did notice a raven that has been circling high above most of the afternoon. Strange behavior, acting like a bird of prey and circling like that, but then the ravens have been given to strange behavior from time to time lately. Other than that, everything is just as it should be. What did you expect?"

Link scanned the sky in the direction the guard indicated before swinging down from his gray.

"Alright, Sire Croaker, I am beginning to think there *is* something to what you have been saying about these birds after all," he said handing the reins of his mount to the guard from the stable, "Brush him down a little before you feed and water him."

"It is not the ravens themselves, it is a presence that is with them that I feel," Croaker corrected, as he handed the reins of Cloud Whisper to the guard, "Our stay will be short, Sire Fairy. A quick brushing will do, while they eat, thank you."

Croaker and Link took only enough time for bread and honey and some hot tea as the guards questioned them about Croaker's apprehension of the raven and the nature of the presence he had referred to.

"I can not explain, Sire Fairy, only that there are times when I feel a foreboding. It is at these times that all is not right with the world," Croaker tried to explain, "All I can say is that at this moment we should all be alert."

"Alert for what, Sire?" one of the guards asked.

"An enemy that is like none you have known!" Croaker's said, his voice stressing the ruthlessness implied by his words as his gaze turned southward.

A long moment of silence passed before Croaker spoke again, "We must leave now. Thank you for your hospitality, but if we are to make Granstone in the time allotted, we can not delay any longer."

"I will have your mounts brought around for you, Sire," a guard standing near the entrance said, and quickly exited for the stable.

As the sun was beginning its descent toward the rolling hills of the west, Croaker and Link departed the checkpoint shelter on the road to Lily Pond with the fairy guards watching them until they disappeared from sight.

The grasses along the road swayed lightly from a light cool breeze, tempering the warm air, as it came off the waters of Lily Pond to the southwest. The scents of the pond it carried reminded Croaker that they were those that he had come to know as home.

Cloud Whisper and the gray padded their way quietly along the hard packed road when Croaker's hand went to his sword, his apprehension growing ever stronger the further south they traveled, an action acutely reflexive as he and Link both searched the sky at the sound of a deep warbling caw from somewhere high above breaking the relative silence.

Cloud Whisper reared and twisted toward the grasses that lined the road as Croaker ducked, his sword slicing up through the air drawing a deep thin red line in the under belly of the rat that exploded through the grasses, leaping at the pair. The brown mass of the rat collapsed to the road, rolling onto its imp rider and crushing him under the rat's weight. At the same moment Link leaped into flight off the back of his mount, a breath before a second rat clamped its jaws on the shoulder of his bush-tail where Link's leg had just been. Bringing his blade down with a swift stroke brought crimson fluid flowing from a gash in the leathery blue-gray flesh that was the imps face a moment ago. The air was filled with the scream of the bush-tail, the squeal of the rats and the guttural roar of their riders as they washed onto the road like a wave from the grasses.

A battle-axe caught Croaker solid in the chest knocking him off Cloud Whisper. The imp that struck the blow sat staring down from his rat, stunned that he had not killed the frog, when Link's blade protruded from his chest and the bat-like face of the imp forming an expression of surprise, his yellow eyes opening wide and the nostrils of his flat triangular nose flaring, before he collapsed.

Link landed along side Croaker, who was regaining his feet, and the two repelled attacker after attacker while maneuvering around the imp and rat bodies littering the road. The smell of warm blood filling their nostrils overwhelmed all other scents that were carried on the light breeze when through the sound of their swords meeting battle-axes the flight of many arrows, suddenly filling the

air, resonated with their distinctive swish as they rained down on
their mark.

◆ ◆ ◆ ◆ ◆

The night had come and gone and after a long morning of
discord between the leaders of the domains, Gribit's patients had
never been tried to this degree and the rawness of his nerves
brought out a harsh side of him that none had ever seen before.

"What must I do to convince you of the urgency of this
situation?" he growled, banging his fist down on the table,
"Fernon, I thought you to be a reasonable sort and Airlein . . . set
aside your youthful naiveté and be the ruler that you were born to
be!"

"Gribit, you go too far. Do you think you can scold us like
children?" Fernon retorted, his indignation coloring his every
word.

"Yes, and why do you think that you can rule the rulers?"
Airlein said, leaning forward to emphasize her indignation, "Come
to think of it, how is it that the frogs were able to set themselves up
as trade administrators and conflict negotiators in the first place?"

"I do not believe you two! I can see why the frogs are in the
position they are!" Puck said, jumping to his feet, a steely glare in
his eyes aimed at the two squabbling leaders, "Since we have
gathered for this summit we have only grown further apart than
when we started. The frogs have always been able to handle things
on our behalf with few problems, unlike the petty self-interests of

some here. Do not let those distract us from seeing what is most important to all of us . . . our mutual security!"

"That was well said, Puck," Isalia said, agreeing with his assessment though she had a hint of doubt tinged her voice, then continued, "Although, they do make a point that there have only been isolated problems . . . granted, the worst of which has taken place in your domain. I am not as certain that the threat is as great as I first thought."

Gribit looked at Isalia in disbelief of what he had just heard, "Are you forgetting our first conversation? And what of the foe Croaker defeated and brought before you?" he asked, "Have you learned nothing from the scrolls of the past or have you forgotten these things already?"

Isalia was about to answer him when a runner entered the hall with seven nymph warriors following behind him. Approaching the delegation, he bowed before addressing Arklan, "Your Majesty. These nymphs bring an urgent message for this delegation," he waved his hand in their direction as they bowed to the King and the other rulers.

"Yes, what is it you have to say?" Arklan asked, looking at the nymph sergeant for her report."

"Your Majesty, I must inform you and my Queen that a great battle has taken place in our domain, near the border of the forest domain," she paused as she scanned the disbelieving looks on the faces of those gathered, "Sire Croaker and Sire Link had been ambushed on the road as they were making their return to Lily Pond."

"Croaker, Link, what of them?" Gribit asked, his apprehension reflecting that of all the others.

"We had noticed a raven circling the road for most of the morning and went to investigate this unusual behavior," she began to explain, "When we were close enough we could hear the sounds of a pitched battle taking place. Sire Croaker and Sire Link had fought off ten of the creatures and their rat mounts and were being set upon by another ten when we arrived. How they had managed to slay so many and still be able to fight I still can not fathom."

"What of them?" Gribit demanded.

"Our mounted archers let loose their arrows on the hoard, killing all but three and their rats as well. Sire Croaker and Sire Link were able to finish them. To see Sire Croaker swing up on that beautiful mount of his and run two of the rats and their riders down, it was like nothing I have ever witnessed before. And Sire Link, he flew after them faster than my best dragonfly could have and dispatched the third. The raven carried a rider and they were able to flee to the southwest."

"They are alright then?" Gribit asked, a look of partial relief at the news they were still alive.

"Yes, Sire. The only casualty was Sire Link's gray, he succumbed to his wounds before night fell."

"Croaker and Link are at Lily Pond then?" Webber asked, wondering why they were not with the nymphs.

"No, Sire. They bid us to accompany them here," the sergeant quickly turned in his direction, "I sent half of my patrol back to Lily Pond with my report and to let my commander know that we would be accompanying them here. We rode through the evening and into this day without stop. They are here, but wished to take some food before appearing before you. They should be here before long."

"Thank you Sergeant. You have done well and with King Arklan's permission," Isalia said, looking at Arklan for his approving nod, "you and your troops may take refreshment and rest yourselves."

"My runner will show you the way," Arklan gave the order and the fairy runner bowed his acknowledgement then led the nymphs from the hall.

CHAPTER TWENTY-SIX

Croaker and Link entered the great hall to the buzz of excited conversation between the rulers, at the news of this new battle and where it had been fought. They were pondering the ramifications of this event for the entire realm of Lily Pond.

"It appears that Gribit and Arklan have been proven out about the severity of the imp threat," Fernon admitted, stroking his chin whiskers between his thumb and index finger, "I for one have to concede to that."

"How was a force of that size able to make its way to the very heart of the realm without detection?" Isalia asked, voicing the others' thoughts.

"I am concerned that this force was intentionally lying in wait for Croaker and Link," Gribit said, indicating to the two as they approached the seated delegation, "I do not believe that they were there to attack any would be travelers that happened along."

"I agree, they must have learned of Croaker's victory over their leader," Arklan said, standing to greet the pair, "Sire Croaker, once again you have been very hard on your tunic I see, as has been Sire Link. Please join us. We have much to discuss with both of you."

Webber, seeing the tattered and blood stained tunics of the pair, jumped to his feet and threw his harms around his friend as they came out of their greeting bow, "If not Old Big Fin, to put yourself in harm's way, then you had to go and find something that was even worse!" he mockingly scolded, then stepping back a step and motioning with his upraised palm at Croaker's attire, "It is best that Lily can not see you in this state. She would finish the job those riders tried to do, just for the scare you would have put her through."

"Webber," Croaker's eyes squinted some when he gave a little chuckle as he envisioned Lily scolding him soundly, before continuing to reassure his friend, "The blood is not ours. We are fine except for some bruises. Link and I will be making full use of the hot pool when we are finished here."

Link nodded his agreement and Croaker continued, "Your Majesties, I am curious about the agreement between the domains that you have arrived at?"

"Sire Croaker, I am sorry to inform you that no agreement has been reached as yet," Arklan informed him.

Surprised by the answer, Croaker looked at Gribit, his eyes showing his astonishment, and asked, "Why?"

"It was not until the report of your recent battle that some here thought the threat was not as severe as they now believe. I am sure we will resolve any minor issues in order to come to an agreement to what must be done," Gribit answered, looking at each of the leaders for their resolve, especially Fernon and Airlein.

"Whatever the agreement, I believe it to be in our best interest that we frogs form an army again. I will lead them if you ask but I believe that their training should be over seen by Link and any he chooses," Croaker informed Gribit and the rest of the delegation.

Link looked at Croaker in surprise since this had never been discussed between them, "When did you come up with this?" then after a quick moment of thought, "I am honored that you would ask this of me."

"The idea came to me at this moment, Link. The training you gave me has allowed me to succeed in the battles that I have been in and I can think of no other that I would want to train my friends and family," Croaker explained.

"So it shall be, Sire Croaker!" Arklan quickly agreed, "Sire Link, you shall be known as Commander Link, of the new frog army, from this moment forward. The stored weapons in the chamber can be issued to the troops you will train."

"In this last battle that Link and I were in, I want to point out that had I been alone I would have perished. It took frog, fairy and nymphs fighting together to defeat the attackers. Do your best to come to agreement soon!" Croaker reminded them.

"It is now up to you, the leaders of the domains, to forge an alliance from the fires of your discord. An alliance that has strength as strong as the alliance of old, between the domains and us frogs, as has been written in the scrolls. It is the differences between each domain that are like the elements added to the molten ore that increases the steels strength, for each society brings something the others need. We have only to hammer it out, this our shield and weapon. We face a foe that has shown that they are devious and with a strength that we have yet to fully discover. We can not wait for them to reveal their true strength before we prepare, for if we do wait it may be too late for us," Gribit said, imploring the delegation to finally come together and take positive action on behalf of the entire realm.

"I will pledge my army and whatever supplies my domain can offer," Isalia said resolutely, standing and looking at the others, challenging them to do the same.

"I will form the militias of the Rolling Hills into a single army and pledge that army and any supplies my domain can offer," Puck quickly followed, "Though it may take me a little longer to bring this about; but it will be done!"

"My domain has much to offer in both supplies and army. I will pledge them to our common cause," Fernon stood, looking at Airlein for the young queen's commitment.

"I would be foolish to stand by myself! I too will pledge army and goods to the common cause of the domains," Airlein agreed, "I do so with the understanding that the domains maintain their sovereignty."

"The question remains, who . . . will lead these armies?" Arklan asked, "I believe that it should be a counsel of the leaders with recommendations from the generals of those armies."

"Again, we can learn from the scrolls. Their rulers and generals in the separate fields of battle had led the armies of the old alliance. They were able to make decisions based on what was happening at the moment, though they kept in contact with the others for the larger picture," Gribit noted information he had gleaned from the scrolls.

"After Link and I have soaked away some of the ache of our bodies and rested, we will return to Lily Pond and bring together a frog army," Croaker said, excusing himself and Link from the delegation, and as the two bowed to the leaders, "By your leave, your Majesties."

"Prepare them well, Commander Link," Airlein smiled.

EPILOGUE

The dark of the night was slowly being washed away extinguishing the bright points of light above until only a faint few in the west could still be seen in the predawn gray as Gribit's booming voice paused for a moment. Only the slight rustle of the grasses from the light breeze that still flowed down from the rolling hills disturbed the quiet hush of those that had been listening to the Sage's story of Croaker.

"The night has been long and the story is only half told. This is how the alliance had been forged but the battle for the realm had yet to be fought and if you return tonight I will tell you of that part of the story. Go to your homes now, for this tired old frog must rest!" Gribit informed them, excusing himself from the storytelling.

AUTHOR'S COMMENTS

Lily Pond is a fantasy adventure on its surface though it is an allegory to the global warming story. The characters Croaker and Webber are launched on a quest by the same basic motivation, though each has a different path to follow, before reaching the same place. In their quest to find truth in the events that are taking place around them, and with each revelation, bringing a new weapon to their arsenal with which to fight the problem they must ultimately confront.

The frogs in this story are those that look beyond their own interests unlike the inhabitants of each of the domains who are blind to the common interest of the entire realm. In order to prepare for the greater challenge that lay before them, the frogs must bring all the domains together in a common effort to avert disaster from this larger and, in many cases, denied threat.

In this allegory the frogs represent the scientists and others trying to warn us of the threat we face if we don't confront how we are doing things that affect our environment. The five domains represent the countries of our world that have mistrust of each other and are worried only about their own needs without looking beyond those.

The Imps represent those that can make a difference but refuse to because of their personal greed while the imp minions, toads and slithers, represent the bad things that happen when the balance is upset. The children in this story that are killed by the slithers represent the future generations that will have to pay the price for the lack of action to prevent the impending disaster.

The city of Lily Pond itself represents our environment with its delicate balance needing to be preserved just as the balance of the water pressure pressing in on the city's dome and the air pressing out against it must be maintained. This constant threat to the city is eased somewhat by the rib structure that is the insurance provided just as the frogs provide some insurance by working to bring the domains together to prevent this problem from overwhelming them, and losing all to the resulting building force, due to inaction.

ABOUT THE AUTHOR

In addition to his writing, Howard A. W. Carson is a National Award winning artist and teaches art at the Veteran's Hospital in Minneapolis, Minnesota. He also volunteers many hours of service to the Skyway Senior Center in Downtown Minneapolis. His works have appeared in numerous venues including the rotunda in the Capitol Building in Washington, D.C.

Made in the USA
San Bernardino, CA
14 March 2016